"Decadent . . . with a Big Easy attitude."

—Paige Shelton, *New York Times* bestselling author of *If Onions Could Spring Leeks*

"A tasty treat for mystery lovers, combining all the right ingredients in a perfectly prepared story that's sure to satisfy."

—B. B. Haywood, national bestselling author of *Town in a Sweet Pickle*

"Jacklyn Brady whips up a delectable mystery layered with great characters and sprinkled with clever plot twists."

—Hannah Reed, author of the Queen Bee Mysteries

"Delicious from start to finish." —*Suspense Magazine*

"[A] lighthearted mystery featuring over-the-top characters and fun dialogue." —Kings River Life Magazine

"The prose is smart, snarky, and possesses as much character and charm as New Orleans itself." —The Season

"[It] wrapped me up in a delectable mystery right from the first page." —Cozy Mystery Book Reviews

"A truly excellent read." —Fresh Fiction

"A heroine wh[illegible] [illegible]nd Reviews

Berkley Prime Crime titles by Jacklyn Brady

A SHEETCAKE NAMED DESIRE
CAKE ON A HOT TIN ROOF
ARSENIC AND OLD CAKE
THE CAKES OF WRATH
REBEL WITHOUT A CAKE
THE CAKES OF MONTE CRISTO

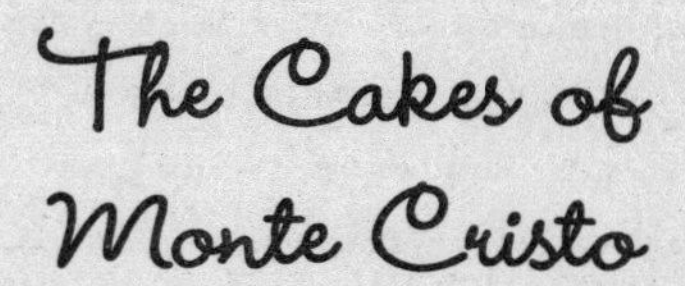

Jacklyn Brady

BERKLEY PRIME CRIME, NEW YORK

An imprint of Penguin Random House LLC
375 Hudson Street, New York, New York 10014

THE CAKES OF MONTE CRISTO

A Berkley Prime Crime Book / published by arrangement with the author

ISBN: 978-0-425-25828-6

PUBLISHING HISTORY
Berkley Prime Crime mass-market paperback edition / January 2016

PRINTED IN THE UNITED STATES OF AMERICA

10 9 8 7 6 5 4 3 2 1

Cover illustration by Chris Lyons.
Cover design by Diana Kolsky.
Interior text design by Laura K. Corless.

PUBLISHER'S NOTE: The recipes contained in this book are to be followed exactly as written. The publisher is not responsible for your specific health or allergy needs that may require medical supervision. The publisher is not responsible for any adverse reactions to the recipes contained in this book.

For all the readers who love Rita,
her friends, and her family,
and who ask for more of their adventures,
a heartfelt thank-you!
For my editor, Shannon Jamieson Vazquez,
for her unfailing faith and her amazing patience with me.
Shannon, you truly are an author's dream.

One

"What do you mean, trouble?" I barked into my cell phone. It was a beautiful January morning in New Orleans. The temperature was cool and the humidity low. It was so nice out that as I left home, I'd rolled down the windows of my brand-new Range Rover to let in the fresh air. The Range Rover, just two months old, still had that new car smell, a scent I'd never enjoyed in a car of my own before. It was the very first brand-new car I'd ever owned and it was mine because I'd totaled my previous ride last fall. (Don't ask.)

I'd enjoyed the spring-like day for exactly twenty-three minutes. That's when I'd been halted by a solid wall of traffic on the freeway. The odor of exhaust began to fill the car, forcing me to roll up the windows as I settled in to wait for traffic to clear. In my book that was trouble enough for a Monday morning. Simone O'Neil's phone call and her cryptic reference to trouble was a complication I didn't want or need.

"Tommy just called," Simone O'Neil explained. "He sounded hysterical."

Simone is a member of the Crescent City Vintage Clothing Society. She and I had been working together for the past couple of months on the upcoming Belle Lune Ball, which the high-end bakery I run, Zydeco Cakes, was catering. The ball was just two weeks away, which meant that the stress was starting to build.

"Tommy always sounds hysterical," I reminded Simone. Tommy Sheridan, the drama queen, was our contact at the Monte Cristo Hotel, the venue for the event. "He loses it on a regular basis."

"He might have good reason this time. Apparently, a water pipe on the third floor broke and the Papillion Ballroom is completely flooded."

My heart dropped like a rock. The Belle Lune Ball was a very big deal and I'd put Zydeco's neck on the line by accepting the contract. We were committed not only to delivering five cakes that would wow the guests, but catering the event as well—something we had never done before. Losing the space we'd planned for might derail us completely.

"How bad is it really?" I asked. "Have you seen it?"

"Not yet," Simone said. "I'm headed there now. Evangeline wants me to check it out."

Evangeline Delahunt, Simone's mother, was a founding member of the Vintage Clothing Society. She's been in charge of coordinating the Belle Lune Ball for two decades, and has definite ideas about how things should work. That makes her a difficult woman to please. Simone's the only one who can do it consistently.

"Tommy swears they can still accommodate us," Simone said. "But Evangeline is concerned that we'll have to cancel. She's not happy. I'm sure you can imagine."

I nodded, but didn't respond out loud. I try not to share my negative thoughts about Evangeline with her daughter. I don't want my big mouth to ruin our budding friendship. "Let's hope the damage isn't as bad as Tommy thinks."

"We can dream," Simone said with a sigh. "He wants us to look at the alternate space right away so we can decide what to do. How soon can you meet me?"

I craned to see past the wall of cars in front of me, but all I could see were more cars. "Judging from the way traffic is moving, maybe tomorrow. Did Tommy tell you what he's thinking?"

I could hear footsteps on Simone's end followed by an electronic signal from inside a car, which probably meant that she was on her way. "No," she said. "He just kept saying that he has a space to show us and promised over and over that we won't have to move to another location."

"I hope he's right. The Monte Cristo isn't that big," I mused. Cars in the lane next to me inched forward and a small space opened up between two of them, but traffic ground to a halt again before I could make a move. "I wonder if they even have another space with the square footage and electrical outlets we need."

"We won't know until we look," Simone said reasonably.

I laughed. "That's true. So I'll meet you as soon as possible. All I have to do is get to the next exit. Then I'll get off the highway and drive the rest of the way through town. I can see the exit from where I sit, but the ramp is packed with cars that don't seem to be moving. Can you stall Tommy until I can get there?"

"I'll try," Simone said. "Both he and Evangeline are chomping at the bit. I don't know how long they'll be willing to wait."

"I get that," I said, "but I don't dare approve any space without checking measurements and traffic flow." I didn't have my notes with me, but I wouldn't waste time stopping at Zydeco to get them. I'd looked at them so often, I figured I could remember most of what I needed to know. If there was something important I couldn't remember, I could always call Ox, my second-in-command at Zydeco.

"I'll get there as soon as I can," I promised Simone. "Try not to make any decisions without me."

Simone agreed and I disconnected, immediately calling Zydeco to let my staff know about the latest development.

The phone rang five times before someone picked up, and then an angry male voice snarled, "Zydeco Cakes."

"Ox? Why are you answering the phone?" Ox is a trained pastry chef, a gifted cake artist, and the one person at Zydeco besides me with enough culinary training to cater an event like the Belle Lune Ball. He had so much on his plate at the moment, he was the last person I expected to answer.

"I answered because it was ringing," he growled. "Somebody had to pick up the damn thing."

Oh good. He was in a mood. I really wanted to know why the temporary receptionist I'd just hired—the third temp in the two months our office manager had been on maternity leave—hadn't answered my call. But since Ox was so full of sunshine, I decided not to pursue the question.

I heard a crash and a cry of dismay in the background, which prompted me to ask, "What was that?"

"Nothing. Where in the hell are you?"

Ox had expected to take over at Zydeco back when my almost-ex-husband (and Zydeco's founder) died. Maybe Ox *should* have been the one in the boss's chair, but my mother-in-law, Miss Frankie, had chosen me instead. Ox has never completely reconciled himself with her choice and sometimes he forgets which one of us calls the shots. But that was another topic I wasn't going to pursue that morning.

"I was on my way, but I got stuck in traffic," I said. "Plus,

I just got a call from Simone. Apparently, there's a major complication at the Monte Cristo so I have to swing by there before I come in."

"What kind of complication?" He sounded suspicious, as if he thought I might be making an excuse to skip out on work. As if I would ever do that.

I refused to let him rattle me. "Broken water pipe. Flooded ballroom. They've told Simone there's an alternate space, but I'm not going to commit without seeing it for myself."

"Does that mean you're not coming in at all this morning?"

"I'll be there," I assured him. "It'll just be a bit later."

Ox let out a heavy breath but when he spoke again his tone was friendlier. "Sorry I got on your case. We've run into a snag of our own over here. Half the fondant on the Grady wedding cake has cracked. We're peeling it off now, but I'm not sure how many of the decorations we'll be able to save."

I moved the Range Rover a foot closer to the exit, where cars had begun to move slowly. "Do your best," I said, although my direction really wasn't necessary. "I'll do what I can to help as soon as I can get there."

Ox mumbled something that I took as agreement and disconnected. I went back to watching traffic and looking for an opening that might let me escape the gridlock. Four lanes of traffic eventually merged into three, and then two. Thirty minutes later, I crept past a couple of banged-up vehicles, an ambulance, and a state trooper car. And just like *that*, traffic began to move again.

I breathed a sigh of relief and concentrated on getting to the Monte Cristo. Thankfully, I'd shoved a tape measure into my glove box after our original inspection and I hadn't gotten around to putting it back where it belonged. Despite what Aunt Yolanda had said when I was growing up, procrastination can sometimes be a good thing.

* * *

Simone was waiting for me in the Monte Cristo's lobby when I came in through the revolving door. The Monte Cristo is a smallish hotel built sometime during the nineteenth century, but of no particular historic significance. Most of it is horribly outdated, including its kitchen, but its age appeals to tourists and to groups like the Vintage Clothing Society.

The Belle Lune Ball has been held at the Monte Cristo for the past nineteen years and I suspected that the society's members would be devastated if we had to change locations at the last minute—assuming we could even find another venue on such short notice. I knew for certain that Evangeline Delahunt would be devastated if we had to leave the Monte Cristo.

Evangeline is one of those people who think the world revolves around them and takes exception to anyone or anything that tries to prove otherwise. Simone is as unlike her mother as possible. She's around my age, tall and thin with short dark hair and a friendly smile. Not only is she aware that she's not the center of the Universe, but she's comfortable with that fact.

On the surface, Simone and I seem to have little in common. She was born into money. I grew up on the wrong side of the tracks. She is unfailingly elegant. I'm what I optimistically refer to as casual. She's happily married. I was married briefly, thought I was happy, but found out differently when my husband walked out on the marriage. Despite the fact that a couple of really great guys had become part of my life, I honestly didn't know if I would ever take the plunge again.

The fact that Simone had once been almost engaged to the man I later married could have driven a wedge between us, but I don't think she'd ever been seriously interested in Philippe (or thankfully, he in her). The proposed union between them had been the brainchild of their mothers. Bucking the wishes of two such strong-willed women had required almost superhuman effort, but they'd done it, clearing the way for me to end up as Mrs. Renier—for a few years anyway.

Even with our differences, I'd liked Simone the minute I met her and she seemed to like me. I refused to let the fact that Evangeline was her mother cast her in a negative light. After all, that hadn't been Simone's choice, and so far at least, it seemed that she'd fallen far from the maternal tree.

During the two months we'd worked together on the Belle Lune Ball, Evangeline had thrown us both a few curveballs. I'd learned from Simone how to take them in stride, and eventually Evangeline had approved my menu and the cake designs. After that, the road had smoothed out and the work had been enjoyable.

Simone waved to make sure I'd seen her and started walking toward me. "Traffic must have been a real bear," she said when we met up in the middle of the lobby. "It's been almost an hour since I called you."

"Fifty-seven minutes," I said. "Sorry. I got here as soon as I could. Have you seen the space?"

She nodded and motioned for me to follow her. "It will work for what I need, but I don't know what y'all need for the food. Tommy's so distraught I promised to show you the space and sent him off to have a stiff drink. We'll have to take the elevator. The stairs are closed because of the flooding."

"So it's really as bad as Tommy says?"

She nodded. "Unfortunately, yes."

I followed her to the elevator, a contraption so old I was never sure it would actually work.

"The space is on the second floor," Simone said as we stepped into the rickety elevator cage. "There's no other area large enough to accommodate us." She pressed the appropriate button and the car began its shaky ascent. "We'll be on the north end of the building in the small ballroom. That means we'll have to put the buffet tables in the hallway, but I think it's plenty wide. Of course, you'll have to see what you think."

Tommy had given us a brief tour of the hotel at our first meeting. I remembered the small ballroom and the hallway outside, but since we hadn't expected to use the space, I hadn't bothered to check the number of available electrical outlets or think about possible traffic patterns. With the stairs out of commission, access from the kitchen was a concern, and I worried that Tommy wouldn't be able to provide a staging area to rival the one we'd originally agreed upon.

"What about the guests on the night of the ball?" I asked. "Will they all have to get up to the second floor on this thing?"

Simone nodded. "I'm afraid so. It will take a while to get two hundred people upstairs, so we may want to push dinner service back by half an hour."

"And pray that the elevator won't break down and trap somebody inside."

Simone looked horrified. "Don't even suggest something like that! Can you imagine how some of our members would react?"

I'd met a few of the society's members in the past few weeks, mostly the ones with complaints or some issue they wanted the society's administration to resolve. I was pretty sure that trapping any one of them in an elevator would result in pandemonium.

We reached the second floor and got off the elevator. The right side of the spacious foyer was blocked off by orange cones, so we turned to our left. "Tommy assures me they'll have a more attractive barrier set up by the time we're here," Simone said, grimacing at the cones. "I understand the ballroom is a complete disaster from the water damage. They have to wait for inspectors and insurance adjusters and who knows who to look at the damage. That could take weeks. After that, it will probably take a minor fortune and a month or more to make the repairs."

We had reached the smaller ballroom and I ran a critical glance around the open space. My first impression was that the foyer would be large enough for the buffet service, but I didn't want to take any chances. I pulled out the tape measure and a notebook and set to work, jotting down measurements, calculating the space necessary for serving stations and traffic patterns, and making a rough sketch of the area, marking the locations of electrical outlets.

When I'd finished there, we moved into the ballroom itself. Simone explained the proposed layout of tables and her suggestions for displaying the cakes and setting up dessert stations. The Belle Lune Ball was a charity event, with proceeds going to benefit various women's causes. The price tag for a ticket to the event was steep enough to make my eyes water, but a large chunk of that money went to funding the event, paying the band and the caterer (that would be me), and renting the hotel space. A big share of the money they donated to charity came from society members who paid big bucks for space to exhibit their wares and a silent auction conducted during the event. All of that meant that we had to squeeze in tables to accommodate them as well.

The rooms weren't as spacious as the original area we'd agreed upon, but after discussing a couple of different configurations, I thought we could work around the few restrictions I'd found. We'd almost finished when Tommy Sheridan surged into the room, his face flushed, dark hair tousled as if he'd been running his fingers through it. He's mid-thirties with a boyish face and soft brown eyes that make him look much younger. "Well?" he said as he advanced toward us. "What do you think? Is it going to work?"

He looked so distraught, I hurried to reassure him. "It will be a bit tight," I said, "but yes, I think it will work just fine."

He stopped walking and clasped both hands to his chest. His dark eyes filled with tears and he sprinted the last few steps toward me. He wrapped me in a hug so enthusiastic I almost lost my balance. "Praise the good Lord! You have no idea how worried I've been. I feel just horrible about this."

I hate to cry and I'm not comfortable when other people do it. Being caught up in Tommy's arms while he sobbed into my neck made me squirm. I tried to disentangle myself, but he held on tight. "It's okay," I assured him. "It's going to be fine. Please don't worry anymore." *And please stop crying!*

He sniffed loudly and finally let me go, digging a handkerchief from his breast pocket and mopping his eyes with it. "Forgive me," he said with an embarrassed laugh. "I'm just so relieved that you are okay with the space."

I put a couple of feet between us, creating a safety zone in case he lost control again. "I do have a few questions about logistics," I said, "but I don't think there's anything we can't work out. My biggest concern is with the staging area. We originally had two rooms that were connected to the ballroom so we had a workspace to get everything set up. I don't see anything like that here."

"There isn't," he said with a slight frown. "But we have what I believe will be an adequate space at the end of the hall. Would you like to see it?"

I said that I would, and we all trooped off together. Tommy unlocked the door to a small meeting room and showed me how that room connected to the one next door. He vowed on his life to provide anything I thought we would need, including the moon and stars. I thought Tommy was going to dissolve into tears again when Simone and I both agreed that the replacement rooms would work for us. To my relief, he held it together long enough for us to sign the paperwork, and less than an hour after I walked through the front doors, Tommy scurried away, leaving Simone and me smiling after him.

"I think that went well," I quipped as Tommy disappeared around the corner. "I'm just glad we didn't have to move to another location entirely."

"You and me both," Simone said. "Evangeline will be so relieved."

I grinned as we started walking toward the elevator. "Good. I like making her happy when I can." And it hadn't even been that difficult.

The two of us made plans to meet for lunch the following day to discuss changes the new venue would make to the decorations and the positioning of the cakes Zydeco would be making for the event, five cakes in the shape of dress forms, each sporting a different style of dress from the 1930s. As I drove away from the Monte Cristo, I was feeling pretty good about how I'd handled that morning's crisis.

It turned out approving the new meeting space was the easiest thing I would do all day.

Two

It was nearly eleven when I pulled into the parking lot behind Zydeco. I nosed the Range Rover into a parking spot and came inside through the loading dock door, which lets directly into the design room. It's my favorite room in the building, probably because I'd imagined it so many times while Philippe and I were in pastry school. Imagine my surprise when I came to New Orleans to get his signature on our divorce papers and found that he'd brought my dream to life.

Zydeco is housed in a graceful antebellum home near the Garden District. It was built sometime in the nineteenth century and was probably magnificent in its heyday. The back half of the house was revamped well before Philippe opened the bakery, but the front half is structurally the same as it was when the house was built. The foyer, complete with sweeping staircase, became our reception area. A large parlor morphed into my office, and the upstairs rooms became meeting and storage areas. The lovely finishes are still there, but most of the original furnishings are long gone, replaced by more utilitarian office furniture.

I've never known much about the building's history but learning about its past is penciled on my to-do list. Unfortunately, something else always takes priority. One of these days, when the sky isn't falling down around my ears, I'll get around to doing the research.

The design room in the back of the house is a huge area connected to a state-of-the-art kitchen. Large windows look out over the parking lot and what remains of the original gardens. On sunny days, light streams into the room, bathing everyone and everything in sunlight.

The only exception is Sparkle Starr, a twenty-something dedicated to all things goth, who had chosen the one corner sunlight never reaches. Sparkle glanced up from her workstation and acknowledged me with a narrowing of her black-rimmed eyes and a slight lift of her chin. I used to think that Sparkle might turn to dust if the sunlight actually touched her, but the recent birth of her nephew, John David, had changed her a lot. She still did her goth thing—black clothes, lips, and fingernails and thick black liner on her eyes—but now she actually smiles on occasion.

Across the room Ox and Isabeau, his significant other, were studying the damaged wedding cake, which appeared to have shed the cracked fondant without trouble. Ox is six feet of well-toned muscle, an African-American Mr. Clean lookalike. He's in his late thirties and he's been a friend since we were in pastry school together. Isabeau is roughly fifteen years younger, short and blond and cheerleader perky.

I couldn't see Dwight Sonntag (another friend from our pastry school days) but I could hear him banging around in the kitchen. Meanwhile Estelle Jergens, fifty-something and the oldest member of Zydeco's staff, hustled out from behind her workstation the instant she noticed me.

Estelle's springy red hair had escaped the bright blue kerchief she was using to hold it in place, and her faded green sweatpants were already bagging at the knees. "Rita? I need to talk to you for a minute. It's important."

Hoping that Estelle wasn't about to hit me with bad news, I stopped walking.

She shooed me toward the front of the house. "Not here," she whispered with a sidelong glance at Ox. "We need privacy."

Uh-oh. I didn't like the sound of that at all. Filled with trepidation, I led her into the front of the house, through the empty reception area, and into my office. I sat behind the desk, and she dropped into another chair, linking her fingers on her lap.

"Is something wrong?" I asked.

"You could say that. Danielle quit this morning."

That wasn't what I'd been expecting her to say. It took a moment for me to process the bombshell since Danielle—our latest temp—had worked at Zydeco for only one day. "Why? What happened?"

Estelle wagged a hand in front of her. "She didn't really say and I didn't think it was my place to ask."

I groaned in dismay. "No wonder Ox is in a mood."

"Oh, he doesn't know," Estelle said. "I haven't told him yet."

He didn't know? Great. That meant his mood would get worse before it got better. "If Danielle didn't tell you why she was leaving, how do you know she quit?"

"I ran into her coming out of the break room and she told me she was quitting."

"Just like that? No explanation?"

"None. She just asked me to tell you."

I sank back in my chair with a sigh. We'd been through three temps in the two months our office manager, Edie Bryce, had been on maternity leave. Number One had been a sweet older woman who was thoroughly baffled by the phone system. Number Two had been a whiz at the computer, but she'd spent most of her time on Twitter and Instagram, leaving work a distant third on her priority list. Now that Number Three had walked out, I wondered if we'd ever find someone who could fill the gap.

"Well, thanks," I said, reaching for the phone. "I guess I'd better call the employment agency and see if they can find us another warm body."

Estelle held up a finger to stop me. "About that . . . I might know somebody who could do the job."

That made me perk up a bit. "You do? Who?"

"My niece, Zoey. She's been looking for work, so she's available right away. I'm sure she could step in and take care of this job with no problem at all."

Estelle was offering me a lifeline, but I didn't jump on the offer right away. Sure, I needed someone at Edie's desk, but I'd had some experience with Estelle's nieces during Mardi Gras the previous year. Frankly, they'd both seemed a bit flighty. Typical for teenage girls, I suppose, but I wasn't sure that either of them was the answer.

Despite my doubts, I didn't want to offend Estelle, so I proceeded with caution. "Aren't they still in school? They're not available to work full-time, are they?"

Estelle gave a little laugh. "I'm not talking about Carmen and Tiffani. They're much too young. Zoey is older. She's my sister Esther's daughter."

As if that would mean anything to me. Estelle had a handful of siblings and she talked about them endlessly. I never could keep them straight, but I didn't want Estelle to know that I hadn't been paying attention, so I nodded as if I knew who she meant. "Then Zoey isn't in school?"

"She graduated four or five years ago. She's twenty-three and like I said, she's been looking for work. She's smart.

And steady. She doesn't spend all her time hanging out with friends or mooning over boys like some girls do. I just know she'd be perfect for the job."

Hope fluttered in my chest. "Does she have any office experience?"

"I'm sure she does, and even if she's not completely up to speed, she's a quick learner."

Translation: Not one minute of experience.

Then again, the three temps we'd hired through the agency had each supposedly had loads of experience and look how they'd turned out.

"Edie's job isn't easy," I said, pointing out the obvious. "We need someone who's highly organized."

"That's Zoey to a T," Estelle assured me. "And she's sharp as a tack." She paused for breath. When I didn't agree immediately, she said, "At least meet her. There's no harm in that, is there?"

She had me there. Other than wasting time if Zoey didn't work out, meeting her wouldn't hurt anything. And maybe, just maybe, this was a blessing in disguise. "I suppose I could talk to her."

A broad smile stretched across Estelle's face. "Perfect! I'll call her. She can be here first thing tomorrow morning. I know she can. And really, Rita, what have you got to lose?"

Actually, I had a lot to lose, but we were shorthanded, and with the Belle Lune Ball coming up so quickly, I didn't have the luxury of second-guessing my decision. Hiring Zoey might be a huge mistake. Training her might put me farther behind than I already was. And if she didn't work out and I had to let her go, would Estelle resent me?

On the other hand, this might be a great solution. Estelle was a dedicated employee and a hard worker. I had to trust that she wouldn't suggest hiring her niece unless she believed that Zoey could do the job.

"All right," I said before I could change my mind. "Give Zoey a call and tell her to come to work. But if she doesn't work out, I'll have to treat her like I would anyone else."

Estelle shot to her feet and bounced a little. "Well, of course you will. I wouldn't expect anything less. Thank you, Rita. Zoey needs this job as much as we need her. You're doing the right thing. Just you wait and see."

"I hope you're right," I said with a smile. "Is there anything else?"

Estelle shook her head and bounced toward the door. "Not a thing."

She disappeared into the reception area, and my stomach gave a nervous flip. I ignored it. I'd learned how to worry from my uncle Nestor, a true master of the art. He could spend days chewing on a subject and tormenting himself with unanswered "what-ifs." I'd seen what worry was doing to his health, and I was determined to take a different path for myself.

Telling myself there was no sense borrowing trouble, I stowed my purse in a desk drawer, grabbed a cup of coffee from the break room, and then headed into the design room, where thousands of gumpaste beads we needed for the beaded evening gown cake were waiting for me to make them. I might not know what would come of hiring Zoey, but I knew for a fact those beads wouldn't make themselves.

By the time I returned to the design room, Ox had moved into the kitchen. While Sparkle applied another layer of crumb-coating buttercream to the damaged cake, Ox directed Dwight and Isabeau as they diced pears and shallots for a chutney recipe we were testing for the Belle Lune Ball.

Unlike Ox, who had initially resisted taking the Belle Lune contract and predicted abject failure, Isabeau had thrown herself into the experience. I suspected that her enthusiasm for learning new and unfamiliar techniques had gone a long way toward softening Ox.

Dwight seemed to be enjoying himself as well. I don't think Dwight has actually seen a barber in several years and he probably won't see one anytime soon. The scraggly whiskers on his chin could have benefited from a trim, but then Dwight always looks rumpled and a little shaggy as if he is perpetually waking up from a long winter's nap. Despite his scruffy appearance, he's one of the most talented cake artists I've ever known.

I looked around for an empty workstation and caught Estelle beaming at me from her station, which made me glad that I'd agreed to give Zoey a chance, and even more hopeful that she'd be the right fit for the job.

I grabbed my chef's jacket from its hook on the wall and managed to get one arm all the way inside a sleeve before Ox noticed me. He motioned for me to join them in the kitchen. I wasn't ready for another distraction. I had too much to do. But he'd been running the show without me all morning, so I finished shrugging into the jacket as I walked.

As soon as I stepped through the door, I realized that Ox, Isabeau, and Dwight weren't alone in the kitchen. Another man, about thirty, leaned against the far counter, arms folded across his chest. He had a dark complexion and deep-set eyes shaded by a ball cap, and he watched closely as the others worked.

I started to ask who he was, but Ox jerked his head again, this time toward the far corner of the cavernous kitchen. I swallowed my curiosity for the moment and tromped over there behind him. Ox doesn't engage in a lot of small talk, so I figured he had something important on his mind.

He got down to business immediately, leaning a shoulder against the kitchen wall and folding his arms across his chest like the mystery man. "Estelle says the new girl quit and you're going to hire her niece instead. Is that true?"

I'm not an expert on body language, but I had a feeling Ox wasn't pleased. I nodded. "I'm going to give her a try."

"What happened to what's her name?"

"Danielle? She quit. That's all I know. Keep your fingers crossed that Zoey is as good as Estelle says she is." I glanced toward the others and lowered my voice so I could ask, "Who's that guy?"

Ox followed my gaze and shrugged. "My cousin, Calvin. Sorry. He showed up a few minutes ago out of the blue. I haven't seen him for years so it didn't seem right to send him away."

I waved that idea away. "Well, of course you couldn't do that. But there's no reason for you to make him stick around here. Why don't you take the rest of the day off? Go spend some time with him. Catch up a little."

Ox started shaking his head before I finished talking. "It's okay. He can wait. We've got too much to do."

"Yeah, but I'm here now, and we're just talking about a few hours. It's fine with me if you want to leave."

"I'll think about it," Ox said in a tone that clearly meant he wouldn't do any such thing. "Tell me, what do you know about this girl?"

I hoped he wasn't getting ready to challenge my decision. I was *so* not in the mood for another round with him. I retrieved a rubber band from my pocket and pulled up my hair, trying to look as if his question didn't bother me. "Not much. Just that she's Estelle's niece. But before you get started, let me just say that I know it's kind of risky, but I don't think Estelle would recommend her if she wasn't up to the job."

Ox quirked an eyebrow. "Maybe you should do a little checking before you commit."

I buttoned my jacket and counted to ten. "I'm sure it will be fine," I said. "How about introducing me to your cousin?"

"In a minute. I'm not sure hiring this girl is the best idea."

My temper sputtered a couple of times. I tried to douse it,

but it flared to life anyway. "Listen, Ox, I know you have your opinions and I know they sometimes aren't the same as mine but it's been more than two years since Miss Frankie made me her partner and we both know I've proved myself. I'm not going to play this game with you every time I make a decision."

My outburst seemed to surprise him. "What game? What is it you think we're doing?"

Was he serious? "You know how much I value your input," I said. "And I wouldn't want to do this job without you. But this"—I waved my hand around as I searched for the word I wanted—"this constant second-guessing me is getting old."

He stood up straight and shoved his hands into his pockets. "I'm not second-guessing you, Rita. I'm just asking what you know about the girl." He glanced around again and lowered his voice. "I only know a couple of Estelle's nieces. Both of them are good kids and all, but if this is someone new, I wonder if that makes her—what was her name?"

"Zoey?"

"Right. If she isn't one of the girls who worked here last year, does that mean she's the niece Estelle was so worried about? If so, that could be a problem."

My stomach dropped with a *kathonk* I swear everyone in the room could hear. "I don't think I heard about that," I admitted. "What was Estelle worried about?"

Ox barked a laugh. "Seriously? Come on, Rita, you *must* have heard about it. She talked about it nonstop for at least a month. Anyone within fifty miles probably heard about it."

It was true that Estelle liked to talk about her family, but that didn't mean I liked to listen. I gave Ox a sheepish smile. "I may not pay strict attention to everything Estelle says. Why don't you remind me?"

Ox rolled his eyes in frustration but his next words took some of the sting out of his irritation. "I don't remember all the details, but I'm sure Isabeau does. What I *do* know is that the kid was dealing with depression. I think she stopped going to church, stayed out late . . . that sort of thing."

I laughed, remembering my own teenage years. "I think that kind of behavior is pretty normal for her age. Is that all? There's nothing worse?"

Ox shrugged. "Her mother was worried. Thought she might be doing drugs at one point. I don't think they ever found proof of that though."

"Then I'm sure there's nothing to worry about. Are you going to introduce me to your cousin?"

Ox looked as if he wanted to argue, but he thought better of it and shrugged. "Sure. Hey, Calvin, come on over here a minute, wouldja?"

Calvin pushed away from the counter and came toward us wearing a friendly grin. He pumped my hand a few times while Ox performed the introductions.

"Calvin's going to be working with our aunt Odessa while he's here," Ox said as he finished.

I'd met Ox's aunt, a voodoo priestess who called herself Mambo Odessa. As voodoo priestesses go, she seemed relatively harmless, but Ox didn't share her beliefs or approve of her practice. In fact, he rarely talked about her at all.

Isabeau looked away from the cutting board covered with pear cubes, a sparkle in her blue eyes. "Isn't that great? I mean, working with Mambo Odessa would be so fun!"

Much to Ox's chagrin, Isabeau was fascinated by his aunt. Unbeknownst to Ox, Isabeau consulted Mambo Odessa regularly. She'd sworn me to secrecy, though. It was a promise I regretted making.

Ox scowled at her. "Good thing you're busy here then."

Calvin ignored Ox and grinned at Isabeau. "I used to help out when I was a kid. I'm looking forward to getting back there." He swept his grin across the rest of us. "If y'all need anything in that line, just come and find me. I'll hook you right up."

Isabeau gave a happy bounce and went back to work. Calvin shifted his attention to me, as if he expected me to place an order for a shrunken head right then and there.

"Thanks," I said, "but I'm not really into voodoo and . . . that kind of thing. Are you from around here?"

Calvin nodded. "Born and raised. Left for a few years after school. Got a great job in Baltimore, but all good things must end so I'm back home for a fresh start. You know how it is."

I knew how it had been for me after my divorce so I nodded. Judging from the scowl on Ox's face, I wondered if Calvin might be escaping some kind of trouble. I was trying to think of a delicate response when my cell phone sang out the familiar ringtone for Zydeco's office manager, Edie Bryce. She's been struggling with her role as a single mother since her son's birth a little over two months ago, so I didn't want to ignore the call.

"Sorry," I said. "I have to take this. It's Edie," I explained to Ox, knowing that he would understand. "It's nice to meet you, Calvin."

"Likewise," he assured me as I scurried away.

I wasn't sorry to cut the conversation with Calvin and Ox short. Family histories can be convoluted, and if there was trouble between the cousins, I didn't want to step into the middle of it. Staying out of other people's business is a rule of mine, taught to me at an early age by the aunt who raised me after my parents died.

Okay, so I didn't follow *all* of Aunt Yolanda's rules. And some of her strictest guidelines were tempered by Uncle Nestor's more pragmatic approach to life. But still, I try to do the right thing. Usually.

Unfortunately, today wasn't the day for avoiding my staff's personal problems. I answered Edie's call and was greeted by a wail so loud I had to hold the phone away from my ear.

"I need help, Rita!" Edie screeched. "And I'm not kidding."

Three

"Did you hear me, Rita?" Edie demanded. "I honestly think I'm drowning here. I'm going under for the third time."

I swallowed a sigh and dredged up a heaping serving of patience. Lately, my conversations with Edie required all I could muster. "What's wrong?"

"Can't you hear?" Edie demanded. "JD has been crying for two solid hours. I don't know what's wrong with him."

Her son, John David, had been born with a healthy set of lungs, and he knew how to use them. But this wasn't the first time he'd exhibited that particular talent, so Edie's reaction seemed a bit over the top to me.

"You've checked all the usual problems? He's clean and dry? Not hungry?"

"Yes. Of course I have. I did all that before I called. He's fine but exhausted, but he won't go to sleep."

I shoved my own concerns onto the back burner and gave Edie my full attention. I even stepped outside onto the loading dock so we wouldn't be interrupted—and partly to keep Sparkle from overhearing my end of the conversation. John David the Unhappy is also her brother River's son, and while the family relations were complicated, I didn't want her to worry.

I don't know River well, but what I do know, I like. Sadly, Edie doesn't know him well either. JD was the product of a one-night stand that was either an ill-timed mistake or an act of fate, depending on which of them you're talking to.

River's clearly in the latter camp and Edie's squarely in the former. And Sparkle tends to get caught in between.

While I didn't have time for a baby breakdown, I couldn't just turn my back on Edie. She was an employee, but she was also a friend. A friend who'd asked me to be JD's godmother. Besides, we'd been limping along without her since the end of October. I needed her back at her desk as soon as humanly possible. Edie is more than just an office manager; she's our anchor. The one who keeps everything together. Without her, organization was in short supply. I figured that the sooner she got motherhood under control, the sooner she'd come back to work.

"I don't know what I was thinking," she moaned in my ear. "I'm so frustrated I don't know what to do. I'm probably the worst mother in the entire world."

"You're a very good mother," I said in my most reassuring tone. "You're just tired and overwhelmed. I know it seems like everything is out of control right now, but it will get better. I promise." It was a big promise and I wasn't entirely convinced about it, but I had to say *something*. Besides, I'd heard Aunt Yolanda say the same thing to other women, and Aunt Yolanda is almost always right.

"That's easy for you to say," Edie said over another unhappy wail from her tiny son. "You don't have to listen to this for hours on end. You don't have to try to figure out why he's so unhappy."

"I know you're out of your comfort zone," I said, raising my voice so she could hear me over the noise. "But believe me, you're doing just fine. You're still in an adjustment period, that's all. Trust me, Edie, if anyone can do this, you can."

"You can say that because you're at work doing what you do best. I'm stuck here surrounded by diapers and bottles and . . . yuck! I spend all my time wiping up poop and spit-up. I haven't slept in days. I haven't eaten a hot meal in two months, and I don't remember the last time I took a shower. Can you come over?"

"Now?" I could feel someone watching me and a quick glance over my shoulder verified it. Ox stood in the open doorway, shamelessly eavesdropping.

"This really isn't a good time," I said, lowering my voice to a near whisper.

"But you're John David's godmother. You *have* to help me before I completely lose my mind!"

"I've been gone all morning," I said. "There's no way I can leave again. Ox would—"

Before I could finish that thought, Ox plucked the phone out of my hand. "She'll be there in half an hour," he told Edie. "Can you hang on that long?"

She must have said yes because he disconnected and thrust the phone at me. "Go on. Get out of here."

"But—"

"It's fine," Ox assured me. "Edie and the baby need you more than we do."

"Don't say a word about this to Sparkle," I warned.

"Not a chance," he assured me. "Now go before Edie has a total meltdown."

This was *so* Ox. He could be a pain in the neck one minute, and a generous, warmhearted friend the next. That's why I would never fire him, even when he gave me a hard time about work. It's also why I'd move heaven and earth to prevent him from quitting if he ever reached the end of his rope. I know it's selfish of me, but I hoped that would never happen.

Edie's apartment looked like a bomb had exploded inside. Clothes, dishes, and baby equipment covered every visible surface. A couple of baby blankets lay curled in the middle of the floor next to an empty pizza box, and the faint smell of urine tickled my nose.

I took one look at Edie's frantic eyes and downturned mouth and decided against asking if anyone had survived the attack. Clearly, she wasn't in the mood.

Edie is short and dark, with a round face and almond-shaped eyes that hint at her Chinese heritage. Her normally shiny chin-length black hair hung in limp, dull strands, and several small white stains dotted the front of her T-shirt.

She's a bit of a control freak, so her appearance and the chaos inside her usually pristine apartment told me more than anything she could have said. Edie believes in having a place for everything and keeping everything in its place, but it was clear that she'd abandoned that method of coping. I could see that her life was completely out of control and she was in desperate need of an intervention. I just wasn't sure that I was the most qualified person to give it to her.

But it was too late to turn back now. I stepped inside and closed the door behind me, bathing the apartment in shadow. I'm not a demonstrative person, and thankfully, neither is Edie. Instead of a hug, which seems to be the traditional greeting of the South, I offered my most supportive smile and said, "I came as soon as I could."

To my surprise, Edie launched herself at me and wrapped her arms around me. "Oh my God, Rita, I'm so glad you're here."

I gave her an awkward squeeze and gently pushed her to

arms' length so I could look at her. "You're being too hard on yourself. You're just tired, that's all."

As if to prove her wrong, John David let out a wail from the other room. Edie's shoulders slumped and the panic in her eyes turned to fear. "He's awake. Again. Why won't he ever sleep?"

I'm no expert on babies, but John David is my godson and I feel it's my responsibility to help Edie with him. Plus, I adore him and have since the minute he was born. "Let me get him," I offered. "You just sit down and catch your breath for a minute."

Edie slid an uncertain glance at the couch, no doubt noticing that there was no place for anyone *to* sit. "I'll move some stuff," she said. "And I'll warm up a bottle. He might be hungry."

I left her to it and hurried into the nursery, where John David had already worked himself up into a fine state—and no wonder. Something nasty had exploded in the nursery as well, leaving brown poo goo on the crib, the baby, and his sleeper.

I'm proud to say that my gag reflex has become slightly less sensitive since JD was born. I stripped off his sleeper and diaper, wrapped him in a spare blanket I found on the floor, and carried him into the bathroom so I could hose him off. There was no way to do that without getting into the shower with him. It was either that or sacrifice my own clothes to the goo, and since I knew nothing in Edie's closet would fit me, I did the only thing I could.

Twenty minutes later, the two of us returned to the living room squeaky clean and relatively happy. The warm water had soothed John David and he hiccupped softly as he cuddled up to me. My mousy brown hair had frizzed up in the shower, but I wasn't planning on going anywhere after I left Edie's, so I didn't worry about it.

I found Edie passed out on the couch and snoring lightly, one hand clutching the bottle she'd made for JD. I swept a pile of clothes from the rocking chair, fed JD, and sang him a couple of songs before he fell asleep just like his mother. I didn't want to risk waking him, so I let him sleep in my arms and marveled at how perfect he was and how beautiful.

I'd grown up an only child, at least technically. My parents died the summer I turned twelve, so I'd then been raised by my aunt and uncle along with their four rowdy boys. Though Uncle Nestor and Aunt Yolanda had never treated me any different than their own kids, and the boys had treated me like a sister, I'd been painfully aware that I didn't really belong.

As a younger woman, I'd nursed dreams of marrying and producing a respectable-sized brood of kids. I'd achieved the first goal, but the marriage hadn't lasted and the kids never materialized. Over time, I'd turned my disappointment into a nonchalant disregard for that old dream, but JD's birth had brought the old longing right back to the surface.

I inhaled JD's freshly bathed baby scent and closed my eyes to savor the moment. They popped right back open again when a man's voice broke the silence.

"Rita? You look tired. Do you want me to take him?"

I stifled a little scream of surprise and focused on JD's dad, River. He's early thirties, tall and trim with short dark hair and a friendly smile. Unlike his sister, Sparkle, River goes for a mainstream look. Even though they have different tastes, I could find plenty of similarities between the two, like the dark eyes that now blinked at me from behind a pair of wire-rimmed glasses.

He took a step toward me, but I shook my head and clutched JD a little closer. "I'm fine," I whispered. "I like holding him while he sleeps."

River stopped moving, but he seemed disappointed. "Yeah. It's great, isn't it? *He's* great."

"He's perfect," I said agreeably and pressed a gentle kiss to the baby's forehead. "Did Edie let you in, or did she finally give you a key?"

River's eyes clouded and he shook his head. "I'm not that lucky. She was still awake when I got here." He glanced at her and a fond smile curved his lips. "I think I'm growing on her, though. She only told me to go away twice before she let me through the door."

I laughed, as I knew he'd meant me to. Edie was still on the defensive where River was concerned, but she'd mellowed a bit over the past couple of months. The fact that he was standing in front of me at all proved that. I just wasn't sure whether letting him stick around today meant that she was ready to let him be part of her life, or if she was simply too tired to fight him.

As if he could read my thoughts, River sank onto the couch near Edie's feet and rubbed his face with one hand. "Do you think I'm making any progress with her?"

I shrugged. I knew he wanted me to say yes, but another of Aunt Yolanda's favorite sayings was that a dishonest opinion has no value. "It's hard to tell with Edie," I said. "Just keep being patient with her."

"That's what you always say."

"Because it's the only way," I said. "If she's going to let you in, she'll have to get there on her own. You can't make Edie do anything she doesn't want to do." JD stirred in my arms and the besotted expression on River's face stirred my heart at the same time. I held out the baby and River took him gladly. "She'd probably kill me for saying this," I said as the two of them settled back on the couch, "but she needs you, and so does John David."

"I'm glad you think so," River said with a weary smile. "I sure wish she would agree with you."

"So do I, but Edie's a hard nut to crack." I smiled gently and stood. "Hold your son," I told him. "I'll see what I can do in the kitchen."

I left the two of them alone and stepped into the kitchen, where I immediately regretted my offer. Dishes lined every inch of available counter space and tilted in stacks on the small table. For the first time, I wondered how long it would really take Edie to pull it together and come back to work.

I spent a few minutes clearing the sink and unloading the few clean dishes still in the dishwasher. I scrubbed and scraped and stacked until I had the dishwasher loaded again, then started it up as I wiped down the table and counters, and nosed around until I found a broom and dustpan. I swept the floor and was reaching for the Swiffer when I heard footsteps scuffing on the floor behind me.

Edie looked around the kitchen and blinked rapidly. "It looks amazing in here." I was afraid she might cry, which would have been awkward for both of us. To my relief, she shook it off and held out her hand for the Swiffer. "I'll do that. You've done enough."

I laughed at the command and checked to make sure there was cleaning fluid in the dispenser. "Sit. Relax. I'm on a roll here. This may never happen again, so accept it while I'm in the mood."

Edie looked like she might argue, but then thought better of it and sat at the table. "The kitchen is clean. The baby is asleep. How can I ever thank you?"

"I didn't do it all," I said. "I'd still be holding JD if River hadn't come by."

Edie stiffened noticeably. "Don't start."

"I'm not starting anything," I assured her. "But it's true. He's a good guy, Edie, and he's utterly besotted with JD. He wants to help."

"I won't deny that, but I'm not getting together with him just because he loves my kid. That would be stupid."

"It's not just JD he cares about."

Edie laughed softly and shook her head. "Whatever. Let's not go there right now. I don't have the energy. I wonder if I'll ever have energy again."

I went over a stubborn stain on the floor with the Swiffer a couple of times. "You'll get back to normal once you're not sleep deprived. Just go with the flow. This is normal for now. Don't waste what energy you do have fighting it."

"I can't just hang around the house forever. I'm going to have to go to work again."

"But not yet. Take whatever time you need. We'll work around you."

Edie's expression sharpened. "What do you mean?"

Her reaction surprised me. "Just what I said. Take whatever time you need."

"You don't want me back?"

I stopped scrubbing the floor and searched her face for some indication that she was joking. I didn't find one. "Of course we want you back. But I want you happy when you come back, and you won't be happy if you're still—" I realized that I might be going the wrong way with that thought and shifted directions. "If you're not ready. That's all I mean."

"I should have known this would happen," Edie said. "Out of sight, out of mind."

Dumbfounded, I leaned the mop against the counter and sat down beside her. I'd been trying to shield her from the reality of life at Zydeco minus Edie, but maybe I'd been wrong. "That's absolutely *not* true," I said. "We're desperate to get you back. We need you. We can't do what we do without you. But I am not going to rush you. I want you back when the time is right."

"I guess this temp person is doing all right then?"

"Hardly." I told her about Danielle quitting and Estelle's idea for a replacement, and then because I'd already told her everything else, I even told her about Ox's concerns. "So I don't know," I said as I wound up. "Zoey might work out and she might not, but we'll keep muddling through until you come back."

Edie sighed deeply, but I thought she seemed a little less worried since I'd been honest with her. "What if Zoey turns out to be amazing?"

I laughed. "I suppose that's possible, but what are the odds? I'm batting oh-for-three in the receptionist arena right now. If she turns out to be amazing, I'll give her a great recommendation when she leaves but she's not taking your job. I promise."

Edie seemed to accept that, so while she made tea, I got up and finished the floor. I left thirty minutes later, utterly exhausted. My arms and legs ached, and my eyes felt gritty with fatigue. It had been a long day, and I hadn't done a single useful thing at work. *Give me physical labor over people problems any day of the week*, I thought as I aimed the Range Rover toward home.

Four

I picked up a burger and fries on my way home from Edie's, ate quickly, and crawled into bed a little after eleven. Even though I was almost dead on my feet, I had so many things on my mind I thought I'd lie awake worrying, but I must have fallen asleep as soon as my head touched the pillow because the next thing I knew my alarm was going off.

The snooze button tempted me, but with payroll figures to pull together before five, a company blog post to write for the Zydeco website, and lunch with Simone—in addition to a few thousand fondant beads to create—I had a busy day ahead. I crawled out of bed reluctantly, put on a pot of coffee, and stepped into the shower while it brewed. I gulped down one cup while I dressed and nursed another as I drove to work.

I'd wanted to get a jump on the day, so it was only a little after seven when I pulled into the parking lot. To my surprise, the employee lot was full; I realized that I was the last to arrive. The staff's dedication to the job is just one of the things I appreciate about them. They've become like family to me since I moved to New Orleans. My evening with Edie and the baby had left me feeling all warm and fuzzy, and looking at the cars in the parking lot that morning ramped the fuzzies up another notch.

I breezed into the design room, and spent a few minutes saying good morning to everyone (except Estelle, who wasn't at her workstation). I verified that Ox and Isabeau would be delivering the restored wedding cake later that morning and then hurried into the front of the house.

One look at the reception area explained why Estelle wasn't in the design room. She was here, pacing in front of Edie's desk and apparently waiting for me. She stopped walking when she saw me and smiled broadly. Her red hair curled all over the place without the kerchief she usually wore to contain it, and her orange shirt clashed wildly with her lime green capris.

"There you are, Rita," she said. "I was starting to think maybe you weren't coming in. You *have* to do something about Ox."

Uh-oh. Ox hadn't looked upset when I said good morning, but maybe I'd missed something. "Why?" I asked cautiously. "What has he done?"

"It's about Zoey," she said with a nod toward the wingback chairs flanking the front window.

My heart sank when I remembered that on top of everything else on my agenda, I had to train Estelle's niece Zoey to do Edie's job, or at least a fraction of it. I did some rapid mental reshuffling as I glanced at the heavyset girl with greasy brown hair who was watching us. The girl—presumably Zoey—wore an oversized T-shirt and jeans that looked at least two sizes too large. Apparently she'd inherited her aunt's fashion sense. When she realized that I'd noticed her, she slumped down so far on her tailbone, it had to hurt.

Not exactly what I'd been expecting. Estelle's other nieces were slim, blond, and bouncy—as if they'd mysteriously fallen from Isabeau's family tree. But Zoey had none of their physical attributes, and it was painfully obvious that she was aware of the difference.

I'd grown up in a poor Hispanic neighborhood without parents of my own and I recognized the look on Zoey's face. It practically screamed, *I don't measure up*, and it tugged at my already fuzzy heartstrings.

"Zoey, say hello to Rita," Estelle instructed.

Zoey glanced up at me from beneath a veil of bangs that obscured her eyes. Her upper lip twitched, which I thought might have been an attempt at a smile. "Hullo."

I'm not the kind of person who routinely takes others under my wing, so the surge of protectiveness I felt for Zoey caught me by surprise. For some reason, I felt an almost overwhelming need to make her feel welcome and appreciated.

I crossed the room toward her and held out a hand. I got some chubby, damp fingers in response. They sat like dead fish in my grip, but I pumped her arm a couple of times and gave her a friendly smile. "We're glad to have you, Zoey. Estelle has told me lots of good things about you."

Zoey's surprised gaze shifted from my face to her aunt's. "You did?"

"Well, of course I did, you silly girl," Estelle chided. "You're smart. You always have been. The only person who doesn't believe that is you."

I knew Estelle meant well, but I didn't think this was the time or the place for such a personal comment. I thought it might bother Zoey but she merely shrugged and looked back at me. "I guess I should say thanks for giving me the chance."

Her enthusiasm was underwhelming but I didn't let it bother me. I didn't know what had hurt Zoey, but I was convinced something had and that cemented the bond I felt for her. I'd spent my early teen years hurt and angry and convinced I didn't belong anywhere. I'd overcome most of those old feelings, but I still struggled with them at times.

"I'm hoping for good things from you," I said warmly. "I'm sure you'll live up to Estelle's predictions."

"Thank goodness someone has good expectations," Estelle said with an irritated glance at the door to the design room. "Ox told her to keep busy until you got here and had the nerve to tell her to move those boxes out of the storage room on the second floor. Can you believe that? It's not even eight in the morning. She's only here this early because she had to ride in with me. Besides, I told him she's not here to do manual labor. She's here to do Edie's job. I told Zoey to sit right down here and wait for you."

"It's okay," Zoey said when Estelle finally took a breath. "I don't mind—"

Estelle cut her off with a flick of her wrist. "I heard what he said yesterday," she said to me. "He doesn't think Zoey can do the job. Or that she *shouldn't* anyway. But I'm not going to let him treat her like . . . like some cheap day labor."

I didn't know which bothered me more, the fact that Estelle had heard Ox talking about Zoey or that she was bringing it up in front of her niece. My protective feelings toward Zoey bubbled up a bit more. I didn't want her to think we'd been talking about her—even if we had.

"That's not what he meant," I assured them both.

"I know *exactly* what he meant," Estelle interrupted. "Really, Rita, I wish you wouldn't try to cover for him."

"I'm not covering for anyone," I insisted. I glanced at Zoey to see how she was reacting to the conversation, but she had embarked on a thorough study of her stubby fingernails. A casual observer might have thought she'd stopped paying attention but I had a feeling she was absorbing every word.

"Obviously there's been a misunderstanding," I said. "Whatever you heard—"

Estelle shook her head so hard a couple of faded red curls tumbled into her eyes. "I won't have Ox acting all high and mighty around my family, Rita. You know how he can get. And the way he told Zoey to start moving boxes like she's some common day labor he hired off the street? He has no right. Just because Zoey is a few pounds overweight—"

Sheesh, Estelle! I cut in before she could make things worse. "Ox wasn't trying to insult Zoey and he doesn't think anything like what you're suggesting. That conversation was private. Whatever part of it you heard was out of context, so let it go, okay?"

Estelle's mouth opened and closed soundlessly a couple of times. "Fine. Whatever. What do you want to do first?"

I wanted to get Zoey away from her aunt's clumsy attempts to boost her self-confidence, but I didn't say so aloud. "I think Zoey and I will be fine on our own. Why don't you go back to work?"

Estelle didn't move until Zoey nodded, and even then, the worried aunt moved off reluctantly. But she did leave us alone, so I counted that as a minor victory.

Zoey stood, hitching up her too-big pants in the process, and spent a moment readjusting her clothes, tugging at her shirt, and wiping the toe of her sneaker on the back of her pant leg, then followed me to Edie's desk. I ran over a few of the basics of the job with her and then left her at the cluttered desk to fill out some paperwork.

Having sorted out both Estelle and Zoey (at least temporarily), I went to my office and booted up my laptop so I could get to work on the payroll figures. I lost myself in numbers for a while and didn't think about Zoey again until a heavy thump overhead snapped me out of my digit-induced stupor. Suddenly aware that I'd left the poor girl sitting at Edie's desk with nothing to do, I hurried into the foyer.

I wasn't surprised to find that Zoey had abandoned Edie's desk but I was embarrassed at my lack of attention. All my good intentions had evaporated the instant Zoey was out of sight. Some mentor I was.

While I stood there chiding myself, I heard a noise above my head. I turned and saw Zoey at the top of the stairs, struggling to hoist a heavy-looking box on top of two others.

"Zoey? What are you doing?"

I must have startled her because she lost her footing and staggered under the weight of the box. She stabilized herself and sent a sheepish grin over the stair railing. "Ox said you needed these boxes moved out of the storage room. I didn't have anything else to do and you were busy, so I thought I could get started."

My cheeks burned with embarrassment. I felt about two inches tall. "Thanks, but you really don't have to do that job. Put those boxes down and we'll start on your training. I'm going to grab a soda. Would you like one? Or maybe some coffee?"

Zoey shrugged. "Sure. Whatever. Soda's fine."

I'd taken only a couple of steps into the hall when I heard Zoey swear, another heavy thud, and a cry of alarm. I made it back to the foyer in time to see Zoey's foot slip from the top step. I watched, frozen in horror, as she tried to catch her balance. The box rocked from side to side, gaining momentum in spite of her efforts to get it under control.

I finally managed to shout a warning and ran toward the stairs, but it felt as if I were moving in slow motion. As I plodded up the first two steps, the box slipped out of Zoey's arms and tumbled toward me. My instinct for self-preservation kicked in and I lunged back downstairs as fast as I could.

Zoey caught the railing and kept herself from falling but the box crashed into the wall, gouging a deep hole in the plaster, and continued down the sweeping staircase toward me. It bounced a few more times, ricocheting between the wall and the railing. Plaster dust and wood splinters flew into the air with every hit.

Zoey staggered away from the edge of the stairs, but in the process she sent another box tumbling. I ducked and covered as the first heavy box bounced past me and the second crashed into the railing with a sickening crunch. Half a dozen newel posts splayed in every direction and a couple of boards on the steps popped up, leaving gaping holes where the stairs should have been.

"Oh my gosh!" Zoey said from somewhere above me. "I can't believe I did that. I'm so *sorry!*"

Both boxes had come to rest on the main floor, sides crushed and tops split wide open. A huge hole gaped in the wall near the top of the stairs, and several beautiful wooden posts leaned out into the room. The damage made my heart sink, but at least I hadn't gotten hurt. I hoped the same was true for Zoey.

"Are you all right?" I called up to her as Estelle, Sparkle, and Dwight burst into the room. No Isabeau or Ox, I noted. They must have been out on the delivery already.

Estelle saw the mess and cried out in alarm. "Zoey! Are you hurt?"

Dwight gaped at the staircase and Sparkle toed one of the boxes experimentally.

Zoey shook her head and took a jerky step away from the edge of the landing, but apparently she'd forgotten that one of the boxes was right behind her. She tripped over it and sprawled into another stack, which sent a third box down the steps toward the rest of us.

This one rolled harmlessly past us, but I didn't want Zoey to do any more damage. "Don't move!" I called up to her. "Just stay put."

Zoey sat up and looked through the railing. Tears filled her dark eyes. "I'm such a klutz!" she wailed. "You must hate me."

Before I could reassure her, Estelle got in my face. "You made her move the boxes?"

"No! I—"

"I did it myself," Zoey wailed. "She was busy and I wanted to be helpful. Don't get mad at Rita."

Dwight muttered something about repairs and turned to me as if he expected me to give him a hammer and nails. Sparkle stepped over one of the boxes and joined him. "What do you want us to do?" she asked.

"Right now?" I glanced around at the damage and sighed. "Go back to work. We'll deal with this later."

Dwight looked surprised. Sparkle shrugged and turned away. Estelle started toward the stairs. "You do *not* have to do the heavy lifting," she said to Zoey.

I wasn't in the mood for that conversation so I tried to divert her attention. "We can sort all of that out later. Zoey isn't hurt and we all have work to do."

"I'm fine, Aunt Estelle," Zoey put in. "Really."

Estelle glared at me mutinously, but in the end she followed Sparkle and Dwight out of the room, leaving Zoey and me alone again.

"Sorry about Aunt Estelle," the girl said. "She's sorta overprotective when it comes to me. So are you going to fire me?"

I stepped over the fallen boxes and piles of plaster and started up the stairs toward her. "Of course not. Accidents happen. The important thing is that everyone's okay."

Zoey sniffed loudly and wiped her nose with the back of her hand. "But the wall! It's ruined. And look what I did to the stairs!"

I was heartsick over the damage to the lovely old building, but I didn't want to make Zoey feel worse than she already did. I kept my face impassive as I stepped over the damaged stairs and sat beside her. "The wall and the stairs can be fixed," I said. "Let's just take a minute to catch our breath and calm down."

Zoey inhaled deeply. Her shoulders rose for a moment and then sagged again. "Aunt Estelle is probably going ballistic."

She might be right, but I gave her my most reassuring smile. "I'm sure she'll calm down soon."

Far from being comforted, Zoey seemed even more dejected. She put her elbows on her knees and rested her chin in her hands. "She loves this place. She told me a dozen times not to screw up this chance, and look what I did on my very first day."

I didn't understand why Zoey seemed so nervous about upsetting her aunt. I'd always considered Estelle harmless enough. *Just another sign of her insecurity*, I thought. "Well, for the record, you didn't screw anything up. I'll vouch for that. And I'm sure you'll do a great job for us."

She slid a look in my direction. I couldn't be sure, but I thought there was a spark of hope in her eyes.

I wanted to see that spark grow and the only way I could help that happen was to show her that I trusted her. "When you're feeling up to it," I said, "I'd like you to go downstairs and check those boxes to see if anything inside was damaged. I'll just make sure the rest of these stacks are sturdy."

"You really aren't going to fire me?"

"Of course not," I assured her again. The smile I gave her felt almost maternal—at least to me. "This is a minor setback, that's all."

For a moment I thought Zoey might hug me, but she just got to her feet and started down the stairs. Instead of going all the way to the first floor, she stopped at the first step with a loosened board and leaned forward curiously. After a moment she hunkered down and pried off the board completely. "Hey, Rita, come and look at this. There's something inside here."

I figured there must be at least a hundred years of dust inside, but since this was the first thing Zoey had shown any real interest in all morning, I moved cautiously down the stairs and craned to see over her shoulder. We were both right. The inside of the step was dusty, but I could also see a lump that clearly wasn't part of the structure.

"What do you think it is?" Zoey said in a hushed voice.

I shifted my position so I could get a better look. "I have no idea. Maybe somebody accidentally left a tool in there."

Zoey frowned up at me. "I don't think so. It looks like it's wrapped up in cloth or something. I think it was put there on purpose. Like maybe somebody wanted to hide it."

She had a point. The lump was nearly a foot long and several inches wide. It was hard to imagine any workman not noticing it there when he nailed the step in place. "Well, then I guess somebody did leave it on purpose," I said. "I wonder why someone wanted to hide it here?"

Honest to goodness excitement lit Zoey's eyes. "I don't know. People do weird things. Wanna see what it is?"

Curiosity has always been one of my weaknesses, but despite what some people think, there's (usually) no harm in it. Besides, I rationalized, a little excitement would do Zoey good. "Sure. Why don't you grab it? We can check it out downstairs."

Without the slightest hesitation, Zoey reached into the opening filled with grime and cobwebs and grabbed the package. Moving it stirred up a cloud of dust that had us both sneezing, but she gamely carried it down the stairs, pausing a couple of times to brush something on a step aside with her foot.

We gathered up a few items that had fallen out of the boxes as they tumbled downstairs, stacked everything in front of Edie's desk, and settled down to check our find. Now that I could see it better, I realized that the package was smaller than I'd first thought. I held the bundle over the trash can, hoping it would catch most of the dust, and gently peeled away a layer of burlap. Beneath it we found a wooden box with an inlaid fleur-de-lis pattern on its lid.

I caught my breath and cut a glance at Zoey, who was leaning forward eagerly. "The workmanship is exquisite," I said. "I think this box was hand-crafted."

"Probably," Zoey agreed. "It looks old, too. It's pretty, isn't it?"

"Very," I agreed. "Now I'm *really* curious. Why would anyone would hide something this beautiful inside a stair?"

Zoey inched forward without lifting her eyes from the box. "Around here, people do weird things all the time. Should we open it?"

I hesitated for a moment. What if somebody had buried a dead pet in the box? I really didn't want to find Fido's skeleton inside. Then again, the box was too small to hold a cat or a dog. A beloved parakeet would easily fit, but who buries a pet inside their house?

Deciding the risk of finding a dead pet was minimal, I tried to open the box. The wood was swollen and stuck tight, but the harder it was for me to get inside, the more curious I became. Not to be defeated, I found a letter opener on Edie's desk and gently eased the sharp point beneath the box lid. It took me several tries but eventually the swollen wood gave way and I was able to pry off the ornate lid.

Inside, another small bundle lay wrapped in a piece of dark blue velvet. "Good grief," I said with a grin. "It's like trying to find the end to a set of Russian nesting dolls."

"Yeah, it's cool. And look at the material. It's velvet, right? So whoever put the box in the stairs must have had money."

"Whoever lived in this house in the first place must have had money," I said with a grin. "This wasn't exactly a pauper's house."

"Whose house was it?"

"I don't know," I said with a shrug. "Researching the history of this house has been on my to-do list for a couple of years, but something else always takes priority." I mentally bumped that research higher on the list.

Zoey laughed and brushed her bangs out of her eyes. "So come *on*. Open it. Let's see what these weird rich people hid."

I removed the velvet, catching glimpses of red as I turned the package in my hands. When the cloth fell away, I gazed in stunned silence at a necklace made up of three rows of red stones varying in size. There must have been a dozen stones, maybe more. The effect was breathtaking.

"Oh. My. Gosh," Zoey said breathlessly. "Are those rubies?"

"No," I said. "I'm sure they're not. It's probably just a piece of costume jewelry." Truthfully, I wasn't sure at all. I don't have much experience with precious stones, but it seemed unlikely that we would stumble across a valuable piece of old jewelry hidden inside the stairs at work. I mean, when does *that* ever happen?

Zoey gave me an odd look. "Why would somebody go to all that trouble to hide a worthless piece of jewelry?"

I gave her a "beats me" shrug and examined the necklace more carefully. "The settings look old. I wonder how long it's been in there."

"Probably since the house was built," Zoey said. "When was that?"

"I'm not sure," I admitted.

"You really don't know anything about this place?"

I shook my head slowly. "I really don't." I would have spent the next hour or two rectifying that on the Internet if the alarm on my phone hadn't chimed just then, reminding me that I was supposed to meet Simone for lunch at noon.

"I don't have time to figure it out right now," I said, disappointed. I wrapped the necklace in the velvet and tucked it back inside the box. "I have a lunch appointment and a lot to do before then, so let me at least show you how to answer the phone while I'm away. I promise I'll train you properly when I get back."

I left Zoey sitting there while I went to the break room for the sodas I'd originally promised. I found a box of beignets on the counter, so I grabbed a couple of those, too. The coffeepot was nearly empty, so I started a fresh pot. Now that the initial shock had passed, I realized that my hands were shaking. The accident must have unnerved me more than I'd realized. I sat for a moment to catch my breath and tried not to think about the damage inflicted on that beautiful old building and whether our insurance would cover the cost of repairs. When my hands stopped trembling, I hurried back to the reception desk.

After handing a soda and a beignet to Zoey, I gave her a crash course on the phone system. She picked it up quickly and didn't seem flustered by the technology, which gave me hope that Estelle had been right about her.

A little while later, I hurried back into my office to gather the files I needed for my lunch appointment. I put the necklace on my desk, promising myself I'd find time to deal with it later.

When I'd rounded up everything I needed, I grabbed my bag and headed for the door but some whisper of caution made me stop. Following instinct or intuition, I went back to my desk and slipped the necklace into my bag. I didn't completely understand why I felt uneasy leaving the necklace behind. I only knew that I'd feel better if I had it with me. Experience had taught me to listen to those little nudges from the voices in my head. They're almost always right.

Five

I arrived a few minutes early for my lunch meeting with Simone, so I sat at the bar while I waited for her, leafing through some of my notes and jotting down ideas for displaying the dress form cakes on the night of the ball. I'd regained my equilibrium after Zoey's unfortunate accident and I was determined to put it and the necklace we'd found out of my mind—at least until later.

I hadn't had time for breakfast that morning, so by the time Simone arrived, a few minutes after noon, I was ravenous. The hotel's restaurant was busy, but Simone has a presence I can't even hope to match. She immediately caught the hostess's eye and a few moments later we were seated at a quiet table far from other diners and the chaos of the kitchen.

We placed our orders—crab bisque (a creamy soup loaded with jumbo lumps of crab meat and pearls of tapioca) followed by pan-seared redfish in red wine matelote sauce for me; roast chestnut ravioli followed by grilled rack of lamb with ricotta *cavatelli* for Simone—and launched into our planning session. While we ate, we adjusted service stations, member exhibits, and silent auction items on paper to fit our new location. Eventually, we worked out all the kinks and settled back to relax.

"So," Simone said as she reached for her water glass. "Tell me what happened this morning. You seem a bit rattled."

"Do I?" And here I thought I'd recovered completely. I wasn't used to having a friend who knew me well so her perception surprised me. "I guess I *am* a bit rattled. We had a new girl start this morning and she had an accident moving some boxes. I guess it threw me."

Simone's eyes clouded with concern. "Nobody hurt, I hope?"

"No, thankfully, but there was some damage to the wall and the staircase. Luckily, we can get by using the back stairs for a few weeks."

It was on the tip of my tongue to tell Simone about finding the necklace, but I held back. I felt like I really should show it to Miss Frankie first, before I told anyone else.

"Of course, this happened at the worst possible time," I added. "We've got the Belle Lune Ball in a couple of weeks and Mardi Gras season is already ramping up. We're going to be swamped for the next couple of months. Not that I'm complaining. I love that Zydeco is doing so well. But having to repair damage to the front stairs is going to make everything harder than it needs to be." I sighed wistfully. "I really need Edie to come back to work."

Simone smiled sympathetically. She'd listened to me vent about the temps who'd come and gone and she knew how much I relied on Edie to keep us organized. "Any chance of that happening soon?"

I shook my head. "I don't think so. I stopped by to see her last night and she's feeling completely overwhelmed. I'd love to have her come back right away, but that's just me being selfish. She needs more time to get used to the whole motherhood thing. But enough about my problems," I said with a determined smile. "What about your day?"

Simone smoothed a small wrinkle from the tablecloth. I knew her well enough by now to read a bit of tension in the action. "Busy, as always. Challenging. I could use a break, but things are only going to get more hectic before the ball is over."

It wasn't like Simone to show signs of stress, and the frown on her usually serene face stirred up my natural tendency to worry. "Is there anything I can help with?"

Simone smiled and shook her head. "It's not a big deal, I swear. I hit this stage every year. About this time in January I vow I'll never work on the ball again, but then I'm right back, front and center, when the next season rolls around."

"I can relate," I said with a laugh. "But I'm here if you need to vent."

"Thanks, but it's just the same old stuff, different year. Crazy society members, old rivalries flaring up. . . the usual stuff. Having to change locations is making it all a bit worse than usual, but it's just a new challenge, right?"

"Right."

"I hope we don't have to do this again," she admitted. "It's really brought the crazies out of the woodwork." She ran her hands over the napkin on her lap and sighed softly. "So how bad is the damage to your staircase? Are you going to be able to get it fixed or is it more serious than that?"

The change of subject surprised me. I wanted to be a sounding board for Simone if she needed one, but I've never had a close girlfriend before and I'm still learning the ropes. I decided to take my cues from her and change the subject.

"I think it can be repaired," I said. "I need to check our insurance, but even if we have a deductible I'm sure we'll be able to afford the work, thanks to the Vintage Clothing

Society. Money's not the big issue, but finding a spare week or two to let workmen swarm all over the place is another matter. Plus, I don't have the time right now to research contractors and find someone who's both good and reliable."

"And qualified to work on a building with historic significance."

"That too." Truthfully, I hadn't even considered that until she mentioned it, and mentally doubled my estimates for repair cost and time.

"If it's not one thing, it's another," Simone sympathized. "If you want a recommendation for a contractor, I could give you a couple of names."

I nodded eagerly. "That would help a lot. Can you e-mail the names to me?"

"No need." Simone dug around in her purse and pulled out a couple of business cards. "This would be my first choice," she said, pushing one of the cards toward me. "We used this firm when we renovated part of the office last year." She handed me a second card, adding, "If they're not available, this guy is almost as good."

Intending to store the contact information on my phone, I reached into my bag. My hand brushed the cool wood of the box and I reconsidered my earlier decision. Simone was a friend. What could it hurt to show her the necklace?

I retrieved my phone and also put the box on the table between us.

Simone arched a delicate eyebrow. "That's exquisite. What is it?"

"Just a little something I found inside one of the broken stairs at Zydeco this morning. You want to see what it is?"

Simone leaned forward eagerly. "What kind of question is that? Of course I want to see."

I opened the box carefully, unwrapped the velvet, and showed her the necklace.

Simone gasped and put a hand to her throat. Her eyes grew wide and darted between my face and the necklace.

"It's not real, of course," I said quickly. "I mean, it couldn't possibly be. But it's pretty, don't you think?"

Simone's eyes landed on my face and stayed there. "I think you're wrong. I think those are rubies—very valuable rubies if I'm not mistaken."

I had started to laugh, but her expression stopped my laughter with a gurgle. I'd never seen a real ruby before, but I was quite sure Simone had. Not that I thought she could value a stone with the naked eye or anything, but she had a better chance of identifying a genuine stone than I did. The only precious stone I'd ever owned was the diamond in my wedding set, and I hadn't worn those rings in years.

"How valuable?" I asked.

"Right now, very. Rubies have become so rare, they're worth more than twice as much as diamonds."

I studied the stones in silence. "If they're real," I said softly, "the necklace must be worth a fortune."

"I'm sure it is," Simone agreed. "It's clearly an antique piece, and it may even have a history that adds value. If I were you, I'd get it appraised. And I'd keep it somewhere safe until you know exactly what you have there."

"I'll do that," I said. "But I want to show it to Miss Frankie before I do anything. She owns the building, so technically, it belongs to her."

"And you say your new temp is the one who noticed it first?"

I nodded slowly. "Yes. Why?"

"Do you think she'll try to claim some kind of finder's fee?"

I hadn't even considered the possibility. "Do you think she might?"

"If she thinks you've found something valuable, she might."

I gave that some thought and finally shook my head. "I

can't imagine her doing such a thing. She's . . . well, she's quiet and unassuming and shy, and besides, she's Estelle's niece."

Simone gave me a look that said she thought I was being naïve. "To the wrong kind of person, a family connection wouldn't mean anything."

I was having trouble enough accepting the idea that we'd stumbled across a valuable piece of jewelry hidden inside the stairs. I was having even more trouble imagining Zoey as someone so greedy she'd try to claim a percentage of the necklace's worth. But suddenly my bag seemed a little heavier and the possibility that I was lugging around a fortune in vintage rubies made my head hurt.

Our server arrived with coffee and we fell silent until she disappeared again.

"Well, I hope you're wrong about Zoey," I said then. "And frankly, I hope you're wrong about the necklace, too."

Simone grinned and stirred cream into her cup. "I swear you're the only person I know who would feel that way. But out of curiosity, where are you headed after this? Back to Zydeco?"

I nodded. "I still have to train Zoey. Why?"

"I need to pick up some pieces from Orra Trussell at the Vintage Vault. She's been in business forever and knows everything there is to know about old jewelry. She might be able to tell you something about the necklace. I just thought you might like to ride over there with me."

I considered the offer, but shook my head reluctantly. "It's tempting," I said, "but I really think I should show it to Miss Frankie first in case there's someone else she'd rather take the necklace to."

"Of course. Miss Frankie knows more people in New Orleans than I do. I'm sure she has a jeweler she trusts."

Just then, something behind me caught Simone's attention.

She lowered her cup to the table and stood. I glanced over my shoulder and spotted a disheveled woman of about thirty winding through tables toward us. It took a moment for me to recognize the woman as Corinne Carver, an employee at the Vintage Clothing Society's French Quarter offices. I'd met her once or twice when I went there for meetings with Simone and her mother, but I wasn't sure what her job was.

"*There* you are," Corinne almost snarled at Simone. "I've been looking all over for you."

Simone gave her a worried smile in return. "Is something wrong, Corinne? You seem upset."

That's my friend, a master of the understatement.

Corinne sighed heavily and made a visible effort to calm down. "You'll never guess who just left my office."

"I won't even try," Simone said. "What happened?"

"Natalie Archer, that's what happened. Do you know what she's done now? She's pushing everybody around, including me. She's not the only person who paid for display space at the ball, but now that the space is smaller, she's demanding that we cut the other displays so she can have the space she wants."

"I'm sure it's a misunderstanding," Simone said in her most soothing voice. "That can't be what she wants. She knows we can't do that."

"It's *not* a misunderstanding," Corinne insisted. "She thinks she's the queen of the world. I told her we couldn't do what she wanted and she threatened to ask the board to fire me."

Simone sighed and nodded toward our table. "Maybe you should sit down and tell me exactly what happened."

Corinne glanced at the table and spotted the necklace, which was still displayed out on the tablecloth. She momentarily fell silent. I hastily retrieved the necklace, wrapped it in the velvet, and slipped the box back into my bag, which had the effect of snapping Corinne out of her stupor.

Simone resumed her seat and Corinne sat sullenly, propping her chin in her hand. "Natalie can't get me fired, can she?"

Simone put a hand on Corinne's arm. "She can ask the board, of course, but there's no reason they would fire you. You're one of the best staff members we have. I haven't heard any complaints about your work, so even if Natalie brought a request like that to the board, I'm sure nothing would come of it."

Corinne relaxed slightly and offered me an apologetic smile. "I'm sorry I barged in on the two of you. Some of our members make me crazy sometimes. Honestly, I don't know who Natalie thinks she is. I've had calls from half a dozen members this morning complaining that she's been trying to bulldoze them into giving up their display space." She shook her head and sighed heavily. "Nobody's going to just hand her a space they paid a thousand dollars for."

A thousand . . . I was growing more used to living in the land of milk and honey, but for a poor Hispanic girl from the wrong side of the tracks, hearing about people paying that much money for a chance to display a few baubles still scrambled my brain.

"Try not to let Natalie bother you. We'll get her calmed down again," Simone said reassuringly. "Rita and I were just having coffee. Would you like to join us? We could figure out the best way to deal with this mess." She looked at me over the top of Corinne's mousy brown hair. "Would you mind, Rita?"

We'd handled all of our business and I couldn't do anything about the necklace until I talked to Miss Frankie, so I assured them both that I didn't mind at all. I finished my coffee while Simone pulled out the notes we'd made earlier and showed Corinne how all the display tables would fit fine.

I listened with half an ear in case they made a decision that would impact Zydeco, but that left my mind free to skitter back to the necklace. I wondered if Simone was right. If the necklace was old and valuable, if the stones were genuine, it could be worth a *lot* of money. But I was more intrigued by the story behind it. Somebody had hidden the necklace inside the staircase, and I wanted to know who . . . and why.

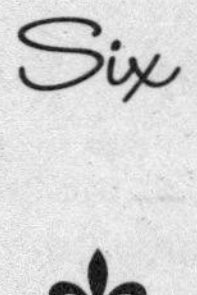

Six

I went back to Zydeco after lunch and spent the afternoon working with Zoey, who peppered me with questions about the computer system and our calendar program, tossing in a question or comment about the necklace every so often. By the time Estelle was ready to leave and came to collect her niece, I was completely worn out and I still had to finish payroll.

Luckily, with everyone else gone, I was able to finish my own work quickly. I zapped the figures to the payroll company and locked up around seven. After twelve long hours, I was ready to curl up with a good book and some Cherry Garcia ice cream, but I didn't want to put off showing Miss Frankie what we'd found. She had friends everyone and I didn't want her to hear about the necklace before I could tell her.

Fog had settled in, so the drive across town took a bit longer than usual. My mother-in-law lives in an upscale neighborhood filled with lots of money and people who don't like to talk about it. Even shrouded in fog, the neighborhood managed to look elite.

I found Miss Frankie standing at the end of her driveway, shining a flashlight on a misshapen cluster of pampas grass. Last time I'd visited, the grass had been roughly eight feet tall and crowned with huge white plumes that fluttered gently whenever there was a breeze. Tonight the bush had shrunk by at least half, and only a couple of white plumes remained.

I parked and got out of the car. "What on earth happened here?"

Miss Frankie glanced at me and gave her head a solemn shake. She was wearing an outfit in winter white, slim pants and a sweater embroidered with gold snowflakes. Even in the near-dark I could see that her auburn hair had been teased and sprayed so well the moisture in the air had no effect on it. Not so for mine; I could feel my hair frizzing a bit more with every passing second.

"Boys from the church," Miss Frankie said sadly. "They came by this afternoon."

"What did they do? Play football in it?"

"No, sugar, they were helping out. Trying to earn money for something. Their youth pastor asked if I had any yard work the boys could do. I wanted to be helpful, of course, so I told them they could trim back a couple of bushes."

I tried not to laugh, but a titter escaped my lips anyway.

Miss Frankie turned toward me with a dejected sigh. "It's hideous, isn't it?"

"I wouldn't say it's hideous," I fibbed. "But it does look a bit sick."

"It looks horrible. They took my money and drove away like nothing was wrong. I didn't even notice it until Bernice came by." Bernice is Miss Frankie's neighbor and dearest friend. I was surprised she'd left Miss Frankie to deal with the

Frankenbush alone. "Can you believe they left it looking like that?"

"I think you should call and tell them to fix it."

Miss Frankie rolled her eyes at my suggestion. "And just how would they do that? Mow it down? Dig it up and burn it?"

I laughed. "Either one might be an improvement."

"A big one," Miss Frankie agreed. She turned away from the bush and squared her shoulders. "What's done is done," she said firmly. "But I've learned my lesson." She tucked a hand into my arm and started walking slowly toward the house. "But let's talk about more pleasant things. What brings you here this evening?"

I pulled my gaze away from that sorry clump of pampas grass and fell into step with her. "I have something to show you. I found it today at Zydeco and there's a good chance it's worth a *lot* of money."

Miss Frankie patted my arm. "That sounds intriguing. Tell me more."

I considered skipping the gory details. Did she really need to know how I'd found it? But I knew I couldn't conceal the damage the boxes had done, and the bad news would be better coming from me so I plunged ahead. "Estelle's niece Zoey started working for us this morning. She was emptying the storage room on the second floor and lost control of a box or two. There are a couple of holes in the wall and there's some damage to the staircase."

Miss Frankie's step faltered, so I hurried to reassure her. "It's not as bad as it sounds. I don't think it will be difficult to fix."

Miss Frankie stopped walking entirely. "How bad is it?"

"Hopefully the cost out of our pockets will be minimal," I said, silently urging her to keep walking. I wanted to get out of this humidity. My hair was so big, I felt like a Chia Pet.

She took the hint, and when we reached the front door,

Miss Frankie ushered me inside and led me into her living room, a large room done entirely in sea foam green and white. She motioned me toward the couch and took a seat beside me.

"I suppose I'll have to come down and see the damage for myself," she said.

"If you want to. Simone O'Neil gave me the names of some contractors. If you have no objection, I'll call for estimates, but I may not be able to get to it until after the Belle Lune Ball." I pulled the necklace in its box from my bag and put it on my lap. "I hope this will make up for it."

Miss Frankie studied the box for a moment and lifted her curious amber eyes to meet mine. "What is it?"

I removed the lid with a flourish and unwrapped the velvet. The stones caught the overhead light and gleamed deep red. The gold setting shimmered and I heard Miss Frankie's quick intake of breath.

Naturally, I understood her reaction completely. I'd known she'd be blown away, too; I'd been looking at the thing all day, and even I had trouble taking it in. It seemed a little more beautiful every time I opened the box. "I know, right? Have you ever seen anything like it?"

"Put it away." Miss Frankie's voice sounded harsh. Clipped. Even angry.

Confused, I frowned up at her. "If you're worried about someone seeing it, I don't think—"

She stood quickly. "I said, put it away. Get that . . . *thing* . . . out of here."

Her reaction was so odd, I had trouble processing it. "Are you talking about the necklace?"

"Of course I am." She wagged a hand at it, then pulled her hand back sharply, as if she'd been burned. "I don't want that thing in my house. I don't want it anywhere near me. Get rid of it immediately."

Was she joking? "Why? What's wrong with you? Do you

have any idea how much it could be worth? It could fund Zydeco's operation for months, if not years!"

My mother-in-law's horrified expression cut off whatever I might have been planning to say next. "Rita, stop. I will not have that necklace in my house, nor will I use it to pay for anything. You shouldn't have it anywhere near you either. If you're smart you'll throw in the river and get rid of it for good."

Except for right after Philippe died, I'd never seen Miss Frankie so agitated. In spite of the fact that curiosity was eating me alive, I wrapped the necklace and returned it to the box, then carried the whole thing out to the car. I wasn't happy about leaving something so potentially valuable unattended, but I reminded myself that Miss Frankie's neighborhood is usually safe. I couldn't keep the necklace in the house—obviously—but I wasn't ready to just drive away without finding out what had prompted Miss Frankie's freak-out.

She had moved into the kitchen by the time I returned to the house. Her hands were wrapped around a glass of iced tea and she stared at the ice cubes as if they'd done something to offend her.

"Okay. It's gone," I said. "Do you mind telling me what that was all about?"

She lifted her gaze and shook her head. "I want you to get rid of that necklace, and I don't mean just put it away somewhere. Do you understand?"

"I understand what you're saying, but I don't know why you're saying it. What's wrong?"

"Nothing. Just do what I say."

My spine stiffened and my jaw clenched. One of the fastest ways to get me angry is to order me around without an explanation. "I'm not just going to toss a clearly valuable antique necklace into the trash," I told her. "And I'm sure not going to throw it into the Mississippi River for no reason. I don't even know if it's even genuine."

"It's genuine all right," Miss Frankie said.

"You can tell just by looking at it?"

"I can tell because I know exactly what that necklace is. I thought it was long gone. Destroyed, I'd hoped. Are you telling me it's been at Zydeco this whole time?"

I sat across the table from her. "It's been there awhile anyway. As long as I've been there. Why would you hope it had been destroyed? It's beautiful."

"It's cursed," Miss Frankie snapped. "If you have that necklace in your possession, something horrible will happen."

I laughed. I couldn't help myself. Miss Frankie is the most practical person I know—at least most of the time. With all the mystical, magical things swirling around New Orleans, her feet remain firmly on solid ground. I didn't know why she was pretending to believe in some curse now, but I wasn't buying her act.

"Very funny," I said. "I've been carrying it around with me all day and nothing bad has happened yet."

"I'm not joking," Miss Frankie barked. She followed that declaration with the sign of the cross, which was really odd since she's not Catholic. "That's the Toussaint necklace. It disappeared in 1885 and it hasn't been seen since."

Confusion made it hard to follow her. "If it's been missing, how do you know what it is?"

"I've seen the painting. I've heard the stories."

"What painting?" I asked. "What stories?"

She waved off my questions. "You don't want to know."

Oh, but I did. She wasn't going to fill me in though, so I switched gears. "So those are actual rubies? For real?"

Miss Frankie let out a shudder that racked her entire body. "Yes, but they're dangerous. They're cursed, Rita. Cursed."

"Surely you don't believe that."

"I most certainly do."

"What kind of curse do you think is on it?"

"I don't think there's a curse, I *know* there is, and that's all I'm going to say on the subject. You get rid of that vile necklace at once and we'll say no more about it."

I opened my mouth to protest, but she held up a hand to stop me. "No, Rita. I'll say no more. I've said too much already. You're just going to have to trust me on this."

I'd never seen Miss Frankie like this but her odd behavior only made me more curious. I could tell that she meant what she said, and I knew better than to push when she'd made up her mind, so I zipped my lip and tucked my questions away for a later time.

"All right," I said. "If you say so."

"You promise you'll get rid of it? Immediately?"

"You'll never have to see it again," I vowed. That seemed to mollify her, but if she really thought that I would throw away the necklace and let the matter rest, she didn't know me very well at all. Miss Frankie might not have to see the necklace again, but I was determined to find out everything I could about it and about the curse that had her so rattled. What Miss Frankie didn't know wouldn't hurt her.

Maybe she wouldn't talk about the necklace, but *someone* would. All I had to do was find the right person.

I left Miss Frankie's house intending to go straight home, but halfway there, I changed my mind and drove to the Dizzy Duke, the Zydeco staff's favorite after-work watering hole. I was in the mood for one of Gabriel Broussard's margaritas. I hoped a little tequila and some time with a hot Cajun might take the edge off after my strange conversation with Miss Frankie.

The Duke is a redbrick building in a rundown neighborhood two blocks east of Zydeco. I stepped into the dimly lit interior and headed straight for the polished wood bar that stretched across one end of the long, narrow room. Most of the round tables surrounding the dance floor were filled, and the house band was playing on the small raised platform at the far end of the room.

Laughter and conversation ebbed and flowed all around me. It was nearly ten so it didn't surprise me when I didn't see anyone from Zydeco in the crowd, but Gabriel was holding court behind the bar and that's all I needed. He's all sorts of male sexiness, from his chocolate brown bedroom eyes to his killer smile and a few other attributes that haven't escaped my notice. One lazy shank of dark hair fell across his forehead. I swear it does that just to make women swoon.

Besides just his physical appeal, Gabriel's easy to talk to. He and I have been dancing around a relationship of sorts for a while now. I'm not sure which of us is holding back more—Gabriel's true intentions are still a mystery, and he's not the only guy in my life, which tends to complicate things.

My insides did their usual flippy thing as I bellied up to the bar. Hoping to have an equal effect on him, I offered my most seductive smile. I'm not sure I succeeded. It felt more like a grimace from my end.

Gabriel slid a coaster onto the bar in front of me and leaned in so close I could feel his breath on my cheek. "You're here late. Long day, *chérie*?"

His voice worked on me like a shot of aged whiskey, warming me from the inside out. I hooked my bag over my knee and swung my legs under the bar's overhang. "That's putting it mildly. Is anybody else still around?"

He slid a glance over the crowd. "One or two people. Were you hoping to get me alone so you could have your way with me?"

We hadn't gotten that far yet, but we liked to flirt about it. I grinned and shook my head. "Another time. You know who I meant. Anyone from Zydeco still around?"

"Dwight was the last man standing and he left about half an hour ago. Something wrong?"

"No, not really. It's just been a weird day. How about making me one of your world famous margaritas? But you'd better make it light," I warned as he turned away. "I'm driving."

He pushed a bowl of peanuts in front of me and went to work blending what is probably the world's finest drink. He is a true master at his craft and his salt-to-rim ratio is absolutely perfect.

I munched happily and glanced around at the other occupants of the bar, most of whom looked familiar even if I didn't know their names. Another couple of years and I might even feel as if I belonged in this neighborhood.

Gabriel was back in a few minutes with my drink, as well as a plate of shrimp and grits. He put both in front of me, followed up with silverware and a napkin, and grinned at the confusion on my face. "I know, I know, you didn't ask for it. But I also know you pretty well. I'm betting you haven't eaten since breakfast."

"Ha!" I said, reaching for the spoon. "I had lunch. Shows what you know."

Gabriel shrugged. "You want me to take it away?"

I wrapped my arm around the plate. "Touch it and die."

The shrimp was perfectly cooked and well seasoned. The grits were prepared just the way I like them, and creamed with Asiago cheese. The sweetness of the shrimp mingled perfectly with the tang of the cheese. I'm not sure, but I think I may have moaned aloud as I ate.

Gabriel watched me for a few minutes while he worked, a grin playing with the edges of his mouth. When he came back to me, he said, "You want to tell me about your day? Or are you going to keep your mouth too full to talk?"

I shrugged and put down the spoon. "There's not much to tell really. Estelle's niece started working at Zydeco today."

"Yeah. I heard. Estelle seemed happy."

"I guess she is," I agreed. "But the thing is, Zoey caused a bit of an accident. Put a hole in the wall. Ripped up a couple of stairs . . ."

"Some accident. You thinking about firing the girl or something?"

I shook my head. "Of course not. It was an unfortunate mishap, that's all." I argued with myself about mentioning the necklace, but decided Gabriel was worth the risk. I glanced around to make sure nobody was paying attention to us and asked, "Have you ever heard of something called the Toussaint necklace?"

One eyebrow shot up beneath that lazy lock of hair. "I've heard of it. Why?"

So it *was* a known thing. Huh. Well, at least he hadn't run away screaming. I was encouraged by that. "What do you know about it?"

Gabriel shrugged. "Not much. Just that it has some kind of mysterious history and that it's been missing for a long time."

"That's it? You don't know anything else?"

He gave me an odd, searching look. "I've heard things."

"What have you heard?"

"This and that. Why the sudden interest?"

If I didn't know better, I'd swear he was trying to avoid answering. "I'm trying to find out if the rumors I've heard are true," I said.

"What rumors would those be?"

I gave an airy wave of my hand. "Nothing major. Just something about a curse." I locked eyes with him and said, "You don't know anything about *that*, do you?"

He gave another shrug, probably trying to look casual, but he kept his eyes locked on mine and didn't even blink. "About a curse? I might have heard a thing or two."

"Well, then, would you mind telling me?" I was over the

game playing. "I think I may have actually found the thing, and if I really do have it, I'd like to know what the story is."

Gabriel broke eye contact and swiped at the bar with a rag. "If you really do have it, you might want to get rid of it. It's supposed to be bad news."

I wanted to hear his take on the story, so I pretended ignorance. "In what way?" When he didn't answer me immediately, I gave up on the innocent act and said, "Come on, Gabriel. I just showed the necklace to Miss Frankie and she wigged out on me. I think I deserve to know why, don't you?"

His shoulders twitched. "You showed it to Miss Frankie and she had that kind of reaction? Where is it now?"

"Someplace safe." To make sure, I checked the strap on my knee.

Gabriel glanced at the people sitting closest to us and lowered his voice. "You have it *here*?"

"What if I do? Does that make you nervous?"

He didn't answer right away. He just strode away, talked to the other bartender for a moment, and then came out from behind the bar. He took me by the arm and tugged me from my stool. "Come on. We're going outside."

In spite of my attraction to Gabriel, I have an aversion to being manhandled. I pulled my arm away and hitched my bag onto my shoulder. "Gee, Gabriel, you sure know how to sweet-talk a lady."

"Yeah, well, good thing I'm not trying to sweet-talk anybody right now." He strode purposefully toward the door and I followed, too curious to argue. A dozen questions danced on my tongue but I held them all in. Gabriel's reaction was as out of character for him as Miss Frankie's had been. I honestly didn't know if that made me nervous or curious. Maybe both. I did know that I was a whole lot more determined to find out what the deal was with the necklace in my bag. I just hoped somebody would be willing to start talking.

Gabriel didn't speak again until we were standing outside in front of the Dizzy Duke and he'd satisfied himself that nobody was within hearing distance. Then he held out one hand and waggled his fingers impatiently. "Let's see this thing."

"Here?" I laughed and shook my head. "I don't think so. You can come by my place later if you want. I'll show it to you there. What's the big deal anyway? Don't tell me you believe in the curse of the necklace."

Gabriel's expression tightened at my mocking tone. "I don't believe or disbelieve," he said, "but I have a healthy respect for things like that. You should, too."

I folded my arms across my chest and lifted my chin defiantly. "It would be a whole lot easier to respect the stupid curse if somebody would tell me what it's all about."

Gabriel let out a breath heavy with impatience and swept the lock of hair from his forehead. It fell back immediately, but he didn't seem to notice. "I don't know that there's an actual curse, but people who have had that necklace in their possession have a bad habit of dying."

My mouth fell open. "Seriously? Like the Hope Diamond or something?"

"Something like that."

"I've been carrying it around all day and I'm still here."

"For now."

The concern in Gabriel's expression was touching, but unwarranted. "How did the necklace get a curse on it?"

Gabriel glanced over his shoulder once more and led the way to a bench on the curb. "My grandmother used to talk about it," he said when we'd settled in. "I don't know if I can remember the whole story, but what I do remember is that a guy named Armand Toussaint had the necklace made for his mistress back in the day."

I interrupted to ask, "What 'day' would that have been?"

"Right around the end of the War Between the States, I

think—what you Yankees like to call the Civil War. Anyway, I guess he promised the necklace to her, then changed his mind and gave it to his wife instead. The mistress was furious."

"Understandably so," I said. "Not that I condone the whole mistress thing, but still, that's a pretty lousy thing to do. A promise is a promise."

"That's what she thought, too, apparently, since I'm told she put a curse on the necklace and within a week both Toussaint and his wife were mysteriously dead."

"No joke? Okay, so that's a bit freaky," I admitted. "So after that people believed in the curse?"

"I'm not sure it was right away," Gabriel said. "According to Grandmère, people didn't really start believing the whole curse thing until a few years later, when Toussaint's nephew inherited the estate and gave the necklace to his bride—who died within a year, shortly after giving birth to their only child."

Even I had to admit that was oddly coincidental. "Is that when the necklace disappeared?"

Gabriel shook his head. "That happened years later, when Toussaint's nephew gave the necklace to his daughter on her wedding day."

I shifted uncomfortably on the cold bench. "Don't tell me she died, too."

"Six months later."

"But c'mon," I argued. "That was a long time ago, when people died from all kinds of things. Medicine wasn't like it is now. They could have contracted some disease making the rounds or . . . whatever."

"Could have," Gabriel agreed. "I don't think we'll ever know for sure. But after the daughter died, the necklace disappeared and nobody has seen it since. Until now."

"Maybe," I reminded him. "I don't know for sure that's the same necklace I found. It could be something else."

Gabriel nodded absently for a moment, staring at something—or nothing—in the shadows. "So what are you going to do about it?"

I thought about Miss Frankie's frightened reaction to the necklace and her insistence that I get rid of it. But I think we both knew I couldn't do that. "I guess the first thing to do is find out if it is actually the Toussaint necklace. Simone gave me the name of an appraiser earlier. I'll take it to her tomorrow."

"And if it is the Toussaint necklace?"

"I don't know," I admitted. "I guess I'll cross that bridge when I come to it. But really, Gabriel, how bad can it be?"

"Just make sure you watch out for yourself, *chérie*." He pulled me into his arms and kissed me thoroughly enough to curl my toes and straighten my hair. I melted and kissed him back. And I told myself that maybe this curse wasn't such a bad thing after all.

But of course, I was wrong.

Seven

I spent the next day at work catching up on everything I'd let get behind. I made edible beads in the morning, rolling gumpaste into strings that would fit into silicone molds, pressing to make sure I got rid of any air bubbles, then scraping away the excess to avoid creating rough edges. Once I had each string perfectly in place, I unmolded the beads and started all over again.

It was mindless work, really, which gave me plenty of time to think. My mind kept ping-ponging between Miss Frankie's reaction to the necklace and Gabriel's story (plus that kiss, of course). I thought about Armand Toussaint, his wife and mistress, and his poor nephew's wife and daughter.

The story of the Toussaint necklace was intriguing, but I still wasn't convinced that the necklace in my purse was the genuine article. I'd made up my mind to take Simone's advice and get it appraised. The Vintage Vault seemed like a reasonable choice if, as Simone claimed, Orra Trussell was knowledgeable about old jewelry. According to the Vault's website, it was open until seven. I planned to slip away after work and get an expert opinion.

Thinking about the necklace, Miss Frankie, and Gabriel was distracting, though. When I unmolded three flawed sets of beads in a row, I tried to put the whole thing about of my mind and concentrate on the job I was being paid to do. That worked for a few minutes until the worried look on Gabriel's face would flash through my head and the whole thing started all over again.

Eventually, I made all the beads I thought we'd need for the evening gown cake (and a few extras for the inevitable mishaps), then dusted them with pearl dust and moved the strings into storage containers to be kept cool and dry until we were ready to apply them to the cake.

With the bead situation under control, I moved into my office to sort through the accumulation of mail that Zoey had put on my desk. I was pleased to see that she'd caught on to the phone system and was adept at taking messages. When Edie took notes during a call from a prospective client, she gathered all the information I might ever need to know plus a little bit more. Zoey's notes were sparser, but the crucial information was there.

She seemed to have recovered from the accident on the stairs the day before, and had even attempted to help with the repairs by researching contractors who specialized in restoring historical properties. I found a file full of information printed from the Internet piled up with the mail on my desk.

Even with so much to do, the hours seemed to crawl by. At last, though, the workday was over and the staff started making noises about meeting at the Dizzy Duke. I begged off, pleading a headache, and waited until I was alone to pull up the GPS directions to Orra Trussell's shop on my phone.

Vintage Vault turned out to be a smallish shop in the middle of a block crowded with numerous mom-and-pop stores. The street in front of the Vintage Vault was blocked by a couple of Dumpsters catching debris from the renovation of a record store two doors down, so I parked three blocks away and walked back to the shop.

That early evening's warm winter sunlight cast dappled shadows on the uneven sidewalks and jazz blared from a stereo somewhere out of sight. Walking around New Orleans isn't always enjoyable for me, mostly because of the heat and humidity—my desert-loving lungs hadn't completely adjusted to living at sea level, and I still felt waterlogged when the humidity rose to fifty percent—but the winter months in Louisiana are my favorites. Cool temperatures and a low level of mugginess made winter feel more like the springs I remembered from childhood.

I wondered what I would do if Orra actually identified the necklace in my bag as the cursed Toussaint necklace. Would I heed Miss Frankie and Gabriel's advice and get rid of it? Or would I take a risk and try to sell it? I didn't think I'd keep it. It was beautiful, but not really my style.

Did I believe in curses? I didn't think so. Aunt Yolanda had raised me on the fear of God, but she had also warned me to keep my distance from anything of the woo-woo variety. She had a strong belief in the divine, but she also believed in hell and everything that went with it. I believed that evil existed, but curses? The jury was still out.

Inside the shop I found a plump woman of around sixty behind a glass counter containing several old-looking pieces of jewelry and some beaded evening bags. A half-buried sign on the counter told me that the Vintage Vault had been in business since 1980, which I found impressive. Who knew a person could make a living for so long selling other people's castoffs?

The rest of the store was cluttered with racks of clothing

and displays of shoes and accessories, but I didn't see any other customers, which was fine with me. I wanted Orra's thoughts on the necklace, but after talking to Miss Frankie and Gabriel, I was ready to err on the side of caution. If I was lugging a possibly valuable and potentially cursed piece of jewelry around New Orleans, I didn't want anyone else to know I had it. Too many people had seen it already.

The woman behind the counter had blunt-cut salt-and-pepper hair and wide pale eyes. She sent me a beaming smile, which plumped up her cheeks and made her look like a garden gnome. "Good evening. How can I be of help?"

"I'm looking for Orra Trussell," I said. "Is she in?"

She bounced up onto the balls of her feet and thrust a hand toward me. "I'm Orra," she said. "And you are?"

"Rita Lucero." I gave her hand a quick shake, surprised by the strength of her grip. "I'm with Zydeco Cakes."

"Rita Lucero. Now why does your name seem familiar? Have you been in to see us before?"

I shook my head. "No, but my bakery is catering the Belle Lune Ball for the Vintage Clothing Society in a couple of weeks. Maybe you've heard of me that way."

"Yes, yes. Of course. I've seen your name on some of the updates I've received." She bustled out from behind the counter. "What can I help you with, Rita? A costume for the ball maybe?"

"No, thanks." I glanced around the shop to make sure we really were alone and drew the wooden box from my bag. "Simone O'Neil suggested that I talk to you. I came across a necklace recently, and she thought you might be able to tell me if the stones are genuine." I didn't mention the curse or give her the Toussaint name. I didn't want to put ideas in her head.

Even so, I saw a jolt of recognition in Orra's expression when she saw the wooden inlay on the box, and heard the sharp intake of her breath when I lifted the lid. Her gaze shot to my face as she demanded, "Where did you get that?"

Weird reaction number three. My heart began to beat a little faster. "Do you know what it is?"

Orra put one hand on her chest and met my gaze. "It looks a great deal like a necklace that's been missing for a century and a half. Where *did* you find it?"

"Hidden inside a staircase," I said without elaborating. I asked the same question I'd asked Miss Frankie. "If it's been missing for so long, how do you recognize it?"

"The portrait, of course." Orra's answer came out a bit sharp. She blushed and smiled apologetically. "You couldn't know, of course, but I've seen the portrait of Beatriz Toussaint, the original owner of the necklace, wearing it. And you say you found it inside a staircase?" At my nod, she let out a breath and returned her attention to the necklace. "I suppose it would have had to be something like that," she mused. "It disappeared so completely, you know."

"That's the trouble," I said. "I don't know. Obviously you're familiar with it. Is this genuine?"

Orra lifted the necklace from the box for a better look. The gems caught the light and glowed deep red. "I can't tell just by looking at it, but I'd be happy to examine it for you. It would take some time, though."

A noise from the back of the shop caught Orra's attention and a young woman came into the showroom carrying an armful of clothing. She was tall and thin with a head of unruly dark hair and so much jewelry on her neck and wrists she jingled when she walked. "I finished sorting the clothes from the Yarborough estate sale," she said as she burst into the room. "There are some valuable pieces, I think, but we'll have to have everything cleaned. The whole collection reeks of moth—" She broke off when she noticed me and gave an embarrassed laugh. "Sorry. I didn't realize we had a customer."

"That's quite all right," Orra told her. "Although perhaps next time you could be sure I'm alone first. My assistant, Dominique Kincaid," she explained with an apologetic smile, and immediately returned to the necklace. "I would say that if this is a reproduction, it's quite a good one." She touched a couple of the stones almost reverently. "But I'll need you to leave it with me for a few days. You're prepared to do that, I assume?"

A frisson of something unpleasant raced up my spine. "Leave it? I don't know if I can do that, but I'd be glad to bring it back when you have more time."

Orra's pale eyes clouded. "Well, of course, if that's what you want. It's just that it's very hard to know when I'll actually have time to look at the piece. It would be much better if you could leave it with me. I'll get to it when I can and let you know when I'm finished."

I wondered if she knew how much the necklace would be worth if it was genuine, and decided she must. "I understand, but I really don't feel comfortable leaving it." From the corner of my eye I noticed Dominique inching closer to where we stood. "The necklace is not actually mine. I'm just making inquiries for the owner." The facts that the actual owner wanted nothing to do with the necklace and hadn't asked me to pursue anything were mere technicalities.

A deep frown furrowed Orra's forehead. "The ownership of that necklace—*if* it's genuine—has been in dispute for some time. I don't know that anyone can rightfully claim ownership without some legal wrangling."

I couldn't hide my confusion. "Are you saying it was stolen?"

Orra shook her head. "Not stolen exactly. You know the story of the piece?"

"A bit of it," I admitted. "I've been told that it might be the Toussaint necklace, but that's about all I know."

At the mention of the Toussaint name, Dominique looked quickly from Orra to me. "Is it?"

"It could be," Orra said. "If so, you have to know that there will be a great deal of interest in it once word gets out—and not only because it's worth serious money. The stones alone are extremely valuable. Rare value, exquisitely cut. But it's the story behind the necklace that really adds to the value."

"I've only heard a little about the family," I said. I'd heard Gabriel's version of the story, but I wanted Orra's. "Can you tell me what the story is?"

Orra smiled and looked pleased at my request. "The piece was commissioned by a man named Armand Toussaint near the end of the Civil War. Even then it was worth a small fortune."

"Who was Armand Toussaint?" I asked. "Someone famous?"

"I wouldn't use that word, but he was wealthy and powerful. The Toussaint family settled here in the middle of the seventeenth century and at one time owned land all along the Mississippi River. Armand married Beatriz de la Hera, whose father was from Spain and probably the only man in the area with more money than Henri Toussaint."

"Henri was Armand's father?"

Orra nodded. "They were fabulously wealthy before the war, but like so many people, the conflict wiped out a great deal of their fortune. Armand still had some money, though—obviously."

"Enough to buy a necklace like this for his wife," I said disingenuously.

"Oh, it wasn't for his wife, dear." Orra's mouth pinched in disapproval. "You must understand the way things were back then. It wasn't unusual for a wealthy white man to . . . dally with a woman of mixed race."

That was a twist Gabriel hadn't previously mentioned. "Are you saying that his mistress was a slave?"

Orra shook her head. "Not a slave. Society had various systems in place back then. *Plaçage* existed to connect white men and free women of color. The men provided generously for the women and they . . . well, I'm sure you can figure out the rest."

"Without any trouble at all," I assured her.

Dominique had stopped near a crowded display of shoes and began tidying as if she was concentrating on work. I suspected she was listening to our conversation very carefully.

"Most wives knew what was going on," Orra said. "They weren't stupid, and the men made no particular effort to hide what they were doing. But well-bred women were expected not to acknowledge their husbands' activities."

I thanked my lucky stars that I hadn't been born back then. I'm not sure I could have conformed to the expectations. "So Armand had a mistress and Beatriz turned a blind eye to his philandering?"

"So the story goes." Orra leaned against the counter, warming to her subject. "Armand commissioned the necklace in question for his mistress, Delphine Mercier, and rumor has it that when Beatriz found out, she raised holy hell. She had plenty of jewels in her own collection, of course, but nothing as fine as that necklace. I guess she didn't mind Armand sleeping with Delphine, but she drew the line at her getting better gifts than those he gave his wife."

"Especially if they'd taken a financial hit during the war," I mused.

"I would say that had a bearing," Orra agreed. "Anyway, the story is that Armand relented and gave the necklace to Beatriz instead. Some people say the necklace is cursed—"

I leaned forward, eager to hear more, but the front door

opened and a large round man rolled inside. He looked to be about forty, with an abundance of facial hair and thick brown hair on his head that curled down to brush his collar.

Orra cut a meaningful look at me and whispered, "Try not to let Sol see the necklace, dear. But if he does see it and offers you money, tell him no. Sol Lehmann is notoriously greedy—*and* cheap. And Miriam, his wife, is even worse. She's a barracuda. Just be warned, Sol won't give you anywhere near what the piece is worth."

With that warning, Orra surged away, arms open wide as if she were greeting her BFF. "Well, Sol Lehmann, I haven't seen you in this neighborhood for months! What brings you our way this evening?"

Sol returned her hug, but I was pretty sure his heart wasn't in it. He extricated himself as soon as he could and started strolling along one of the aisles. "Don't worry about me, Orra. I can see you have a customer. I'm fine to look around on my own."

Orra gave him a playful slap on the arm. "Don't be silly, Sol. I'll be right here in case you have any questions. Dominique is finishing up with Ms. Lucero so you have my full attention."

Dominique stopped sorting shoes and started toward me.

Sol acknowledged Orra's offer with a dip of his head. "Very well. I heard a rumor that you picked up the Yarborough estate sale. I thought I'd stop in to see what you've found. Naturally, I want the first option on anything of value."

He seemed to be paying attention to Orra, but I could see him eyeing my box on the counter curiously. If the necklace really was valuable, maybe letting Sol Lehmann see it wasn't such a bad thing. Orra had been recommended to me, but that didn't mean I had to trust whatever offer she made me. A little competition might drive up the price. Still, with her warning ringing in my ears, I started to wrap the necklace back in the velvet. But as I went to place the necklace into the box, I had second thoughts.

I'd warmed to Orra, and the truth was, I didn't have time to schlep the necklace all over town looking for someone who could appraise it while I waited. It made sense to take Orra up on her offer.

"Was there something else?" Dominique asked as she slid behind the counter.

"Yes, I'm going to leave this with Orra after all. Do you think she'll have time to do the appraisal this week?"

Dominique held out her hand for the box. "I'm sure she will. We're busy getting ready for the Belle Lune Ball, but I'm sure she'll work in an appraisal soon." She pulled out an order pad and pushed it across the counter toward me along with a pen. "If you'll just fill in your contact information—"

I wrote down my name and cell number and gave the pad back to her. Dominique filled in the rest of the form with a flourish and handed me a copy. "Give us a few days. We'll get back with you as soon as Orra has had a chance to look the necklace over."

I tucked the receipt into my bag and waved to Orra as I left the Vintage Vault. I suspected that she knew more about the Toussaints, but clearly she hadn't wanted Sol to overhear our conversation. I'd just have to be patient and wait for my next chance to talk with her alone.

Eight

Dusk was settling over the city as I left the Vintage Vault, and the temperature had dropped at least ten degrees while I was inside. With nothing to do that evening, I strolled back toward the Range Rover, checking out the shops on the street and letting my imagination run wild with guesstimates about how much I thought the necklace might be worth.

We'd had a rough go at Zydeco after Philippe died, and Miss Frankie had sacrificed to keep the company afloat. I'd love the chance to contribute to the bakery's financial well-being. Surely she wouldn't object to my selling the rubies and using the money to fund our operation.

I'd gone about a block when a tall black man in a suit stepped out of a recessed doorway right in front of me. I swerved to step around him but he moved in the same direction. We did an awkward little dance on the sidewalk, each of us trying to avoid impact. I was paying more attention to the uneven concrete than to my dance partner, so when he let out a whoop, I jerked backward and nearly fell.

He grabbed my arms to steady me. "Rita, right? It's Calvin." He put a hand on his chest and tried again. "Ox's cousin, remember? We met the other day."

"Yes, of course. I'm sorry. I didn't recognize you." I was a little embarrassed, but in my defense, Calvin looked completely different than he had the first time I saw him. When we'd met at Zydeco, he'd been wearing worn jeans, a T-shirt and a ball cap. He'd also been sporting two days' growth of whiskers. Today, he was clean shaven and wearing a silk suit that looked as if it had been tailored to fit.

"Are you okay?" he asked. "Did I hurt you?"

I shook my head quickly and smiled to prove that I was hale and hearty. "I'm fine. No harm done." And then, because I felt awkward just standing there smiling, I asked, "Is this your day off? You're not helping Mambo Odessa today?"

He looked confused by my first question, but his expression cleared in response to my second. "No. Yeah. I'm not working today. Just taking care of a little personal business and about to have dinner." He stuffed his hands into his pockets and glanced down the sidewalk. "I don't suppose you're free? You wouldn't want to join me, would you?"

The offer caught me by surprise. "For dinner?"

He shrugged. "Unless you have other plans. Nothing fancy. I was just gonna grab a bite at Mama June's around the corner. It's kind of a dive, but it's got great food and I'd much rather have someone to talk to than eat alone."

It was on the tip of my tongue to refuse, but I caught myself before I could. I wasn't in the habit of accepting dinner invitations from strange men, but Calvin wasn't exactly a stranger and it wasn't as if he was asking me for a date or as if I had other plans. In fact, my social calendar—if I'd had such a thing—would have been glaringly empty.

"Sounds great," I told him. "Lead the way."

We made small talk until we reached Mama June's, a small white brick building sporting a chalkboard menu on the sidewalk. Today's special: crawfish po'boys. Once inside, we were shown to a small table in the middle of a large nearly empty dining room featuring Formica-topped tables and mismatched chairs. Paper napkin dispensers and bottles of hot sauce served as centerpieces, and posters for jazz festivals from years past completed the décor.

Calvin held my chair while I sat, then made himself comfortable on a plastic chair, stretching his long legs out in front of him. "Welcome to Mama June's," he said. "I haven't been here in years. I hope the food's still as good as it was."

I took an appreciative whiff of the odors filling the room. "If it tastes anything like it smells, it should be wonderful. It's pretty well hidden, though. How did you find this place?"

Calvin handed me a plastic-covered menu. "Auntie Odessa used to bring us kids here when we were little. She lives just a couple of blocks away so it was close enough to walk." He gave me an assessing look and added, "I'm surprised Ox hasn't told you about it. It was his favorite back in the day."

"He's a private person," I said. "He doesn't talk much about the past. Which of you is older?"

"I am, by about three years. And believe me, I never let Ox forget it."

I mentally adjusted his age upward by a decade. "Don't take this the wrong way," I said, "but you look younger. Not a day over thirty."

He flashed a grin. "That's because I'm so much better looking."

I laughed and glanced quickly over the menu. Mama June's offered simple fare, but everything on the menu sounded delicious. "Are there a lot of cousins in your family?" I asked to keep conversation flowing while I pondered my choices.

"It's a big family," Calvin said, setting his menu aside. "There are around twenty of us on Mama's side. I've lost count on Daddy's." He tapped a picture on the menu with his finger. "If you like po'boys, try the special. It oughta knock your socks off. And get a side of the fries. They're the best in town."

I decided to take his advice and added a Diet Coke to my wish list. He left me long enough to place our orders at the counter, where a bearded man strummed a guitar between customers, and came back carrying a beer for himself and my soda in a plastic cup exactly like the ones my *abuela*'d had when I was a girl. My grandmother had died just a couple of years after my parents' accident, and most of my memories of her had faded with time. I hugged that one close as we settled in to wait for our food.

"Ox tells me you're new to the city," Calvin said, turning the conversation on me. "How do you like it so far?"

"I guess I'm still considered a newcomer," I said, "even though I've been here for over two years. It's different from what I was used to, but so far I like it a lot."

"And what were you used to?"

"I grew up in Albuquerque, and I lived in Chicago while I was in pastry school. That's where Ox and I met."

"New Mexico and Illinois," Calvin said thoughtfully. "What brought you to New Orleans?"

I told him about Philippe dying and Miss Frankie offering me the partnership at Zydeco, skipping the gory details about our separation and the divorce that never happened. I almost left it at that, but decided that Calvin might have some insight into his cousin that could help our relationship. "I think Ox was disappointed," I said. "He was here for Philippe from the beginning, and I know he wanted to step up when Philippe died. Sometimes I wonder if he . . ." I let the words trail off as I realized that there was no good way to end that sentence.

"If he resents you for having the job that should have been his?"

Apparently Calvin was fully capable of filling in the blank. Heat crept into my cheeks. I nodded and reached for my comforting plastic cup. "Something like that. Don't get me wrong, I'm not complaining. I'd just like to find a way to undo whatever damage has been done. Assuming there's been damage, that is." I sighed in frustration and eked out a rueful grin. "Has he ever said anything to you?"

The guitar player delivered two plastic baskets filled with our sandwiches and overflowing with fries so hot they were still sizzling.

Calvin popped a couple into his mouth and swallowed them as if they were lukewarm before answering my question. "You're asking if Ox has confided in me?"

"Something like that," I admitted. "Ox is a great friend, but I can't help feeling as if something got a little broken between us."

Calvin unwrapped his sandwich and shook hot sauce over his crawfish. "Ox and I were close when we were kids, but we aren't like that now. I left town to do my thing. He went off to learn about food. I hadn't even seen him in at least ten years." He smiled. "Even back then, our deepest conversations were about women and the Saints." He ate more fries and ran an assessing glance across my face while he chewed. "You want me to talk to him or something?"

I shook my head quickly. "No. No!" I shuddered at the thought and grimaced with embarrassment. "Forget it. I shouldn't have said anything. It's just that I consider Ox a good friend, and if there's anything wrong between us that I could fix, I'd like to know how to do it. But if you said anything to him, it would probably just make things worse."

We ate in silence for a few minutes. The po'boy was incredibly good, the bread crusty on the outside and soft on the inside, the remoulade sauce just spicy enough to tingle gently on my tongue, the crawfish fried to perfection.

"I wouldn't worry about it too much," Calvin said after he'd polished off half his sandwich. "Ox is big on family. We both are. He knows your mother-in-law made the only decision she could have. So even if he was disappointed, he'd be okay with it."

I smiled, grateful for the effort. "And how do you know that?"

"He's still there, isn't he?"

My smile grew a bit wider. "Yeah. He is."

"So there you have it." Calvin picked up the second half of his sandwich but paused before biting. "You wouldn't happen to have any job openings, would you?"

I hadn't been expecting that. "At Zydeco?"

"Unless you've got another business I don't know about."

"Nope. Zydeco's it. I just didn't realize you knew anything about cake."

"I know it's delicious," Calvin said with a grin. "What else is there to know?"

I laughed and shook my head. "I guess that means you have no formal training."

"Naw, but I can do other stuff. Lift. Tote. Wash dishes. Clean."

I might have expected that from him the day we met, but tonight, wearing that suit and looking as if he should be running his own business, the offer surprised me. "What happened to Mambo Odessa's?"

"I'm still there, but she only needs me a couple of days a week. I've gotta find more work than that if I'm going to make ends meet. Do you think you could hook me up? Ox said you were shorthanded."

"We were," I said, "but only because our office manager is out on maternity leave. I just hired someone to fill in for her."

He looked so disappointed, I felt like a jerk. I liked Calvin, and wanted to help if I could.

"That isn't a 'no,'" I assured him. "We have a huge job coming up in a couple of weeks, and it will be Mardi Gras season right after that. I might be able to find something temporary for the next few weeks, but I can't promise."

The disappointment on his face morphed into a grin. "Hey, that's cool. Whatever you can do. I've done a little construction in my day, if you need help. It looks like your place is pretty torn up."

I grimaced. "Yeah, but I can't worry about that until things slow down again." I tried a fry and realized they were seasoned with chili powder and garlic—along with a few other spices I couldn't immediately identify.

"Okay. Well, keep me in mind," he said and then changed the subject. "What are you doing in this part of town? Do you live around here?"

I shook my head. "No, I just had to drop something off at a shop down the street. I'm glad I ran into you. I might never have found Mama June's otherwise."

"Glad to help," Calvin said. "It's just as good as it used to be. It's nice to see that some things don't change."

He looked so wistful, I felt a slight tug on my heart. Like Calvin, I'd left home to make my way in the world and there were times when I missed it so much it hurt. I'd gone home for Thanksgiving and I'd been blown away by the changes to the city and comforted by the familiar. Remembering that made me want to do what I could to help. I'd talk to Ox in the morning, I decided. Together we'd figure out a way to put Calvin to work.

After my dinner with Calvin, I drove home, took a hot shower, and climbed into bed with an Elizabeth Peters mystery and a contented sigh. I'd just spent the evening with good food and good conversation, and I had a great house to come home to at the end of every day. What more could a woman ask for?

I didn't get a chance to answer that question because the doorbell rang, startling a surprised squeak out of me. I tossed my book aside and jumped out of bed, peeking out my window, which gave me a truncated view of the front porch.

There was a shadow standing in front of the door, but to my relief it was a familiar one. He must have known I'd be looking because he glanced up at my window and sketched a salute.

My heart jumped and a silly grin crept across my face. Liam Sullivan and I were as close to a "thing" as I'd been in a long time, but between my schedule at Zydeco and his as a homicide detective with the New Orleans Police Department, we sometimes went weeks without seeing each other. Not to mention where Gabriel fit in; he was a complication I hadn't quite worked out yet.

I thundered down the stairs in my most ladylike imitation of a herd of buffalo, flipped the deadbolt, and threw open the door. I only hoped he was as excited to see me as I was to see him.

He came into the room, six feet of muscle and Southern charm, but the somber look on his face made my giddiness evaporate just like *that*. I knew his cop face only too well.

"What's wrong?" I asked as I closed the door behind him.

He stopped just inside the foyer, his blue eyes dark with something that made my breath catch. "I just came from the scene of a robbery," he said. "I'm here because we found your name on a receipt there. You were at the Vintage Vault this afternoon?"

I could only stare at him while I tried to understand what he'd just asked me. "Orra was robbed?"

He nodded slowly. "Someone broke into her store a couple of hours ago. We got a 911 call asking for an ambulance from a woman who identified herself as Orra Trussell. She told the operator that someone was trying to rob her and said she thought she was having a heart attack."

"Poor Orra. Is she all right? Was it really a heart attack?"

Sullivan nodded. "That's what it looks like right now, but we won't know for sure until we get the autopsy results."

I inhaled sharply. "Orra's *dead*?" My voice sounded high and childish, and I was having a hard time taking a deep breath. I envisioned Orra's big smile and her garden gnome cheeks, and my heart skipped a beat or two. "Are you sure?"

Sullivan put a steadying arm around my shoulders and led me into the living room, making sure I was breathing in and out before he left me to grab a throw from the basket in the corner. I curled up on the couch, tucking my feet beneath me while he covered me.

When he was satisfied that I wasn't about to pass out, he sat beside me. "Orra Trussell was a friend of yours?"

I shook my head slowly. "No, I just met her this evening, but it's still a shock. What happened?"

"Near as we can figure, she was working late and somebody broke in through the front door. The storefront was dark. Whoever it was probably thought the store was empty. Orra must have gone up front to see what was going on and ran into the burglar. She placed the 911 call, but by the time paramedics arrived, she was dead on the scene."

My eyes misted with tears and a lump the size of Texas filled my throat. "Why would somebody break in to her store? She didn't have anything really valuable there."

"She must have had something," Sullivan said. "The 911 operator thought she mentioned a necklace, but Mrs. Trussell was having trouble talking. The operator isn't sure what she was trying to say."

My head shot up and my shock took on an almost eerie shape. "What necklace?"

"We don't know yet. We don't even know for sure that

she was talking about a necklace. Although—" He broke off and shook his head.

"Although what?"

"Nothing, really," he said, but he didn't meet my eyes so I didn't believe him.

"*I* left a necklace with her," I said, "but you already know that, don't you? Was she talking about *my* necklace?" *The one with the curse on it? Was her death a result of the curse?* I pulled the throw up to my chin, but I still felt chilled to the bone.

"I don't know if it was yours," Sullivan said. "And even if I did, I can't discuss details of the case with you."

"Then why are you here?" I narrowed my eyes in suspicion. "And if Orra's death wasn't a homicide, why were *you* there at all?"

He let out a heavy breath and rubbed his face with both hands. "A friend of mine caught the case. He called me because he recognized your name. I stopped by to see what was happening and then came straight here. I wanted to let you know and make sure you were all right."

"Well, as you can see, I'm fine." I tried to relax against the sofa cushion but I couldn't stop thinking about Orra the way she'd been that afternoon. I didn't want to imagine her so frightened that her heart had stopped, but that possibility was better than thinking that the curse had gotten her. "Does your friend have any idea who broke into her store?"

"Not yet," Sullivan admitted. "She had in-store security, but apparently she hadn't yet armed it for the night, and it doesn't include video surveillance anyway. I don't know if there's video from any other businesses nearby."

I hoped there was. Whoever broke in deserved to be caught. "What did the thief take?"

Another shrug. "We won't know that until her assistant has a chance to take a complete inventory. My friend said it wasn't clear whether or not anything was taken, but the store is apparently pretty cluttered so it's hard to tell."

"I wonder if the Toussaint necklace was taken during the robbery," I mused aloud.

"Is that the piece you left at the Vintage Vault?"

I nodded. "Orra was going to appraise it and tell me whether it was genuine or a fake."

"What is it? A family piece?"

"Not exactly," I said, "but I do have some claim to it." I explained about the accident with Zoey and the boxes, and about finding the necklace hidden inside the stairs. "I showed it to Miss Frankie," I said as I wrapped up. "She wigged out when she saw it. Said it was cursed. I couldn't get her to tell me anything more, but I've done a little research since then. It seems that everyone who has owned the necklace since the time of the Civil War has died. It disappeared for a century or so and then we found it. And now this."

Sullivan listened intently as I talked, but laughed when I got to the end. "Don't tell me you believe the necklace is dangerous."

"Not really," I said sheepishly. "But you have to admit it's a little spooky to hear about the curse and then be told that Orra Trussell died while she had the thing in her possession."

"Coincidence."

An involuntary shudder racked my body. I wrote it off as another chill and got to my feet. "If you say so. I'm going to make some coffee. Would you like some?"

"I wouldn't say no," Sullivan said with a grin. "You have any of those shortbread cookies?"

"I might." I wouldn't have admitted it for the world, but after learning that pecan shortbread cookies were Sullivan's favorite, I made a point of always having a few on hand—just in case. He followed me into the kitchen and we chatted about inconsequential things while I got the coffee started and arranged cookies on a plate. I didn't return to the subject of the robbery and Orra's death until I put creamer and sugar on the table and sat across from Sullivan.

"The 911 call is on tape, right? Can they listen to it again and find out what Orra said?"

"I'm sure they will," Sullivan said as he reached for a cookie. As his gaze raked across my face, I caught a look in his eye that set off a buzz in the back of my head. I'd seen that expression on his face before—usually when he was trying to keep something from me.

"What?" I asked.

The look disappeared and one of supreme innocence replaced it. "The cookies," he said. "They're good, as always."

"Nice try, Sullivan. What aren't you telling me?"

He popped the cookie into his mouth and shook his head, pantomiming his inability to answer with his mouth full.

I laughed but I wasn't amused. "You know something, don't you? You might as well come clean. I won't give up until you tell me. You should know that by now." He reached for another cookie but I snatched the plate away before he could take one. "Talk or the cookies go back into the jar."

He grimaced good-naturedly. "You drive a hard bargain, Lucero."

"Yeah. I've been taking lessons. What are you trying to hide?"

He leaned back in his chair and laced his fingers over his stomach. "Your necklace wasn't stolen."

I felt a rush of relief followed closely by a cloud of confusion. "Well, that's great, but why didn't you just tell me that to begin with?"

"Because the investigating officers found it in Orra Trussell's hand. She was holding it when she died."

That unsettled feeling in my stomach grew stronger. "So you think that's what she was talking about when she placed her 911 call?"

"I think it's a good possibility."

"But the thief didn't take it."

"No, but that doesn't mean he—or she—wasn't after it. It looks like Orra collapsed on top of it."

"To protect it?"

"It's possible."

"So you think the thief broke in and tried to steal my necklace, but Orra died before he could get it?"

Sullivan shrugged. "I think it's a possibility. The police have taken it into evidence and it could be a while before you see it again, but I think you should be alert for the next little while. We have no way of knowing what the thief was really after, or whether he'll try again to get it. I really don't think you're in danger, but I do think you should be cautious until we're sure what caused Mrs. Trussell's death."

I sighed unhappily. "Thanks for the warning. What about her family? How are they taking the news?"

Sullivan shook his head. "She didn't have any that we can find. According to her assistant, Mrs. Trussell was a widow. No children. We're still looking for next of kin."

"She was all alone? That's horrible! I hate thinking there's nobody waiting for her to come home. It makes me feel even worse about her death. Are the police going to follow up on the burglary? Find out who frightened her so badly? Because it seems to me that whoever broke into her store is responsible for her death."

Sullivan's mouth curved downward at the edges. "Look, Rita, I know you care about people. I like the fact that you care. But don't get yourself all worked up over this. In all likelihood, the woman had a heart attack. At first glance, it doesn't appear that anything was actually taken from the store, and in reality the cops who caught the case probably aren't going to have time to track down someone who *didn't* rob the place."

"You're saying the police aren't going to do anything?"

"That's not exactly what I said," he said with a weary smile. "I just want you to be prepared for reality, and the reality is that this case probably isn't going to be a high priority."

"So whoever broke in and frightened Orra to death is going to get away with it?"

He leaned forward, holding my gaze steadily. "Come on, Rita. You know how it works. Cases go unsolved all the time. The police force is understaffed and overworked, and we can only give a case our full attention for so long. An attempted robbery is going to get bumped off the list within a day or two, tops."

It sounded so cynical when he said it like that, but I knew it was true. I'd listened to him complain about this very thing in the past, watched him deal with his own frustrations when a case had to fall off his radar because another case suddenly took priority.

I understood, but that didn't mean I liked it. I knew that the thief who broke into Orra's store probably hadn't murdered her, but I couldn't help thinking that he—or she—was still responsible for bringing on the heart attack that killed that poor woman. Because if I didn't think that, I might start thinking that the cursed necklace had something to do with Orra's death, and I really didn't want to go there.

Sullivan finished his coffee, kissed me good night, and left me to get some sleep before his next shift started. I understood that, too, but I didn't like it either. I cleaned up in the kitchen, scrubbed my face, and crawled into bed an hour later, but I was still thinking about Orra's heart attack and wondering if her death really would be written off as an unfortunate coincidence.

One thing I knew for sure, though. I wasn't going to tell Miss Frankie about the burglary or Orra's unfortunate demise. Most of all, I wasn't going to tell her that I'd taken the necklace to Orra that evening. Because if I did, Miss Frankie would almost certainly blame the necklace for both.

Nine

I dozed off and on all night after Sullivan's visit. I kept thinking about Orra and the necklace and wondering whether the thief had been after the Toussaint rubies when he broke into the Vintage Vault. Only a handful of people had even known that we'd found the necklace, so it seemed unlikely. It was an unfortunate coincidence, that's all.

At least that's what I told myself.

But that didn't stop me from trying to remember who might've seen the necklace while I had it in my possession. There was Zoey, of course. And Simone. Corinne Carver had spotted it briefly when she'd barged in on my lunch meeting with Simone. And, of course, I'd told Gabriel about it.

I couldn't seriously think of Zoey, Simone, or Gabriel as thief material, but I supposed Corinne might have been a possibility. She'd always seemed fairly quiet and somewhat mousy to me, but she'd been wound up pretty tightly when she interrupted our lunch at the Monte Cristo.

I had to assume that by now everyone at Zydeco knew about the necklace, but I wouldn't even consider one of my staff as the would-be thief.

Miss Frankie knew about the necklace, and she might have been capable of breaking into the Vintage Vault under the right (or wrong?) circumstances, but she'd been so upset by just the sight of the necklace that I could not truly believe there was any way she'd have gone after it. Though she might've mentioned it to someone else. Someone who wanted to get their hands on those rubies . . . But even if Miss Frankie had told everyone she knew about it, she couldn't have known that I'd taken the necklace to Orra.

Which brought me to the Vintage Vault itself. Orra certainly hadn't broken into her own shop, but what about Dominique? Although it seemed unlikely that she'd have needed to break in if she'd wanted to steal the necklace; she could have just waited for Orra to go home.

Sol Lehmann was a definite possibility. Orra had told me he was greedy. Maybe he'd returned to the Vintage Vault after Orra closed, determined to get his hands on pieces from the estate sale he'd been asking Orra about. Maybe the Toussaint necklace wasn't even a factor in the burglary. I wanted desperately to believe that. The alternative made me feel too guilty.

By the time a little gray began to creep into the night sky, I gave up trying to sleep and threw on a pair of comfy jeans and a favorite old T-shirt. I pulled my hair up so I wouldn't have to spend time doing anything else to it, brushed on a skiff of eye shadow and a little mascara, and I was good to go.

The streetlights were just starting to blink off as I pulled into the employee parking lot behind Zydeco. I dragged myself onto the loading dock and coerced myself into the break room with the promise of caffeine. By the time the coffee finished brewing, Ox and Isabeau had arrived, so I carried a cup with me into the design room hoping they'd help distract me from thoughts about Orra.

Isabeau bounced around the room leaking cheerleader perkiness all over as she got her workstation ready for the day. Ox was a bit more subdued, eyeing my coffee as if I might hand it over if he looked pathetic enough.

It wasn't going to happen.

I wanted to tell them about Orra's death and the break-in at the Vintage Vault, but I didn't want them to get the wrong idea. A few months earlier, the entire staff had staged an intervention of sorts, hoping to convince me not to get involved when odd situations crossed my path. I wasn't in the mood for another lecture, so I decided to keep last night's news to myself.

I gathered the things I'd need to make fondant peacock feathers and set up my workstation while Ox got his own caffeine infusion. I waited until he'd had half a cup, which usually made him almost approachable, then decided to see how he felt about hiring his cousin.

"Guess who I had dinner with last night," I said as I dusted my table top with cornstarch.

Ox glanced at me over the rim of his cup and made a noise in his throat, which I interpreted as a request for the answer.

"Calvin. I ran into him as I was leaving the Vintage Vault. He told me that your aunt lives nearby there. I guess he's staying with her?"

Ox lowered his cup slowly. "She does. And I guess he probably is. I don't really know." His eyebrows drew together over the bridge of his nose. "You two had dinner together?"

"Yeah. He was going to a place called Mama June's and I didn't have plans so he invited me to join him. The food was delicious, by the way. I can't believe you haven't told me about it before."

Ox's eyebrows beetled even closer to one another. "I haven't been there in a while. What did he want?"

I pulled a ball of green fondant from its container and began to knead it so it would be the right consistency when I rolled it out. "What makes you think he wanted something?"

"Are you saying he didn't?"

"He asked me about a job," I admitted reluctantly. "But that's not all we talked about."

Ox snorted a laugh and swallowed the rest of his coffee. "What did you tell him?"

"I said that I'd see if we could find something for him, but I wanted to talk to you before I made any promises." I stopped kneading and reached for my rolling pin. "And I warned him that even if we could find him a job during our busy season, it would only be temporary."

Ox didn't say anything to that, but one eyebrow arched suspiciously.

"Is there some reason I *shouldn't* give him a job?"

Ox shrugged. "I suppose not."

Hardly a glowing recommendation, but Ox never had been one to gush about people, "Good. Because I thought that with the Belle Lune Ball coming up and Mardi Gras right after that, we could really use some help. We always hire temps at this time of year, and I don't know why your cousin couldn't be one of them."

Ox buttoned his chef's jacket before he responded. "Fine with me. He's all right." He glanced at me from the corner of his eye. "Did he say anything about how long he's planning to stick around?"

"No, he just said he needs the work if he's going to make ends meet." I began to roll the fondant, aiming for a thickness of about one-eighth of an inch. "Is that something I should be worried about?"

Ox shrugged. "I wish I knew." He expelled a heavy breath and sat on a metal stool. "I have no reason not to trust the guy, if that's what you're asking. I just haven't seen him in a while, that's all."

Clearly, something was bothering Ox, but I didn't want to push for an explanation—Ox tends to clam up under pressure. "That works for me," I said with a grin. "And it's not as if I'm relying on him to stay around. We're just talking about a matter of a few weeks."

Ox grunted his agreement, but didn't say anything more.

Maybe I should have let the subject drop, but my curiosity had been stirred so I asked, "What kind of work does he usually do?"

Ox gave me another shrug. "I have no idea. He's been in Baltimore for a while. That's really all I know."

"The two of you aren't close?"

"Not anymore." Ox went to one of the metal supply shelves and rummaged around for a moment. "We played together as kids, but we lost touch when we got older." He found a revolving cake stand and turned to face me. "What's with the twenty questions? If you want to hire him, do it."

I turned the fondant and rolled it in the other direction. "You really wouldn't mind?"

"I said I didn't, and I don't. But if you're asking for a recommendation, I don't know him well enough to give you one."

"Well, great. I'm sure we can find enough to keep him busy two or three days a week. I'll let him know—unless you'd like to be the one to tell him."

"Go ahead."

Sparkle arrived for work and Ox went into the kitchen, returning with a cart bearing half a dozen white cakes, which he would stack and secure before carving them into the shape of a female dress form. He spent a few minutes squaring himself away and situating the tools he needed before he asked, "What were you doing at the Vintage Vault last night?"

With the fondant rolled out to the perfect thickness, I reached for a large leaf-shaped cookie cutter and pressed it into the fondant. Hoping I looked nonchalant, I said, "I'm assuming you've heard about the necklace I found."

"Isn't Zoey the one who found it?" Isabeau piped up.

"She spotted the bundle inside the stair," I admitted, wondering if Simone had been right to wonder if Zoey would claim a finder's fee. I channeled my inner Scarlett O'Hara and decided to think about that later. "We opened it together."

"Well, whoever did what, I'm dying to see it," Isabeau said.

Sparkle, decked out in a filmy black tunic and slacks, perched on a stool and applied a fresh layer of black lipstick. "You don't want to see it," she warned. "It's cursed."

"It's not cursed," I said firmly. "But I can't show it to you. I don't have it. Anyway," I said, returning to Ox's question, "Simone suggested that I take it to the Vintage Vault and have Orra Trussell appraise it for me."

Isabeau left her workstation and moved closer. "What's that about a curse?"

"It's just a rumor," I said.

"There's no curse," Ox said, backing me.

Isabeau's blue eyes darkened with concern. "And you took it to the Vintage Vault? I think something bad happened there last night. I heard something on the news this morning but I'll admit I wasn't really paying attention."

"I heard it, too," Sparkle said from her shadowy corner. "Didn't somebody die?"

So much for keeping my mouth shut. "Yes, unfortunately," I admitted. "Somebody broke into the shop last night. Orra called for help, but Sullivan says it looks like she had a heart attack before anyone could get there."

Isabeau gasped. "Do they know who frightened that poor woman to death?"

"No," I said, "but she said something about a necklace to the 911 operator, and I can't help wondering, what if she was talking about *my* necklace—the one we found, I mean? And what if the burglar was after it?"

"Don't get any big ideas," Ox warned.

"I'm not getting *any* ideas," I assured him. "Big or small. I'm just feeling guilty, I guess. If I hadn't taken the necklace to Orra, she might still be alive."

"Or she might be just as dead as she is right now." Ox gently picked up a cake and prepared to stack it on top of the others. "It sounds like the woman had a bad heart, which means that she would probably have had a heart attack even without the robbery."

Sparkle rotated back and forth on her stool. "I don't know. Maybe it was the curse."

"It was *not* the curse," I insisted. "But maybe somebody was after the necklace I left with her, and maybe that frightened her so badly her heart gave out."

"I'll bet that's what happened," Isabeau said in hushed tones. "No wonder you're upset, Rita. I would be, too."

I sent her a grateful smile. "And I just know that Miss Frankie is going to blame the curse for it anyway. I don't intend to tell her, but you know how she is. She knows everybody in this city. Somebody's bound to tell her."

Ox stopped working and locked eyes with me. "There's no curse. And as for Orra's death, maybe she would have had a heart attack anyway. Maybe she wouldn't. But we're never going to know, are we? Racking yourself with guilt isn't going to make one bit of difference to Orra or her family."

"She doesn't have a family," I said, "which somehow makes it all worse."

Isabeau gave a little mew of sympathy. Even Sparkle seemed disturbed by that piece of news.

Ox shot a warning look at both of them. "It doesn't change anything."

"Whatever." I turned back to the fondant and cut out a few more leaves. "Technically, I suppose you're right, Ox, but that doesn't mean I can just flip a switch and change how I feel. And I do feel responsible for the necklace. After all, I'm the one who found it."

"Put the blame on Zoey," Ox said with a grin. "Then it's not your responsibility at all and we can stop talking about it."

His flippant attitude annoyed me, but Isabeau stepped in before I could respond. "Quit being such a grouch, Ox. I know exactly where Rita is coming from. And yes, Zoey might have been the one to find the necklace, but it was hidden here in this house, which means it belongs to Rita and Miss Frankie."

Exactly my point. It was nice to know that someone understood. And since Miss Frankie had washed her hands of it, the necklace was my responsibility.

Isabeau moved a little closer to me and lowered her voice. "You know who you need to talk to, don't you? Mambo Odessa could probably tell you everything you need to know. Zoey was trying to find out more about the necklace online yesterday, but there's practically nothing on the Internet except something about an old painting. But Mambo Odessa knows all about local history, especially anything supernatural. I'll bet she'd know all about the curse."

"Good idea," Sparkle said. "She might even know how to counteract the curse. That could be good information to have."

Ox's frown tugged at the corners of his mouth. "There *is* no curse," he said again. "And don't go dragging my aunt into the middle of this."

Isabeau sighed dramatically. "I don't know why you're

so set against letting Mambo Odessa use her gifts. She's remarkable. You're just unsupportive."

"I'm not unsupportive," he argued. "I'm practical. I'm realistic. I love Auntie Odessa, but I'm not going to say that she's psychic or has some kind of otherworldly power. And I sure as hell don't want you asking her to play around with some made-up curse."

"You can deny it all you want," Isabeau retorted. "But Mambo Odessa *knows* stuff. You're just too stubborn to admit it. She knows things that regular people couldn't possibly know. And what if there really *is* a curse on the necklace? Wouldn't it be better to know what you're dealing with than to bury your head in the sand?"

This last was directed at me. "I don't know . . ." I said with an uneasy glance at Ox. "I mean it's not as if I believe there's actually a curse on the necklace, but it certainly upset Miss Frankie. Mambo Odessa might be able to tell me about the rumors."

"No!" Ox said, jabbing a finger at me. He wagged it at Isabeau next. "No. You know how I feel about that stuff." And to Sparkle, "Quit egging her on. I mean it."

Sparkle rolled her eyes and mumbled, "Whatever."

Isabeau lifted her chin and glared up at him. "Yeah. I do know how you feel, but that doesn't mean you're right." The top of her perky blond head barely reaches Ox's armpit, but she didn't let the fact that he had almost a foot in height and a hundred pounds on her get in the way. "Maybe there's not a curse on the necklace, but if people believe there is one, isn't that what matters? If somebody tried to steal it from the Vintage Vault, it's because of the curse. You know that, too."

Ox's nostrils flared. "That doesn't mean that Rita has to get herself involved."

"I'm not getting involved in the robbery investigation," I said stiffly. "There probably isn't going to be one anyway. But once the police are done with the necklace, they're going to give it back to me and I'd really like to know what I'm dealing with before they do. And if I decide to talk to Mambo Odessa, I will. I don't need your permission."

Ox made a noise low in his throat that sounded suspiciously like a growl. He wasn't happy, but he seemed to realize that he'd lost that argument. "Do what you want," he snapped. "Just don't call me when things go bad."

"You have my solemn vow."

The thing was, I hadn't been sold on talking to Mambo Odessa until Ox forbade me to do it. Now I was determined to pay her a visit. Was it a good idea? Maybe. Maybe not. Right then, I didn't particularly care.

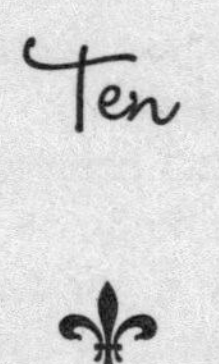

Ten

If I hadn't been a responsible adult, I would have left for Mambo Odessa's shop right then and there. Instead, I stayed at Zydeco and tried my best to focus on making several hundred peacock feathers out of fondant, layering green, blue, and lavender leaf-shaped cutouts on top of one another then using a plastic modeling tool to press indentations into the bottom two layers to create a feathery appearance. It wasn't particularly grueling work, but it did take time and patience.

I broke once to answer a call from Tommy Sheridan at the Monte Cristo Hotel, who wanted to make sure he'd answered all of my questions about the new location. I assured him that all was well and promised again to let him know if I needed anything.

By the time noon rolled around, I was more than ready to meet Edie for our lunch date. She had suggested meeting me at Zydeco, but I'd discouraged that idea mostly because the reception area was still a disaster. Zoey had spent the previous day organizing the piles of paper currently covering Edie's desk into stacks she and I would eventually have to work through, but I still wasn't anxious for Edie to see the backed-up work, the holes in the wall, and the broken stair railing. The whole idea of our lunch date was to make her feel better, not worse.

It also meant that I couldn't tell the others about our lunch plans. If I did, they would certainly have wanted Edie and John David to stop in. I knew a visit was inevitable, but I hoped to put it off at least until we found the surface of Edie's desk.

I put away the remaining fondant and stored the peacock feathers I'd made that morning before I checked in with Zoey and made some admiring noises over her progress. Then I grabbed my bag and headed for the front door.

I'd let Edie choose the restaurant and she'd picked Rubio's Ribs, a local favorite within easy walking distance for me. She and John David were waiting just inside the front door when I arrived. Edie looked better than she had the other night. Her hair was clean and shiny and she'd even managed a bit of makeup. Only one small white splotch high on her shoulder marred her appearance, and I didn't know whether to mention it or keep my big mouth shut.

JD was fussing a bit, so I gave Edie a quick hug and took the baby carrier from her to give her a break. While we waited to be seated, I cooed and gurgled and made all the appropriate noises, which got JD's attention and, I swear, even earned a smile from the baby.

Unfortunately, her son's good humor put a scowl on Edie's face. "Why does he like you better than me?"

I managed to suppress the grin I'd been giving JD as I looked up at her. I didn't want to make her feel worse. "He doesn't like me better than you," I assured her. "I think he feels your stress and reacts to that. I'm not as stressed as you are." Which might not have been entirely true. Edie had motherhood to deal with, but I was plenty stressed at work, and now

I was also carrying around guilt over Orra Trussell's untimely death. My stress didn't have anything to do with John David, though, which probably made the difference.

"I don't resent you for being able to handle him, Rita. Really I don't. I just wish he'd calm down for me like he does for you."

I didn't know what to say to her, so I went with an optimistic prediction. "He will in time. Has he been sleeping any better?"

She gave her hand a so-so waggle. "A bit, I guess. He actually took a nap yesterday *and* he slept for four solid hours last night. I think that's a personal best for him."

"That's progress! Everyone says it gets easier as they get older."

Edie's expression turned pensive. "It had better be true," she said. "I don't know how much more of this I can take."

Luckily, just then the restaurant's hostess appeared, and I hoisted the baby carrier to trail her and Edie to a table near the window. We spent a few minutes settling the baby and the diaper bag around us, and eventually got ourselves seated as well.

"Thanks for suggesting this," Edie said as she plucked her napkin from the table. "I feel almost like a real live girl."

"Good," I said with a smile. "That was my intention."

Edie's lips curved slightly in response. She reached for her menu and gave it a cursory glance. "How are things at work?"

I wasn't sure how much to say, so I went with a generic, "Fine."

Her eyes narrowed in suspicion. "What's wrong?"

"Nothing. We're busy, of course. And Zoey is just settling in, so that's a bit of an adjustment, but really, we're all fine."

"Oh?" She looked back at her menu, but her expression was far too innocent. "Sparkle said there'd been some trouble. Something about damage to one of the walls?"

I gave myself a mental kick for trying to be coy. I should

have known that someone would fill her in on the gossip, but I hadn't expected Sparkle to gab. She and Edie had had a few issues in the past, but I kept forgetting that since JD's birth, they'd been thick as thieves. I still hadn't adjusted to the new dynamic.

"It's nothing major," I said. "I just haven't started repairs yet because we have so much work to do in the next couple of months. We can't have workmen underfoot while we're trying to get everything done."

"That's all?"

"Well, mostly," I admitted just as a bubbly young waitress bounced over to our table. "Let's order before JD gets fussy again. We can talk while we eat."

We spent the next few minutes listening to Bubbles enthuse about the daily specials. JD stirred fitfully a couple of times, but we managed to place our orders and send our server away without disturbing him too much.

I thought the interruption might have distracted Edie, but she'd caught the scent of a story, and she wasn't letting go. "Sparkle also said that you'd found something interesting. A necklace, I think she said?"

I laughed and gave up trying to shield Edie from the trouble at work. "Obviously you know the story already, so why don't you just tell me what else you want to know."

"Anything there is to tell. Sparkle only knows that you and Zoey found a necklace, but she doesn't know anything else." She paused while Bubbles put our drink choices on the table. "Apparently, Estelle is being very tight-lipped about the whole thing," she said when we were alone again.

That didn't sound like Estelle at all. Again I wondered if Zoey might assert a claim to the necklace. "I don't think Sparkle knows much," I said. "We only talked about it for a few minutes this morning. So here's the story in a nutshell: Zoey—you know, Estelle's niece—dropped a few boxes, and they damaged the stairs. Inside one of the loose steps, she spotted a bundle, which turned out to be a box, and inside the box was a ruby necklace. Which is gorgeous, by the way. I'm still trying to figure out whether it's genuine or costume, and that's really all there is to know."

Edie regarded me critically over the rim of her sweet tea glass. "Are you sure? Sparkle made it sound like there was something mysterious about the necklace."

"There's rumor and gossip, but nothing concrete. Why, what did she say?"

"Just that there's supposedly a curse on the necklace and that some lady died last night while she was holding it in her hand." She put her glass down and scowled at me. "I thought we were friends, Rita. Why didn't you tell me any of this?"

"I didn't want to tell *anybody* about any of this," I said with a guilty wince. "I feel horrible about Orra Trussell's death and I was hoping to keep the connection between the Toussaint necklace and Orra's heart attack—if there *is* a connection at all—under wraps."

Edie reached for her phone, did a bit of swiping and one-finger typing, and shoved the screen at me. "I think the cat is out of the bag."

I glanced at the screen and groaned. CURSED NECKLACE REAPPEARS AFTER 100 YEARS, the screen shouted. It followed with a story by a local journalist all about Beatriz and Armand Toussaint, and Armand's ill-fated relationship with Delphine Mercier. It wasn't posted on a major news outlet, but Edie had seen it, which made me wonder just how far and fast the story would spread.

With a sigh, I gave Edie's phone back to her. "How did they find out about it so fast?"

Edie shrugged. "Who knows? Nothing stays private these days. You know that."

"Yeah. I guess." I can't say that I'd embraced social media, but we did have a nodding acquaintance. I maintained a business blog, a company Facebook account, and I kept up with old friends and my New Mexico family on a personal account, but I didn't spend as much time online as most people.

"So? Tell me," Edie said. "What's going on? And this time don't leave anything out."

"There really isn't a lot to tell. Sullivan came over last night and told me about Orra Trussell's death—but it's not as if she was murdered or anything. She died of a heart attack."

Edie looked almost disappointed. "Really? It wasn't murder?"

"No, and you might try to appear sorry. Dead is dead, no matter how it happens."

Edie assumed a solemn expression—or at least she tried. "What about the curse the article mentions?"

A brittle laugh escaped my lips. "Don't tell me you believe that rumor?" Edie shrugged but didn't say anything, which caused me to laugh again. "Seriously? You really think there's a curse?"

"The lady died, didn't she?"

"Yes, but only because she was frightened by a burglar. It wasn't because of the necklace."

"You don't know the necklace had nothing to do with her heart attack," Edie said. "You said yourself there might be a connection."

"Not the kind of connection you're suggesting." We were interrupted by the arrival of our orders—two trays filled with Rubio's famous ribs and coleslaw. We shifted things around to make room for everything. JD stirred again but didn't wake up, and the two of us dug in like we'd both been starving for days.

"Look, Edie, I need you to keep quiet about this," I said after we'd munched in silence for a few minutes. "The very last thing we need is for word of a supposed curse to get out and have it associated in any way with Zydeco. It could be the ruin of the business."

"Or the making of it," Edie suggested. "This is New Orleans, Rita. Around here, something like that might get the bakery a lot of attention."

"Attention, we need," I agreed, "but that's hardly the right kind. The kind of people who can afford our cakes aren't going to be impressed by some hundred-year-old voodoo curse."

"Are you sure about that?"

"You think they will be?" I tried to imagine someone like Evangeline Delahunt getting excited about a cursed necklace, but the image wouldn't form. I kept seeing the look on Miss Frankie's face instead.

"I think it's the kind of thing that stirs up interest," Edie said. "And I don't think it matters much who you are or how much money you have. It's the kind of story that will grab anyone's attention. I'm not saying we should play it up or anything. I just don't think you should worry about word getting out. I don't think it would hurt business."

"Maybe." I turned Edie's argument over in my mind, but I still had a bad feeling about the whole thing. "The point is, a woman died last night. I don't want to do anything that would make it seem as if we're trying to capitalize on her death, especially since we'll be hanging out with her associates at the Belle Lune Ball."

"I'm not suggesting that we should," Edie insisted. She might have said more, but John David began to stir again and this time he was fussy enough to distract his mother. Maybe she was right, but the whole subject made me increasingly uneasy. The journalist might have picked up the story of the burglary from the police, but since they hadn't seemed overly interested in the Toussaint rubies, I doubted very much they'd mentioned the curse.

But someone clearly had, and I couldn't help wondering who.

Eleven

After trying unsuccessfully to calm JD, Edie hurried away with her squalling infant and the diaper bag. I signaled our server for a refill of Edie's sweet tea so it would be waiting for her when she got back to the table, and I gave myself a pat on the back for being thoughtful.

I still wasn't used to seeing Edie in full motherhood mode and I wondered whether having JD waiting for her at home would change her when she came back to work. JD's birth had reignited my own old longing for children, but he had also raised questions about my ability to juggle motherhood and a career. I wondered how easy it would be for Edie to handle the challenge.

"Ms. Lucero?"

I'd been so lost in thought, I hadn't heard anyone approach the table, and the deep voice so close to my ear startled me. I shifted in my seat and found a furry face just a few inches behind my shoulder.

It took a moment for me to recognize Sol Lehmann after my brief encounter with him at the Vintage Vault.

"It is Ms. Lucero, isn't it?" he asked. "Or have I mistaken you for someone else?"

"No. Yes." I laughed and pulled myself together. "Yes, I'm Rita Lucero. And you're—?" Since we hadn't actually been introduced, I thought I should play it safe.

"Sol Lehmann." He waved a beefy hand toward one of the free chairs at my table. "Would you mind if I join you for a moment?"

Well, yes and no. It seemed like an audacious request since we didn't know each other, but I couldn't think of any reason besides the necklace that he might want to talk to me and I really wanted to hear what he had to say. "I can give you a minute," I said. "I'm having lunch with someone."

"I know. I saw her leave with her baby a moment ago. It will only take a few minutes . . . if you don't mind."

I nodded toward the chair. "What can I do for you?"

He sat and tugged his vest down over his substantial belly. "I don't know if you remember me. We didn't actually meet, but I was at Orra's shop yesterday at the same time you were."

"I remember." A dozen questions formed on the tip of my tongue, but I swallowed them all.

"I suppose you've heard about Orra's heart attack?"

I nodded. "Yes. It's awful, isn't it? How did you find out?"

Sol folded his hands together on the table. "Dominique called me this morning. She called several of us who are—*were*—Orra's colleagues, to let us know. She was a good lady and she really knew the business. She'll be missed."

I liked thinking that someone would miss her, but if Sol was feeling real grief, I wasn't picking up on it. "She wasn't very old, was she?"

"Sixty, sixty-five. I'm not sure." He gave me a sad smile.

"I knew her for years, but I know better than to ask a lady her age. Even if I'd asked, Orra wouldn't have told me."

His smile faded slowly. An expression I couldn't read darted across his bearded face, but I didn't miss the cool glint in his eyes. "Dominique told me that you left a necklace with Orra to be appraised. She was under the impression that it might have been the famous Toussaint necklace."

Well, that didn't take long. "That possibility has been suggested," I admitted, "but if you're asking me to confirm or deny, I'm afraid I can't do that. I have no idea if the necklace is genuine."

"I know this is a bad time to bring it up, but when I saw you sitting here, I decided to take a chance. Now that Orra's gone . . ." He broke off, wiped his face with one hand, and tried again. "If you still need that appraisal, I'd be happy to look at the piece for you." He reached into a pocket and produced a business card.

I slipped the card into my back pocket. "Thank you, Mr. Lehmann, but I don't have the necklace at the moment."

"Oh? Is it . . . What I mean is, is the piece at the Vintage Vault? I could pick it up if you'd like. Save time. I'm sure you're busy."

He certainly was eager. Which made me cautious. "That's generous of you, but it's actually in police custody. I don't know when—or even if—I'll get it back."

Disappointment clouded his eyes. "The police have it. I hadn't even thought of that."

"Apparently it's evidence in last night's break-in. I'm sure I'll get it back at some point, but I really don't know when that will be."

"Oh. Yes. Of course. I hadn't thought," he said again. He cleared his throat. "Well, the offer stands. I'd be happy to appraise it for you when the time comes. It's a shame, don't you think? I was hoping I might persuade you to let me add it to my exhibit at the Belle Lune Ball."

I blinked a couple of times in surprise. "You want to exhibit the Toussaint necklace?"

"Of course. Putting that piece on display would be a major coup for any vintage dealer. You should know that. I'm sure you'll find lots of interest in the necklace now that it's been found." He glanced around furtively and lowered his voice. "Where did you find it, if you don't mind my asking?"

Lots of interest. Oh, goody. "I'm really not ready to talk about it," I said. "I'm sure you understand."

"Of course. But I would be honored if you'd let me be the one to show it. When the time is right."

Of course. I could tell just how concerned he was about me. "Judging from your own interest, I have to assume you know the necklace's purported history?"

Sol nodded eagerly. "Certainly. It's a colorful one, that's for sure."

"So you know it's rumored to be cursed."

A gravelly laugh emanated from his throat. "Absolutely. That's the most interesting thing about it." He sobered and put a beefy hand on my elbow. "But listen, if the curse frightens you, I'd be happy to take the necklace off your hands. I'd make you a generous offer—if it turns out to be the real thing, of course."

Just as Orra had predicted. I could almost feel the excitement vibrating off of his body.

"I'll keep that offer in mind, too," I said, politely pulling my arm away from his hand. "But I wouldn't get your hopes up about showing the necklace at the Belle Lune Ball. The ball is a little over a week away. It would take a minor miracle to get the wheels of bureaucracy turning that fast."

"One can always hope," he said. "Just don't forget about me.

You have my number. Let me know if you need my services."

I said that I would and Sol lumbered away as Edie made her way back to our table.

I held out my hands for JD and Edie put him in my arms. "Who was that?" she asked with a glance at Sol's retreating figure.

"A vintage dealer named Sol Lehmann. He was at the Vintage Vault yesterday when I dropped off the necklace."

Edie handed me a bottle for the baby. "Oh? What did he want with you today?"

"He wants the Toussaint necklace," I said after JD began to eat. "He offered to appraise it now that Orra's gone, but he also admitted that he wants to show it at the Belle Lune Ball. And he mentioned that he'd be interested in buying it."

"Really?" Edie took another look at Sol and frowned thoughtfully. "He certainly is aggressive."

"That's what I thought, too." JD squirmed, so I readjusted my hold on him. "Doesn't it seem odd that he'd bring it up today? I mean, Orra hasn't even been dead for twenty-four hours and he's already trying to get his hands on the necklace. You don't suppose—"

"That he tried to steal it last night?" Edie shook her head slowly. "Anything is possible, I guess. But if you'd just broken into someone's store and she died right in front of you, wouldn't you want to keep a low profile?"

I shrugged. "Sure, but I wouldn't break in to begin with, so we can't rely on what I'd do." I kissed JD's forehead and watched his eyes close sleepily. "Mr. Lehmann said I'd probably hear from lots of people who are interested in the necklace. I hope he's wrong."

"I wouldn't get my hopes up," Edie warned. "If that guy's any indication, I think you'll have your hands full of treasure hunters."

I groaned softly. "Maybe it's a good thing the police took it as evidence. At least it gives me a good excuse to just send everybody away."

"For the time being. But sooner or later you're going to have to do something with it. You realize that, of course."

"I vote for later. And let's not get ahead of ourselves. We still don't know if the necklace we found is the Toussaint necklace. It might be something else entirely."

Edie cut a glance at me. "Seriously? You still think there's a chance it's just a piece of junk someone took the trouble to hide in your staircase?"

I made a face at her. "It's possible."

"You're probably the only person on the planet who thinks that," Edie scoffed. "But at least you can always tell people you can't make a decision without Miss Frankie. That will buy you some time."

My head snapped up so fast I heard my neck pop. "Oh my goodness," I said. "I've been so focused on the break-in and Orra's heart attack, it didn't even occur to me that people might be calling Miss Frankie!"

"You don't have to worry about her," Edie said. "She's tough as nails."

"Not this time." I removed the bottle from JD's mouth and moved him to my shoulder for a mid-meal burp. "Miss Frankie was really upset about this whole cursed necklace thing. I probably should check on her."

Edie's confusion was evident, but she took JD and his bottle from me. "Then call her."

I dialed Miss Frankie's number twice before we finished eating but didn't get an answer either time. In itself that wasn't unusual. Miss Frankie doesn't own a cell phone and rarely even checks her answering machine. I tried talking myself down by listing all the places she could have been. Like at a charity luncheon, or visiting her neighbor and best friend, Bernice. She could be shopping in town. Or she could be barricaded inside her house, curled up in the fetal position. It was impossible to tell from where I was.

By the time Edie and I finished lunch, I was trying not to worry.

Edie shooed me out the door, knowing I wouldn't relax until I could touch base with my mother-in-law. "Call me," she called after me. "I want to know what's happening."

I waved a hand over my head to show that I'd heard her and headed back to Zydeco for my car. I felt guilty about leaving work to check on Miss Frankie. I'd made less than half the peacock feathers we needed for the ball gown cake and I couldn't afford to lose several hours of work that afternoon. But the thought that Miss Frankie might be as upset as she'd been the night I showed her the Toussaint necklace spurred me on.

Twelve

Back at Zydeco, I waved distractedly at Zoey as I let myself inside and headed straight for my office to retrieve my car keys. Before I could get there, she stepped in front of me and wagged a handful of message slips in my face.

"These are for you. Sorry, but your voice mail is full. I had to start writing them down."

Gulp! This was bad. This was *really* bad. "I'm sorry," I said, trying to dodge past her. "I'm in a hurry. Hang on to those for now. I'll get them from you later."

"But everybody wants to talk to you," she said, jerking her head toward the phone. "They all want to ask about the necklace we found."

We? Hmmm.

She glanced through the messages in her hand and held one up. "This guy is offering a whole lot of money for it. I mean *serious* money." She plucked another note from the stack. "And this guy, Carlo Mancini, wants to interview us for TV."

"Us?"

"We found it together," Zoey said with a subtle straightening of her shoulders. "And when I told him that, he said he wanted to talk to us together."

She looked so pleased, I almost hated to throw cold water on the idea. "I'm not sure that's a good idea," I said cautiously.

Zoey's smile drooped. "Why not?"

"We don't even know if the necklace is the real thing yet," I reminded her.

"It *has* to be. And anyway, we could be famous!"

Seriously? My worry about Miss Frankie reacted badly with Zoey's desire for fifteen minutes of fame. I rounded on her, taking out my frustrations with the rest of the world. "Has everyone gone insane? A woman is dead. She's not even cold yet and people are trying to get rich?" I snatched the message slips out of her hand and reeled them off one by one. "No! No, no, no and no." I tossed the rest at her. "Tell them *all* no. That's my final answer."

Clearly hurt and confused, Zoey scrambled to pick up the messages from the floor. She looked up at me and tucked a strand of limp hair behind her ear. "If you don't want to do it, I could talk to him myself."

The prospect of Zoey giving an interview about a supposedly cursed piece of jewelry, speaking on Zydeco's behalf, made me feel queasy. "I don't think either of us should be giving interviews just now," I said. "In fact, I'd rather you didn't talk to anyone about the necklace, at least not until we know what we're dealing with."

"But why not? I mean, it's so exciting. The necklace is worth a whole lot of money, Rita. And what if it actually *is* cursed?"

"It's not cursed," I said automatically.

"You don't know that," Zoey argued. "It could be. I know you don't like to think so, but that stuff is real. My friend?

Jennifer? Her mom knows all about the supernatural. That's why I showed her the picture."

The feeling of queasiness grew stronger. I held up a hand to stop the flow of words. Zoey sputtered a bit and finally stopped talking completely. "What picture?" I asked.

"I'll show you." Zoey strode back to her desk, tapped a couple of keys on the keyboard, and turned her computer screen so I could see it. An image of the necklace on its bed of velvet filled the screen. Even in a snapshot, the necklace was breathtaking. "I took it the day we found it. When you went to get the sodas? I put it up on Instagram and shared it on Facebook. Then I remembered Jennifer's mom, so I tagged Jen and asked her to show it to her mom."

I groaned and dropped into one of the chairs facing Zoey's desk. It hadn't even occurred to me that she might take a picture and post it online during those few minutes I was out of the room. I'm aware that most phones have cameras in them. I haven't been living under a rock. But I don't use mine very often, and Instagram hasn't made its way into my radar yet.

"I really wish you had asked me first," I said.

Zoey's dark eyes clouded. "Did I do something wrong? Again?"

Seeing the look on her face made me regret my sharp tone. I hadn't meant to hurt her feelings. "No. Not really. It's just . . ." I broke off, unsure how to explain what I was thinking. "It's not your fault. I should have asked you not to say anything to anyone."

"I didn't think it would cause trouble," Zoey whined.

"Obviously, neither did I." I slumped down in the chair and leaned my head back so that I was staring at the chandelier overhead. "Is there any way to get rid of the picture on your Instagram?"

"Sure," Zoey said. I couldn't see her, but she sounded tentative. "But, I mean, what would be the point? It's out there now. People have shared it and probably saved it to their own computers."

Of course. I knew that, too. Once something's online, it's there forever. Asking Zoey to delete her original picture wouldn't do any good. Better to focus on things I could do something about. I made a mental note to save the picture to my own computer in case I needed it for any reason and changed the subject. "I know you've had a lot of calls," I said, "but do you know if my mother-in-law was one of them? Miss Frankie?"

Zoey shook her head. "I don't think so, but I don't really remember."

I didn't know if that was good news or bad. It might mean that Miss Frankie was still blissfully unaware of the latest developments, but I had a hard time making myself believe that. "Tell Ox I've gone to see Miss Frankie," I said, standing up. "And tell him I'll be back as soon as I can. I'm sure he'll understand."

I wasn't really sure at all, but I didn't see any other option. I couldn't just blithely make peacock feathers out of fondant while Miss Frankie was dealing with a subject she desperately wanted to avoid. If someone pushed too hard and she wigged out again, I'd never forgive myself.

Miss Frankie didn't answer her door when I rang the bell, but I hadn't really expected her to. I rang twice more, then hurried around the house and peeked inside the garage window to see if her car was there.

It wasn't.

Okay. Still not time to panic. Maybe there was a perfectly innocent explanation for why she wasn't home. Usually when something upset her, she called me. She hadn't tried my cell and Zoey was almost certain she hadn't called Zydeco. That was a good sign, right? But since I clearly hadn't taken her advice to toss the necklace into the Mississippi, she might have decided to bypass me this time.

Thinking about her on the loose in the city, hysterical, ramped up my worry another notch. I went back to the front door and knocked, in case her doorbell wasn't working. Making a mental note to insist on getting a key to Miss Frankie's house, I hurried down the driveway and across the lawn to Bernice's house. There was a chance I'd find Miss Frankie quietly sipping coffee or iced tea in Bernice's kitchen, but I thought it unlikely.

I rang the bell, expecting to discover Bernice gone as well. To my surprise, she answered almost immediately and a wave of relief almost knocked my knees out from under me.

Bernice is a sweet woman with a round face and a puff of white hair. She smiled broadly when she saw me. "Rita! What a nice surprise. I was just fixing coffee. Would you like some?"

"I'm not sure," I said. "I'm looking for Miss Frankie. Is she here?"

"Here?" Bernice seemed surprised. "No. I haven't seen her. Is something wrong?"

"I'm not sure," I said again. "Do you have any idea where she is?"

Bernice's smile faded. She stepped aside and motioned for me through the door. "I'm afraid I don't. I think you'd better come in. You look fit to be tied."

I hesitated, but only for a moment. Racing off with no clear direction wouldn't do any good. It might be more productive to find out what—if anything—Bernice knew.

She led me into her kitchen and set about making the coffee. "What's this all about, Rita?"

"It's a long story," I said. "Have you talked to Miss Frankie today?"

"Earlier this morning," Bernice said. "But it was only for

a minute. We were supposed to have lunch, but she called to cancel."

My heart sank. "Did she say why?"

"No, she didn't. She was in a hurry, I think." With the coffee started, she sat at the table across from me. "Now tell me what's going on, Rita. You seem upset."

"I am, a little," I admitted. "But I'm not sure if there's any reason to be. Has Miss Frankie said anything to you about . . . anything?"

"She's said a lot to me about a lot of things," Bernice replied with a laugh. "You're going to have to be more specific than that."

I didn't want to upset Bernice like I had Miss Frankie, but my current line of questioning was getting me nowhere, fast. I took a deep breath and blurted, "Has she said anything to you about me finding the Toussaint necklace?"

Bernice nodded firmly. "Oh, that? Yes. She said you'd found it, and honey, she wasn't happy."

"Yeah. So I gathered. She told me to get rid of it."

"And you should," Bernice chided. "That thing is bad news, mark my words."

"I suppose she heard about Orra Trussell . . ."

"The woman who died last night?" Bernice glanced at the TV on the wall as if it might magically turn itself on and spew forth information. "She said something about her, but I'm afraid I didn't understand what she was talking about." Bernice's eyes narrowed and her mouth pursed. "Are you saying that awful necklace had something to do with her death?"

"No! That's *not* what I'm saying. But I'm afraid Miss Frankie may think it did. I've been getting phone calls all day from people who want to buy the necklace or see the necklace or interview me about the necklace, and it just occurred to me that they might have been calling Miss Frankie, too."

Bernice stood slowly, carefully working the stiffness out of her knees before going back to the coffeemaker. "I don't know about that. I talked to Frances early this morning, right after the early news report. That's when she told me she was canceling our lunch."

I wanted to believe the two things weren't related, but I couldn't stretch my connection to reality that thin. "And she didn't say where she was going?"

Bernice shook her head. "No, she only said she had to see someone."

"She didn't say who?"

"No and she hung up before I could ask."

Bernice didn't seem especially worried. I tried to find comfort in that. "You know her better than anyone else," I said. "What do you think she's doing?"

Bernice gave a surprised laugh as she poured coffee into two mugs and brought them both to the table. "Oh, my dear, I couldn't even begin to guess. You know how Frances is."

Yeah. I did. That was the problem. Since running out on that cup of coffee would have been rude, I decided to bring up the thing that had been troubling me the most. "When I showed Miss Frankie the necklace, she got really upset. She kept saying it was cursed, which is so unlike her. You know Miss Frankie is usually the first person to say that spirits and so forth are all nonsense. What's so different about this?"

"You know the story behind the necklace?" Bernice asked.

"I know about Armand Toussaint and his wife and his mistress," I said. "Armand commissioned the necklace for his mistress, Delphine, but gave it to his wife, Beatriz, instead and all hell broke loose. Is there more?"

"Did you know Delphine was with child at the time?"

"I didn't," I admitted. "But how does that factor in?"

Bernice stirred sugar into her cup and sipped. "The story goes that Delphine thought the necklace would provide some security for her children. When Armand gave the rubies to Beatriz instead, Delphine was furious. It wasn't the necklace that was so important to her; it was the future of her children. Even though Armand had already given her the deed to her house, his decision about the necklace was the ultimate betrayal."

I gave that some thought. "I guess she felt that Armand was turning his back on her and their children. They were his, I assume?"

"All three were his," Bernice confirmed. "She had been under his protection for years when all of the necklace business happened. You see, Delphine was a free woman of color, but that didn't guarantee her descendants a good life. A necklace like that, she could've sold if push came to shove," Bernice said. "That's the story I've heard, though God only knows whether it's true or not. Facts can get twisted around in a hundred years."

I laughed at her understatement. "They can get twisted around in ten minutes. Why do you think Armand changed his mind?"

Bernice gave me a knowing look. "Can't you guess?"

I shook my head quickly. "No. I mean he must have known about Delphine's baby—" I cut myself off as an idea occurred to me. "You think Beatriz was pregnant, too?"

Bernice touched the end of her nose with a finger. "Bingo! It makes sense, doesn't it?"

"It does," I agreed, "but that doesn't mean it's true. I wish there were somewhere I could learn about all of this in Delphine's own words. And Beatriz's. Both of them were victims of an awful system. Men allowed to cheat and wives not allowed to say anything about it. Women like Delphine forced to hand themselves over to some rich jerk just to survive. Either way, I'm not sure I could have survived back then without calling up a few curses of my own."

Bernice laughed. "That makes two of us. That's one of the reasons my daddy taught me how to shoot straight."

"Armand should count himself lucky that he didn't end up with us in his stable." I took a jolt of really terrific coffee and sighed. "I'm worried about Miss Frankie. I don't want her to do something reckless."

"I'm sure she's fine," Bernice assured me. She studied her cup for a long moment and said, "Now that I think about it, she could be paying calls on some of Armand's descendants. She'll want to make sure they know the necklace has been found."

"You mean there are some of his descendants still living around here?"

Bernice nodded. "Well, of course, they'd be descendants of Armand's nephew, Gustave, but the family is very much in evidence."

"But I thought Gustave's daughter died six months after her wedding."

"She did, but Gustave married again later and had other children," Bernice said. "Two sons and another daughter, if I remember right."

"Do you know where I could find them?"

Bernice laughed softly. "Me? No. But I'm sure there are records. You could check with the Daughters of the Confederacy. I'm sure they'd have some genealogy you could look through. Or maybe talk to someone at the voodoo museum. They have Beatriz's portrait. They may have other information."

"I'll keep that in mind," I said. But secretly I hoped Miss Frankie would turn up before I had to take that step. I'd love to see the portrait everyone kept talking about, but searching for Gustave Toussaint's descendants in a hundred years' of genealogical records would be like searching for a needle . . . in a stack of needles. Not only did the thought of it make my eyes glaze, but I had other things I should be doing. Things like working so I could keep my employees happy with a paycheck.

I hugged Bernice good-bye and extracted a promise that she'd call me the minute she heard a peep out of Miss Frankie. Feeling confident that I'd done everything I could reasonably do, I hurried back to Miss Frankie's, where my Range Rover lounged in the driveway waiting for me to come back. There was still no sign of her, but talking to Bernice had helped calm my nerves. Miss Frankie had survived without me before. I had to trust that she could get along without me now.

Thirteen

I spent the rest of the afternoon at Zydeco with my nose to the grindstone and ignoring the unusually high number of incoming calls. I wanted to believe they were all business calls, but I'm not naïve. I had to trust Zoey to take messages where necessary and transfer any calls that were actually about cake to the appropriate person. I fielded a couple of calls about the Belle Lune Ball and checked in with Simone to make sure all was well at her end. As far as I could tell, Zoey was doing a good job deflecting calls about the necklace, and that let me focus on the work I was supposed to be doing.

By six, I had two hundred fondant peacock feathers stored in airtight containers, which was a major accomplishment. My neck ached from hours spent hunched over my worktable and the muscles in my fingers were stiff, but I gave myself a mental high-five and drove home in a reasonably good mood.

Sullivan called while I was on the road, which lifted my

spirits even further. His schedule makes it hard to plan in advance, so in spite of the advice Aunt Yolanda had given me as a girl to keep the guys guessing, most of my dates with Sullivan were arranged on the spur of the moment.

He suggested dinner out; I countered with an offer of an evening in. I thought staying in might be more relaxing, but that wasn't my real motive for wanting to stay home. I wanted to stay close to my home phone in case Miss Frankie called. She has my cell number, of course, but she prefers using a landline whenever she can.

Luckily, Sullivan liked the idea of staying in and offered to grab takeout on his way. I hurried home, gave everything in the house a quick once-over, stuffing junk mail into a decorative box that was already overflowing with stuff I'd been ignoring, and running my sleeve over the end tables to remove the dust.

I hopped into the shower just long enough to wash the day away and back out in time to change into black pants and a sheer black shirt paired with a teal tank top. I hooked matching earrings into my ears, piled my hair on top of my head, and gave my face a quick swipe with eye shadow and blush before the doorbell rang.

Sullivan looked great when I opened the door. Either he'd showered at work or stopped at home for a few minutes. I could smell his soap and aftershave, both pleasant and manly. The scents of garlic and oregano told me he'd brought Italian. My stomach growled in appreciation. "Well, hello," he said with a seductive eyebrow waggle.

My insides forgot about food and flipped around for a few seconds before his eyebrows did a quirky thing that helped me remember to invite him in. "Sorry to keep you standing there. It's been a long day."

"Trouble at work?"

"Sort of," I said with a sigh. "But nothing work-related.

I spent half of the afternoon looking for Miss Frankie and I still haven't heard from her. I have no idea where she is."

Sullivan closed the door behind him, put the food down, and pulled me in for a hug. "She's probably just out shopping with Bernice."

"That's the one thing I know she's *not* doing," I said as I took a deep breath and let the scents that had come inside with him wipe away the remaining knots of tension in my shoulders. "Bernice doesn't know where she is either."

Sullivan slid a curious glance at me. "You sound worried."

"I am a little, I guess. I keep telling myself she's fine, but it's that stupid necklace. We got inundated with calls at work today from people wanting to talk about it. After the first couple of calls came in, every time the phone rang, I felt a little more edgy." I stepped away from him and he grabbed the food. We moved together toward the kitchen. "It seems like everybody wants to talk about the Toussaint necklace and I have to assume that if they're calling me at Zydeco, they're also calling Miss Frankie. It's no secret that she's part owner of the bakery."

"I'm sure she can handle it," Sullivan said. "She's tougher than you think."

"I hope you're right," I said. "Anyway, that's one of the reasons I wanted to stay in. I hope you don't mind."

Sullivan grinned. "I get to be here alone with you. What's to mind?" While I pulled plates from the cupboard, he made himself at home, finding a bottle of wine and holding it up for my approval before getting to work on the cork. He handed me a glass and I savored the warmth as it spread through my body. "You worry too much. Miss Frankie is just out on the town. She'll call. You'll see."

I grabbed utensils and carried everything to the table. "I want to believe you," I said, "but you didn't see her the night I showed her the necklace. I've never seen her so upset, except when Philippe died. I even checked with Bernice this afternoon. She hadn't seen Miss Frankie either, but she did suggest that Miss Frankie might be visiting some of Armand Toussaint's living relatives. Which is either a comforting thought or an even bigger reason to worry. She's been out of touch for such a long time now, all I can think about is the trouble she could be getting into."

Sullivan laughed softly. "She's a character, all right. But she's also all grown up. She doesn't need a babysitter."

"I don't want to babysit her," I said with a roll of my eyes. He was probably right, but on previous occasions, he'd been just as concerned about Miss Frankie as I was. I didn't know what had brought about this change in him.

Sullivan studied me for a long moment before putting his hand on top of mine. "Really, Rita. She's fine."

The feel of his hand on mine made me feel marginally better. I turned my hand over and wove my fingers through his. "Thanks. That helps. I'd just feel better if I heard from her. I'm sure she's heard about the break-in at the Vintage Vault and Orra Trussell's death. She canceled her lunch plans with Bernice right after the morning news. And since it's no secret that the Toussaint necklace was there—thanks to my newest employee and social media—she's probably convinced the necklace killed poor Orra."

I sighed and rolled my head on my neck. "At least tell me there's good news about the investigation. Have the police found any leads? Do they have a suspect?"

Sullivan's expression didn't change, but his hand went utterly still for a moment and I suspected that I'd asked a question he didn't want to answer. "It's not my case," he said. "I don't know what's going on."

"Really. Hmmm. You haven't talked to your friend who caught the case? You expect me to believe that?"

Sullivan shrugged and rubbed his thumb gently over the back of my hand—as if he thought I'd lose interest in his obvious white lie if he upped the sexual tension. "We're in two different departments," he said at last. "We don't see that much of each other."

"Hmmm," I said again, as if I were giving that serious consideration. "Interesting. So you don't know whether there was anything missing from the store? You don't know the thief actually took something from the Vintage Vault after he frightened poor Orra into a heart attack?"

Sullivan expelled a heavy breath and gave me an exasperated look. "Nothing was missing," he said firmly. "At least not according to Ms. Trussell's assistant."

"So you've talked to Dominique then?"

"No."

"Ah. I see. Well, however you got wind of her statement, it doesn't sound as if you believe her."

Sullivan's thumb stopped moving. "I don't have any reason *not* to believe her. I didn't talk to her myself, and I won't, so get that gleam out of your eye."

"My eyes aren't gleaming," I said. "I'm interested, that's all. And before you say anything else, I happen to know there's no law against curiosity—especially since it was *my* necklace the thief was after."

"You don't know that," Sullivan reminded me.

I waved his reminder away with an impatient flick of the wrist that wasn't currently under his control. "No, I don't *know* that, but we both recognize the truth. Under the circumstances, I think I have a right to know what's happening with the investigation."

I could feel tension radiating down Sullivan's arm. "Nothing's happening," he said. "It's a nothing case, Rita. Nothing was actually stolen. Robbery Division isn't going to spend any more time on it."

"But a woman is dead," I protested. "Surely that's worth somebody's attention."

"People die every day in this city." I would have pulled my hand away from his, but he anticipated the move and tightened his grip. "I know that sounds callous, but it's not. Orra Trussell died of a heart attack."

"Even if that's true, the heart attack was caused by the thief. He scared her to death."

"It would take a whole lot more evidence than the department has to prove that in a court of law. Robbery Division has bigger cases on its docket and new ones coming in all the time. I'm sorry, Rita, but since all we really have is broken glass in the front door, this one's just not going to get any more attention."

I gaped at him. "The case is closed?"

"It will be tomorrow."

"But that's horrible." I managed to extricate my hand from his and reached for my wineglass to keep him from grabbing it again. "How can they just close the book on poor Orra?"

"There *isn't* a book," Sullivan said. "That's the whole point."

"So what does that mean? What happens to the necklace?"

"It will be released from evidence. You'll probably get a call in a day or two telling you to pick it up at the station."

Assuming, of course, I wanted it back. It had been nothing but trouble since Zoey and I found it. "And that will be that, I suppose. I wonder if things would be different if Orra had a family to make some noise about this. Or money. The police would probably pay more attention if she was rich, wouldn't they?"

Sullivan scowled and sat back in his chair. "Don't start, Rita. Bad things happen to good people. It's a fact of life. We do our best, but we can't fix everything. And you—" He shook his finger at me. "You can't fix this."

"Well, somebody should," I said. "Oh, don't worry," I said in response to his frown. "I'm not going to rush out and look for the would-be thief on my own. I just hate thinking of that poor woman dying without anyone to care what happened to her. Simply because it happens every day doesn't make it right."

"I won't argue with that," Sullivan conceded. He looked into my eyes and I saw the worry and frustration in his morph into something warm and suggestive. "And now how about changing the subject. I didn't ask to see you so we could talk about heart attacks and burglaries. I don't even want to talk about curses or family."

My insides flipped again. With a silent apology to Orra, I held up both hands in a gesture of surrender. "Okay. You're right. I'm sorry. What would you like to talk about?"

Sullivan half stood and leaned across the table, so close I could feel his breath on my cheek. "Who said anything about talking?" he asked and planted one doozy of a kiss on my lips.

It would have taken a stronger woman than me to resist the pull of that kiss, and I didn't even try. What can I say? It was the first time all day something had been able to drive Orra Trussell and the Toussaint necklace out of my mind.

Fourteen

Sullivan left around midnight and I fell into a deep and dreamless sleep. I woke up Friday morning feeling almost chipper, but my good mood lasted only as long as it took me to realize I still hadn't heard from my missing mother-in-law. Even with Sullivan's reassurances, I knew I wouldn't be able to concentrate if I didn't check on her first. I dressed quickly and drove through town, stopping for coffee and a bagel on my way.

Half an hour later, I held my breath as I pulled into Miss Frankie's neighborhood. I let it out in a big fat sigh of relief when I saw her car in the driveway. Even her ravaged patch of pampas grass looked happier.

For half a heartbeat, I considered driving past the house and heading straight to work but I wanted to reassure myself that Miss Frankie wasn't having some kind of breakdown. And, of course, I wanted to know where she'd been the day before. She needed to know that it wasn't okay to just disappear without a word.

I parked behind her car and hurried up the walk, shivering slightly in the cool morning breeze.

Miss Frankie answered the door looking relatively normal. No dark circles under her eyes, no wild expression on her face. She gave me a brief hug—also normal—and ushered me inside as if she hadn't disappeared for an entire day.

"You're up and about early," she said as I followed her into the kitchen. "I haven't started breakfast yet, but it will only take a minute."

"It's sweet of you to offer," I said, "but I've already eaten. I just came by to make sure you're okay."

She stopped with one hand on the refrigerator door and looked back at me in surprise. "Why wouldn't I be okay?"

"I called you several times yesterday," I said. "You didn't answer and you weren't here when I stopped by."

She laughed and pulled open the fridge door. "Well, for goodness' sakes, Rita. As you can see, I'm just fine." She pulled out a pitcher of juice and put it on the counter. "Surely you didn't worry because I had a day out."

"It wasn't that," I assured her. "It was *why* you went out that had me worried. Bernice said that you canceled your lunch plans with her, but she didn't know why."

"Bernice is a dear friend, but she's not my keeper and I certainly don't have to explain every step I take—to her *or* to you. I couldn't make lunch, it was as simple as that."

Nothing is ever that simple with my mother-in-law, but I know that with her I have to pick my battles. I decided to give that one a rest, at least for the time being. "Well, I'm glad you're home safe and sound. Did you at least have a good day?"

She shrugged as she poured juice into a glass. She spilled a little on the countertop, which was unlike her, and made me think she wasn't as pulled together as she wanted me to believe. After wiping up the spill, she filled a second glass and carried both to the table. Only then did she finally get around to answering my question. "It was a productive day. And yours?"

If I hadn't known Miss Frankie so well, I might have been lulled into a false sense of security by her responses. I let her think that was the case. "Not as productive as I would have liked," I said. "But a couple of good days will catch us up again." I sipped juice and made some noises about how good it was, which seemed to please Miss Frankie. I thought maybe she'd relaxed enough for another question or two, so I tried my luck. "I understand that you don't want to tell Bernice what you were doing yesterday, but are you going to tell me?"

She wasn't a bit fooled. "Is there some reason I should?"

"I was worried about you," I said. "Bernice said you called her right after the morning news and I worried that you'd heard something that upset you."

She widened her eyes and tried to look innocently confused. "Such as?"

I was quickly running out of patience so I decided to take a direct approach. "Such as the story about the break-in at the Vintage Vault."

Miss Frankie patted the back of her hair with one hand. "Why would *that* upset me?"

"Because Orra Trussell died of a heart attack that night, and I'm pretty sure I know what you're thinking."

Her eyes narrowed and the innocence evaporated from her expression. "You couldn't possibly know what I'm thinking. But since you brought it up, I heard that she was holding that horrid necklace when she died. After I *told* you to get rid of it. After I *warned* you it was dangerous. I can't imagine how it ended up at the Vintage Vault."

"Of course you can," I said. "I gave it to her."

Miss Frankie sighed heavily. "Oh, Rita, what *were* you thinking?"

"I was thinking I should get the necklace appraised and

find out whether it was even genuine. *And* I was thinking that the stupid thing couldn't possibly be cursed because there's no such thing as a curse."

Miss Frankie sighed dramatically. "Well, you know better now."

"No, I don't," I said firmly. "What I do know is that someone wants to get their hands on that necklace—probably because the story of the curse has made it extremely valuable. And whoever it was frightened Orra so badly her heart gave out. That's tragic, but it's not evidence of a curse."

"Deny it if you want," Miss Frankie said with a sniff, "but the truth is evident."

I buried my head in my hands, too frustrated to speak for a moment. When I found my voice again, I asked, "What is it with you and this curse? Usually you're the first person to laugh at any talk of the supernatural."

"I don't laugh," Miss Frankie said stiffly. "I just don't believe all the superstitions."

"So what's different about this one?"

To my surprise, Miss Frankie's eyes filled with tears. She dashed them away with the back of her hand and shook her head. "I didn't believe in the curse until you showed up here with that necklace in your hand. You said you found it at Zydeco and I thought *my* heart had stopped."

"Why?"

"Oh, Rita, don't you see? Philippe died there, right after he bought that place."

The look on her face broke my heart but suddenly the fog began to lift. "Philippe died two years after he bought the building," I reminded her gently. "And he didn't die because of the necklace."

"You don't know that. The only reason Philippe was able to buy that house was because old Miss Cassie had just died and her family was eager to unload the property." She snorted softly. "I suppose we know why. And then Philippe died. And suddenly there you were holding that . . . *thing* in your hands and I knew what had happened."

I chose my words carefully. "Was Miss Cassie's death suspicious?"

"No. She was old and she'd lived a long, full life. But her husband died in a traffic accident only a few years before her."

"People die all the time, Miss Frankie. It's natural and it's inevitable. Miss Cassie might have died, but if she was old . . . well, it happens." I sounded uncomfortably like Sullivan had the night before, but I tried not to think about that.

"Philippe's death wasn't natural," Miss Frankie snapped. "Don't you dare try to claim that."

I shook my head emphatically. "No, it wasn't. But his death had nothing at all to do with the necklace. You must know that's true."

"What I know is that my son died at *that* house while *that* necklace was hidden there."

"That's true, but—"

"But nothing, Rita. That necklace is cursed. It's not just Philippe's death either. Look how close the two of you came to getting divorced. And all the nasty business that's crossed your path since you took over? No, my family has suffered because of it and I *won't* have anything else happen because you're too stubborn to get rid of it. Promise me you'll destroy it."

Her vehemence made more sense to me now, but that didn't mean I agreed with it. She was watching me expectantly, but I wasn't about to make a promise I couldn't—or wouldn't—keep, so I detoured around it. "I can't do anything with the necklace," I said. "I don't have it. The police took it into evidence."

Relief slowly washed across Miss Frankie's face as my words sank in. "You don't have it?"

"I don't."

She sank back in her chair. "Well, thank the Lord for that."

Okay, so I'd probably have it back in a day or two. That information was on a need-to-know basis, and I saw no reason that Miss Frankie needed to know anything about it. Besides, I hoped that by the time the necklace was in my possession again, I'd have thought of a way to dispel the rumors of a curse.

"Just try not to let your imagination run away with you," I said. "Sure, we've had some bad luck, but we've had good things happen, too. What about Edie's baby? And Sparkle finding her brother? You can't count either of those things as bad luck."

Miss Frankie tilted her head to one side. "I suppose you're right. I'm just so relieved that you're all safe."

"And we are," I assured her. "Absolutely."

"You don't know how much better that makes me feel."

Guilt stirred around inside and made me squirm, but I kept a smile on my face. "Good. I'm glad."

"I can't wait to tell that reporter. Once he knows you don't have the necklace any longer, he'll have to leave us both alone."

The guilt in my stomach turned sour. "You've been talking to a reporter?"

"No, but he's been calling since early yesterday morning. What's his name?" She tapped her chin with one finger. "Carlo, I think. Carlo Mancini."

The same reporter Zoey had mentioned. Of all the nerve. "You haven't given him an interview, have you?"

"Of course not. I don't talk to the press. But he left a message saying that he would be calling you. Have you talked to him?"

"Not yet, but I will. He tried to reach me yesterday. So far I've managed to avoid him. What does he want?"

Miss Frankie got up and went back to the fridge, seeming more like her old self. She pulled out an egg and cracked it into a small bowl, adding a splash of milk. "I'm sure it's about the necklace," she said as she whisked the egg and milk into a froth. "And the feud, no doubt. That whole thing will be stirred up, too, I'm sure."

I started to nod before her words had a chance to sink in. "Wait a minute. What? What feud?"

"Between the Toussaints and the Merciers, of course. There's been bad blood between the two families since Armand and Beatriz died. But that's silly, really, since the two families are actually one." She pulled out a pan and put it on a burner. "Not that they have ever thought of themselves in that way."

"Right. So the two families are feuding? Like the Hatfields and the McCoys?"

Miss Frankie poured her mixture into the pan and seasoned it with salt and pepper. "Not exactly. It's not as if the two families have been killing each other off. But there have certainly been disagreements and bad feelings. The Merciers feel that they were betrayed. The story is that Delphine attempted to get the necklace back from Gustave Toussaint more than once before she died."

"Obviously she failed."

Miss Frankie nodded. "Are you sure you aren't hungry?"

I shook my head. "I guess it makes sense. If the Toussaints believed that they'd been cursed, I guess they'd be upset."

"Relations between the two branches of the family became more strained with every failure. Delphine had worked up quite a hatred for the Toussaints by the time she passed."

"And from there the . . . misunderstanding escalated to talk of a curse. How do you think the necklace ended up in the staircase at Zydeco? How long has it been there, and who put it there?"

Miss Frankie stirred the eggs in the pan and lowered the heat. "I imagine it was someone who thought that hiding it could stop the curse."

"Maybe," I said. "But if that was the case, why hide it in

the house? Why not throw it into the river like you told me to do? Squirreling it away seems like an odd choice for someone who really believed the necklace was cursed. That should make you feel better about it."

Miss Frankie frowned at me over her shoulder. "Why should it?"

"Because obviously whoever hid the necklace wasn't concerned about dropping dead. It sounds like he or she was more worried about the wrong person finding it." My phone let out a soft chime, and instinctively I glanced at the screen. When I saw the time, I let out a little yelp and stood. "I didn't realize how late it was," I said. "Sorry, but I need to get to work."

Miss Frankie walked me to the front door, asking a few questions about the work and our progress, but I could tell she wasn't really interested. I hated seeing her so worried, but I had no idea how to set her mind at ease. I'd start by convincing Carlo Mancini to leave her alone. Somehow. I was almost certain a plan for doing that would occur to me at some point.

After that, time would tell. Eventually, after I repeatedly didn't die in a freak accident, Miss Frankie would realize that the necklace wasn't bringing me bad luck. Until then, however, I'd have to be more cautious than usual. In her current state of mind, even a hangnail might send her over the edge.

Fifteen

The call from the police came that afternoon. I'd been up to my eyeballs in work all day, first holding a staff meeting so we could get our ducks in a row before the Belle Lune Ball next week, then returning business calls and setting appointments with potential new clients, and finally getting the opportunity to offer Calvin a part-time job until after Mardi Gras. After the holiday, we'd see about letting him stay on.

On the plus side, I was so busy I hadn't had time to think about curses or feuds. Another plus was that Zoey had cut the stacks of paper on Edie's desk substantially. Maybe I could actually stop worrying about keeping someone at Edie's desk until she came back.

I'd just finished a preliminary phone consult with a potential client when Zoey popped into my office, wide-eyed and breathing hard. Her hair was clean and shiny, her eyes clear and bright. I liked thinking that the job was having such a positive effect on her. "It's the police," she whispered, as if she was afraid someone would hear her. "It's about the necklace. It has to be. Anyway, it's a woman. The cop, that is. She wants to talk to you."

I wasn't sure why Zoey was so excited, but I was starting to think that necklace was going to be the death of me—just not in the way Miss Frankie thought. "Thanks," I said. "Did you get a name?"

"Of—? Oh!" Zoey's head snapped this way and that as she glanced at her desk and back at me. "You mean of the lady who's calling? I think she told me, but I don't remember. Did I mess up?"

I shook my head and reached for the receiver, pausing when I saw that two lines were lit. "Which line?"

Zoey inched forward and scowled at the phone on my desk. "Line two. I think. No, I'm sure. Line two."

Okay, so maybe Zoey wasn't fully up to speed yet. But she was doing okay, and okay was a whole lot better than her predecessors had done.

I picked up the call with my perkiest "Rita Lucero," expecting that Zoey would go back to work. To my surprise, she waited just inside the door while I listened to the officer's spiel about how the police no longer needed the necklace. I tried to put off retrieving it until after next week's craziness was behind us, but the woman was insistent that I pick it up right away. Maybe she'd heard about the curse.

I arranged to pick up the necklace by the end of business, then hung up the phone. Zoey was still hovering by the door, so I turned a smile on her. "All taken care of. Is there something else on your mind?"

She shook her head uncertainly. "No. I guess not. Only—" She took a deep breath and let her next words out in a rush. "You're not going alone, are you? Because I don't think you should."

"I was planning to. Is there some reason I shouldn't?"

"Well, yeah!" She came a few steps into my office. "I mean, think about it. That necklace is worth a *lot* of money and a whole bunch of people are interested in it. It's probably not smart to just walk around with it in your purse. You should take somebody with you."

The independent side of me wanted to ignore her advice, but Miss Independence had never owned anything valuable in her life. Besides, Zoey seemed to be clearly angling for an invitation to go along—and since she *had* found the necklace, maybe I owed it to her.

"You want to come?" I said with a grin. "That's all right with me."

"Me?" Zoey's eyes filled with horror. "No. I wouldn't—I couldn't—what I mean is, you ought to take somebody . . . you know . . . strong."

"You mean like a bodyguard?" She looked so serious, I tried not to laugh. "Do you really think that's necessary?"

"Somebody broke into the Vintage Vault and tried to steal it, didn't they?"

I'd been making that same argument for a couple of days, but now that Zoey was using it against me, I felt myself waffling. "We don't know that for sure. The necklace probably wasn't even an issue."

"But it was," Zoey protested. "You know it was."

I shut down my laptop and stood. "The thief *might* have been after the necklace, but the police don't think so. And I'll be fine. Nobody will even know I've picked it up."

Zoey gave me a stern look. "You should take Ox. Nobody would try anything if he was with you."

"Ox has too much to do," I said. "Actually, so do I, but somebody has to go and I guess I'm elected." I crossed the room and put a hand on her shoulder. "It's nice of you to worry about me, Zoey, but nobody is going to try anything. I'll be fine. How are you coming with the notes from the staff meeting? Are you having any trouble?"

"I'm almost finished," she said, her mouth puckering with disappointment. "I'll e-mail a draft to you as soon as I have it."

"Sounds great," I said, and moved past her on my way to the design room.

Zoey trailed me into the brightly colored room, where the rest of the staff was hard at work. The minute she stepped through the door, she hustled over to Estelle's worktable. Estelle was trying to restabilize one of the dress form cakes on its metal stand, a task which apparently required a great deal of concentration. She didn't notice Zoey until the frustrated girl shifted her weight a couple of times and let out a heavy sigh. "Aunt Estelle, I need to talk to you."

Thanking my lucky stars that Zoey had stopped worrying about me, I went to the kitchen for a white sheetcake and a tub of buttercream so I could start sculpting a pair of mule-style shoes. Eventually, I'd cover the shoes with emerald green fondant and adorn them with fondant peacock feathers, staging them at the foot of the peacock feather dress cake, accompanied by a peacock feather fan and matching hat.

Normally, I would have put off this step until closer to the event, but with five dress cakes and their accessories to finish in less than a week, we had to do everything that could reasonably be done in advance. The schedule we'd put together in the staff meeting called for all five cakes and their edible accessories to be completed by the middle of next week so we could spend the remaining few days cooking for the banquet itself. Time was quickly running out.

Ox was rolling a sheet of brown fondant large enough to become the skirt for a 1930s ladies' business suit while Isabeau fussed over a matching sheet that she was molding onto a tube of rice cereal treat to create one sleeve for the jacket.

Sparkle absently flicked a spike on her leather choker with one black-tipped finger while she studied the placement of the black fondant beads I'd created on the evening gown cake. Dwight hummed tunelessly as he calculated the first cut in a stacked cake that would ultimately become dress form cake number four.

The sheer volume of work ahead of us threatened to overwhelm me at times, and as I watched the staff, all busy and focused and (mostly) silent, I felt a wave of near-panic wash over me. Don't get me wrong, the staff is great. When it's time to work, they work and work hard. But they rarely do so without talking. The fact that they weren't chatting while they rolled and cut and painted and molded made me wonder if I'd walked into the wrong design room.

I loaded up everything I needed from the kitchen and carried it back into the design room. The crew that had been so hard at work only a few minutes earlier had stopped working completely and every eye in the room was trained on me. Every eye except Ox's. He was still rolling fondant with steely determination.

I stopped in my tracks. "What?"

"You're going to pick up the necklace," Isabeau said accusingly. "And you're not even going to take somebody else with you?"

I shot a look at Zoey, who lifted her chin and stared back at me. "I just thought they should know since you wouldn't listen to me."

"Nobody likes a tattletale, Zoey," I said lightly, annoyed but not wanting to offend the sensitive girl. "And the rest of you can calm down, too. I'll be fine. It's no big deal."

Estelle put both hands on her hips and glared at me. Her curls had escaped the yellow kerchief she'd used to restrain them, and her round cheeks turned an alarming shade of red. "Zoey wasn't tattling. She's concerned about you—and she's right to be. There are too many people who know that that necklace has resurfaced."

Isabeau nodded, sending her perky blond ponytail into gyrations. "And a whole lot of people who want to get their hands on it."

Even Sparkle piped up from her corner in the shadows. She gave me a stern look; or maybe it was just the black liner around her eyes and the black lipstick on her mouth that made her look so disapproving. "Much as it pains me to admit this, I agree. You shouldn't go alone."

I tried to laugh off their concerns. "You want me to put somebody else at risk from the curse? Wouldn't that be irresponsible?"

Dwight scratched absently at his beard guard then moved on to a particularly wrinkled spot on his T-shirt. "I don't think they're actually worried about the curse," he said, glancing from one coworker to another in turn.

Obviously, they'd been talking while I was out of the room and apparently they all knew about the alleged curse.

"I think they just want to make sure you're safe," he went on. "If the necklace is all that valuable, somebody might want it." He stopped scratching. "Is it? Valuable?"

"It must be. Somebody already tried to steal it once," Isabeau reminded me.

"She has a point," Sparkle said.

"We don't know that for sure," I protested limply as I continued on to my workstation. I put down the load of stuff I'd grabbed from the kitchen and frowned around the room.

Ox looked away from his work for the first time. He stretched out a few kinks in his broad shoulders and put his hands on his hips, accentuating his resemblance to Mr. Clean. "You might as well just do what they want," he said to me. "You're not going to convince them. Believe me, I've tried."

"It's not that big a deal," I said. "And besides, that would mean taking two of us away from the work here. Doing that would put us even further behind schedule."

"Not if you took Calvin," Estelle said. She turned to Ox before I could respond. "Didn't you say he'd be coming in this afternoon?"

Ox gave me a sympathetic look and went back to work. "Yeah. He called a little while ago and said he'd be here at four to fill out the paperwork."

"Then there you go," Isabeau said, as if she and the others had settled something between them. "Take Calvin."

I groaned aloud, but I didn't want to waste any more time arguing. "Fine. I'll ask Calvin to go with me. But it's not necessary. Really."

"Just do it, okay?" Isabeau said, flapping her hand and going back to work.

"Yeah, yeah, yeah." I picked up a knife and sliced the cake on my table in half with a satisfying *whack,* then swiped a thin layer of buttercream over one of the pieces. In all honesty, I was only mildly annoyed. I didn't like being backed into a corner, and I hated it when they ambushed me . . . but it was nice to know they cared.

Calvin showed up promptly at four and he proved to be not only willing, but almost eager to go with me to the police station. Isabeau and Estelle peppered us both with warnings to be careful and the two of us dutifully trotted ourselves out to the Range Rover and buckled ourselves in.

Calvin was back to wearing jeans and a black T-shirt, with neon yellow athletic shoes so bright their reflection danced around on the windshield. I tried to ignore the distraction and nosed into traffic, which was already rush-hour thick.

"Thanks for coming with me," I said. "It really isn't necessary, but I had to agree to let you come or my employees would have grounded me for a month."

Calvin grinned and shifted around in the seat, trying to get comfortable. "It's all right with me. I get to feel useful and earn a few points with Ox."

"You need points?"

He flicked something from his sleeve. "Points are always a good thing. Don't ever let anyone tell you they're not."

I laughed, relaxing in his company. "I guess they are at that." I switched lanes so I could pass a slow-moving truck. A white SUV copied my maneuver, sliding in behind me when I switched lanes again. Calvin fell silent, concentrating on his phone. My thoughts drifted back to the necklace we were going to retrieve.

"This stupid necklace has turned out to be more trouble than it's worth," I grumbled.

Calvin glanced away from his phone. "You say something?"

"Yeah, but it's nothing important. Just whining to myself."

Calvin tucked his phone into a pocket. "You want to whine to me? Go ahead. I got nowhere else to go."

I laughed again and slowed to make a right turn. The white SUV did, too. *Weird.* "It's just the necklace that Zoey and I found. You've heard about that, I suppose."

"Yeah. Looks like the place is still pretty torn up."

"It is. But we'll get it fixed."

"So the necklace? Is it real?"

I shrugged. "I don't know yet. I was having it appraised but then it was evidence in a break-in so the police took it. I'll have to find another appraiser but there's no time now until after the Belle Lune Ball. Apparently, it has an interesting history—if it's the genuine article, that is."

"So I've heard."

"So then you've heard the rumors that there's a curse on it?"

Calvin gave me an odd look followed by a shrug. "I've heard a little."

"Not that I believe in curses," I said to clarify my position.

"Maybe you should. I've spent enough time with Auntie Odessa to know there's some real mojo out there. You oughta show it to her. If there's a curse, she'll be able to tell you."

"I might do that if I find out that the stones are genuine," I said. "But I'll worry about that if I need to. My bet is that an appraiser will tell me the thing is worthless and that will be the end of it."

Calvin wagged his head slowly. "You really haven't been in New Orleans long, have you? Around here, you find something like that hidden away? It's worth something and you've got yourself a story to tell."

"Well, you know more about it than I do," I conceded. "I don't mind a story—as long as the story doesn't include things that go bump in the night."

Calvin laughed. "You got a lot to learn about New Orleans, sis. Practically every story is about something that goes bump in the night. This city was built on ghosts and spirits and secrets."

"So that's why it's such a big deal? Somebody might have tried to steal it, my mother-in-law is going crazy because of it, and there's even a reporter who wants to talk to us, but I don't know that much about it, and even if I did, why would I talk to him?"

"The guy's got a job to do," Calvin said reasonably. "That necklace has some history behind it. I guess it's the kind of thing people want to read about."

"I guess," I grudgingly agreed.

"Face it, scandal sells."

"So does sex," I said. "And that necklace has both."

"Right." Calvin shifted in his seat. "So what are you going to do with it now that the police are giving it back?"

"I honestly don't know," I admitted. "Miss Frankie thinks I should toss it into the river and be done with it."

"She wants you to do what? Why?"

"She believes in the curse. She's convinced that it's bad luck. She thinks the only way to make sure nothing else tragic happens is to get rid of it for good." I smiled and watched the SUV in the rearview mirror. It certainly was staying close. "I don't know. Maybe she's right."

"Don't you think it probably belongs to somebody? Family. Right?"

I squeezed between two cars so I could make another right turn. "I haven't heard anything from the Toussaint family. Though I have had interest from a few vintage dealers and jewelers who want to buy the necklace. And that reporter. His name's Carlo Mancini. Have you ever heard of him?"

Calvin shook his head. "I don't think so."

At the last minute, the SUV changed lanes to get behind me, earning an irritated blare of the horn from another driver. An uncomfortable feeling scratched around inside. Was the driver following me, or was I just being paranoid?

"Why the Toussaint family?" Calvin asked. "Shouldn't the necklace go to Delphine's kin?"

I dragged my attention away from the SUV. "Delphine never owned the necklace," I said. "The story is that Armand was originally going to give it to her, but since he actually gave it to Beatriz instead, it's always been in the Toussaint family."

"That's what caused all the trouble in the first place," Calvin pointed out. "Maybe if the necklace goes back to where it was meant to go in the first place, maybe then the curse will end."

"First of all," I said, "the curse is baloney. None of the Toussaints were killed. They died. Period. Armand and

Beatriz probably caught some disease that was making the rounds. And then when Gustave's wife and his daughter both died, people started imagining connections that weren't actually there."

Calvin didn't say anything for a block or two, and I wondered if I'd offended him. I hoped not, but even for the sake of our brand-new friendship, I wasn't going to pretend to believe in a curse.

The SUV was still behind me, but a car had moved between us and the SUV's driver hadn't tried to pass it. My uneasiness faded.

"You're not from New Orleans," Calvin said at last. "You don't know how things work. But believe me, if Delphine Mercier put a curse on that necklace, the thing is cursed to this day."

"Let's say the curse is real," I said. "Just for the sake of argument. Do you think Delphine knew that Beatriz was expecting a baby when she put the curse on the necklace? I mean, it's bad enough to want the adults dead, but somehow it seems so much worse with a baby involved. Two babies, actually. They were both pregnant at the same time."

Calvin shrugged. "Armand's old lady didn't care about Delphine's baby, so maybe she figured it evened the score."

I couldn't believe my ears. "How do you figure that? Beatriz was Armand's *wife*. She had every right to object to him giving another woman a gift like that. Any gift, really. Beatriz just took what should have been hers in the first place."

"She took a lot more than that," Calvin said. "Armand could have tossed Delphine aside like yesterday's garbage anytime he wanted to. How was she supposed to take care of herself and her kids? Who were *his* kids, by the way. It's not like she would get alimony or palimony or . . . whatever."

His response surprised me, but I had to admit he had a point. Plus, I kind of liked the way he stuck up for Delphine rather than take the man's side. "I think it's fair to say that both women were treated badly by that system," I said. "The whole situation was unfair. I can't imagine living in a world where my husband could have a whole second family and nobody would think twice about it. And even if I hated it, I'd be expected to keep my mouth shut and look the other way. It's cruel and demeaning to the women on both sides."

"Yeah. I guess you're right," Calvin said. "But you can't blame Delphine too much. She had to look out for her family, didn't she? Family's the most important thing there is. And she did it the only way she knew how."

I braked for a red light and sighed. "For what it's worth, I can't even begin to understand how difficult Delphine's life was. Or Beatriz's either. And the truth is that if I'd been in Delphine's shoes, I might have been tempted to cast a curse or two myself."

Calvin grinned. "I knew you were reasonable. I told Ox so, too."

I laughed. "Well, thanks. Did he agree with you?"

"Of course! He's not stupid."

Half a block later, I pulled into a parking lot near the police station. I watched as the white SUV drove on by and convinced myself that it hadn't been following me. We spent the next hour in a waiting room that smelled of stale coffee and unwashed bodies, although except for one middle-aged woman sobbing noisily in one corner and a resigned-looking businessman who checked his phone every few minutes, we had the place to ourselves.

Eventually, the officer at the front desk produced some paperwork for me to review and sign, which took all of five minutes. Once I'd finished, we went back to waiting. I didn't want to talk about the necklace in that room where anybody could hear, and to my relief, Calvin had either run out of things to say or he picked up on my feelings.

We chatted for a bit about inconsequential things until,

after what felt like forever, a tall young man in uniform came over. He was probably mid-twenties with dark hair and an engaging smile. He introduced himself as Officer Reagan, and led us into a small, musty-smelling room. In the center was a wobbly table with a scarred top, and around it were four industrial-looking plastic chairs. All the comforts of home.

After Calvin and I made ourselves relatively comfortable, Officer Reagan put a cardboard box on the table in front of us. "I need you to look over the property and make sure everything is there," he said. "Then you'll sign the inventory form and you're free to leave."

"This shouldn't take long," I said with a dubious glance at the box. "I only have one thing to pick up."

Officer Reagan took the lid off the box and motioned for me to look inside. The wooden box I'd come to know rested inside, its fleur-de-lis pattern gleaming even in the glow of the overhead fluorescent bulb. I checked inside it to make sure that the ruby necklace was there.

"This is it," I said, barely repressing a shudder at the thought of Orra Trussell clutching the necklace in her hand as she died. "Is there anything else you need from me?"

Reagan handed over another form. "I just need you to sign one more thing," he said. "Then we're done."

I glanced over the form to make sure I wasn't signing my life away or confessing to some unsolved crime, then scribbled my signature in all the appropriate places. "You wouldn't happen to know if they've figured out who broke in to the Vintage Vault, would you?"

"I thought the case was closed," Calvin said.

Officer Reagan took the form from me and tossed it into the empty cardboard box. "It is. That's why we're returning the evidence."

"It's only been a couple of days," I protested. "Have you even looked for the burglar?"

"Of course," Reagan assured me. "To the best of my knowledge, it was a cold case to begin with. No evidence. No leads other than the second 911 call, and that didn't pan out."

I'd been about to pick up the wooden box, but I snatched my hand back quickly. "What second 911 call?"

Guilt flashed across Reagan's boyish face. "I probably shouldn't say anything—"

"You already did," I pointed out. "Come on. It's not as if you're talking about an ongoing investigation. So what's the harm in answering a couple of questions, right? Who made the second 911 call?"

Reagan shook his head, resigned. "It came from a pay phone about a block away from the Vintage Vault. We have no idea who placed it."

"Male or female?"

"Don't even know. Could have been either. The voice was whispering."

I waited for him to say more. He didn't.

"That's it? That's all you've got?"

"That's it," Reagan said firmly. His gaze flashed on my face and away before he could make eye contact. "Why do you think we closed the case?"

"Did you even try to find a witness? Did anyone see the person who made that second call?" Officer Reagan was inching toward the door. "Exactly what did the caller say?"

Reagan stopped inching. "He—or she—just said that there was a woman in distress at the Vintage Vault on Andorra. That's all. The call disconnected before the operator could ask for more information."

"Obviously it was someone who saw Orra inside the store," I said. "There were no witnesses to the robbery, so it had to be the thief who called."

"Not necessarily. It might just have been a Good Samaritan—somebody who saw that Mrs. Trussell was in trouble and called for help, but who didn't want to get involved. You'd be surprised how often that kind of thing happens. And even if you *are* right," he said, cutting me off before I could argue, "we have no evidence or witnesses pointing to the caller as the burglar. I'm sorry, ma'am, but it's a dead end. Now if there's nothing else . . ."

There was plenty more I wanted to say, but I recognized a lost cause when I saw it. I told myself to be happy with the information he'd given me and stuffed the wooden box into my bag. "No. Nothing else." I shot a look at Calvin. "Are you coming, or not?"

He scrambled to his feet, followed me out the door, and all the way back across town, he listened to me vent about the police and the halfhearted job they'd done investigating the burglary. He didn't even interrupt me once. Is that a friend, or what?

Sixteen

Calvin asked me to drop him at the Dizzy Duke so he could catch a ride home with Ox. I figured, why not join him? The rest of the staff was probably there, and I could use a chance to unwind. Not that there was anything at home to keep me wound up, but it wouldn't hurt to let my concerned coworkers see that I'd made it all the way to the police station and back unharmed.

Luck was with me for once. I snagged a parking spot just half a block from the Duke, and Calvin and I trotted inside. The band hadn't started playing yet but the jukebox was blaring a tune loud enough to make conversation difficult. Which was fine with me. I didn't want to talk about the trip to the police station anyway.

I checked behind the bar to see if Gabriel was working, but the relief bartender was on duty. I stifled my disappointment and dragged a chair to the table that was already crowded with Zydeco folk. Even Zoey had decided to join the others, which I took as a sign that she was fitting in.

"You made it!" Isabeau shouted when she saw me.

"Safe and sound," I shouted back. "Calvin could have stayed behind."

"I didn't mind," he assured me, straddling an empty chair. "It's all good."

"And you got it okay?" Isabeau asked. "The you-know-what?"

Not exactly subtle but at least it didn't seem like anyone was paying attention to us. "Everything's fine," I said. "Let's move on."

Sparkle treated Isabeau to a dark scowl. "Why don't you wave a banner over her head and paint an X on her back?"

Isabeau flounced in her seat and frowned back. "Why don't you lighten up?"

"Why don't we all talk about something else?" I shouted just as the music died away. The question reverberated in the relative quiet, and heads from nearby tables swiveled in our direction. Yeah, I was that cool.

Thankfully, Sparkle stepped up and drew the attention from me by passing around a tablet containing some pictures she'd taken of JD on her last visit. We all spent some time oohing and ahhing over them and then got down to the business of rehashing the day. I'd just started to relax when I saw Ox focus on something over my shoulder. His expression tightened and he flicked a look at me.

I glanced behind me and saw a man of around forty, around my height but sturdy, with dark hair and a goatee-mustache combo that gave him a slightly unsavory look. He looked kind of familiar, but I couldn't place him. "Rita Lucero?"

From the corner of my eye I saw Ox give the guy a chin jerk. "Who wants to know?"

"Carlo Mancini." He addressed his answer to me. "Sorry to bother you here, but I've left several messages and I haven't heard back."

Ahh, so that's why he looked familiar. I'd seen him on the news but never paid enough attention to link the face with the name. "That's because I'm not giving interviews," I said. "Now if you'll excuse us . . ."

I didn't really expect him to give up easily, and he didn't surprise me. Instead of bowing out with a *mea culpa*, he dragged a chair up to our table.

Estelle looked up from the table and gave Zoey a nudge with her elbow. Zoey's posture straightened abruptly and a flush tinted her round cheeks. Isabeau fluffed her ponytail and looked around, probably to see if he'd brought a camera crew with him. Ox glared at him and Dwight went for a more casual reaction, leaning back in his chair and flipping his coaster over and over on the table. Calvin scooted his chair closer to mine. Only Sparkle seemed unaffected.

"I understand you found the famous Toussaint necklace," Mancini said. "I'd like to get a sound bite for our viewers."

"Sorry," I said with a thin smile. "You're wasting your time."

Mancini gave me a sickeningly friendly smile. "Oh, come on, Ms. Lucero. It's a great story. Old world feud. A cursed necklace. I promise I won't take up much of your time."

Ox half stood, ready to leap to my defense. I waved him back into his chair, determined to prove that I didn't need to be protected. "Look, Mr. Mancini, I understand that this is the kind of story some people want to hear about, but there's really nothing to tell. In order to make the story exciting enough for TV, you'd have to fabricate most of it and I'm not going to help you do that."

"So it's not true? You didn't find the necklace?"

"Oh, we found it all right," Zoey said from the other end of the table. "Rita and me. We found it together."

I shot her a "shut up" look, which she pointedly ignored. "I'm the one you've talked to when you call the bakery," she said. "And *I* think it's exciting. I've got a picture of it and everything."

I groaned aloud—I think. The sound was smothered by the music on the jukebox. "Zoey—"

"What? Why can't I tell him about it? It's not going to hurt anything."

Estelle gave me a round-eyed look. "You can't really forbid her to talk to this guy, Rita. It's a free country."

I swore under my breath and stood. "Fine. You want an interview? Let's go." I jerked my head toward the door. "I'll give you five minutes."

Mancini flashed a triumphant smile and got to his feet. "Terrific. What say we have your friend come along?"

I shook my head. It wasn't that I wanted to rob Zoey of her moment in the sun, but I had no idea what she might say and I wanted to contain the damage as much as humanly possible. "Just me," I said. "Otherwise, it's no deal."

Zoey crumpled under the weight of holding her spine straight and slumped back in her chair looking mutinous. I hated putting that look on her face, but I had to consider Miss Frankie and Zydeco. My decision was for the Greater Good.

I could see Mancini weighing his options for a moment. On the one hand, Zoey was almost certain to give him a more interesting interview than I would, but as Zydeco's owner, my version would probably carry more weight. It was a crap shoot, and I wasn't sure I'd win, but eventually he dipped his head and turned away from the table.

He motioned for me to go ahead, and I did, clutching my bag close to my side. First thing tomorrow I was taking the necklace to the bank and locking it in a safe-deposit box. I checked over my shoulder every few seconds to make sure he hadn't doubled back to get a one-on-one with Zoey. When we finally stepped outside, I saw that a thick fog had settled in, shrouding the neighborhood in mist.

Now that we were alone, I started to get a little nervous. I'd seen Carlo Mancini on TV, but what did I really know about him? I glanced around to see if anybody else was out and about, but my visibility was down to almost nothing.

I did my best not to look nervous. "You got a camera crew hiding out somewhere?"

Mancini nodded. "They're here. I'll bring them over in a minute. But first, tell me the story. How did you find the necklace?"

"Before we get to that," I said, "I also want your word that you'll leave my mother-in-law alone."

"Mrs. Renier? I don't know if I can agree to that. She's pretty well known. A lot of people will want to hear what she has to say."

"That's too bad," I said. "I need your word that you'll stop bothering her."

Mancini stroked his chin thoughtfully. "You're awfully demanding. I don't need to agree to any of your terms, you know."

"Maybe not. But you will. Miss Frankie will not be giving you an interview, no matter how many times you call. You might as well back off and save both of you some grief."

He conceded that point with a dip of his head. "What about your friend inside the bar?"

"She was involved for all of five minutes," I said. "She doesn't have much of a story to tell. I'm the one you want to talk to."

"Okay then. Talk. How did you find the necklace?"

"It was an accident," I said. "We were moving some boxes and a couple of them fell down the stairs. In the process they opened up a hole in the wall and ripped up some of the floorboards on the steps. That's where we found the necklace."

He scribbled something on a notepad and grinned at me. "What did you do then?"

I shrugged. "Nothing."

"Then how did the necklace end up at the Vintage Vault the night Mrs. Trussell died?"

"I took it to her for an appraisal."

"So . . . not exactly 'nothing' then."

"Not exactly 'something' either. I dropped the necklace off with her and went home. End of story."

"What do you say to people who think the necklace is cursed?"

"There's no such thing as a curse," I said. "And there certainly isn't one on the Toussaint necklace—*if* that's the necklace we found at Zydeco. We don't even know for sure that's what we found, or even whether our necklace is genuine."

"According to Dominique Kincaid, it is."

That caught me by surprise and I could tell Mancini knew it had. "How would she know?"

"Apparently Mrs. Trussell called her the night she died, and told Ms. Kincaid that the necklace was the real deal."

"Dominique told you and not me?" I tried to look amused. "You expect me to believe that?"

Mancini did a better job of looking amused than I had. "You can believe whatever you like, Ms. Lucero. So what do you plan to do with the necklace now that you have it back?"

Surprise number two. The guy was a jerk, but a jerk who was good at his job. Maybe some people would admire that, but I was stuck on the part where he was a first-class jerk. "What makes you think I have it back?"

"You went to the police station today. I assume you picked up the evidence."

Lights went on inside my head and that itchy feeling I'd had earlier came back, stronger than before. *The white SUV.* "You followed me?"

Mancini shrugged. "A reporter's gotta do what he's gotta do. So what are your plans?"

"I don't have any," I snapped. Maybe not the best response, considering I was talking to a man who had access to microphones and cameras, but he was seriously beginning to tick me off. "You wanted to know how I found the necklace and I've told you. Your five minutes are up."

I thought Mancini would try to stop me from leaving, but he just stood there with his arms folded across his chest and a smile playing across his lips as I strode back into the Dizzy Duke. I stopped just inside the door and watched as a couple of guys moved out of the fog to join him. One had a video camera on his shoulder and the other held a clipboard filled with papers. He laughed as if they'd just scored the coup of the century, and I tried desperately to convince myself I hadn't said anything I wouldn't want broadcast to the world.

Carlo Mancini had just earned himself a spot on my list of least favorite people. The trouble was, I didn't think he'd care.

I didn't sleep well that night. Snippets of my interview with Carlo Mancini kept playing through my head and I kept seeing Zoey's sullen face and Estelle's disapproving glances when I went back into the Dizzy Duke. Carlo Mancini's interruption had put a damper on the group's mood—or maybe it was me. In any case, I wasn't in the mood to party so I'd excused myself and hurried home.

By the time morning broke, I was no longer sure what I'd actually said to anybody. Part of me wanted to stay home and watch whatever station Carlo Mancini worked for until I saw what he'd done with our conversation. The other part wanted to pretend that last night had never happened. That's the part that won.

I brewed a travel mug of coffee and hopped into the Range Rover a few minutes before eight. Instead of driving to Zydeco, I aimed myself at the bank . . . until I remembered that it was Saturday and the bank would be closed. I didn't want to lug the necklace around with me, but there weren't many options available. I couldn't ask Miss Frankie to hold it. Bernice might say yes, but she'd almost certainly tell Miss Frankie and I'd have to dredge the river to find it again. Not that I believed in the curse, but I didn't want to ask one of my staff to hold on to it either.

My phone chimed a reminder so I checked it at the next stoplight. Meet Simone. In all the recent hullabaloo, I'd almost forgotten that Simone had asked me to stop by so we could touch base. Finding a safe place for the necklace would have to wait.

Touching base isn't my favorite part of the job, but it's a necessary one. When the client is as gracious as Simone, it's almost pleasant. She greeted me with a broad smile and led me into her office, where I found an array of fresh fruit and pastries. The room was redolent with the aroma of good-quality strong coffee.

I filled a plate and a cup and we settled down to business. We chatted amiably about space and decorations, about progress on the cakes and last-minute alterations to the menu. I don't know how long we'd been at it when Corinne Carver poked her head into the room. She looked better than the last time I'd seen her at the Monte Cristo. Her hair was done, her makeup flawless, but an unhappy expression dragged at the corners of her mouth.

"Excuse me, Simone, but Natalie Archer is here and she's demanding to see you. I've tried reasoning with her, but she just won't listen to me."

Simone's expression didn't change, but a flash of irritation appeared in her dark eyes. "Tell her I'm in a meeting, please. I'll be happy to call her when I'm through here."

"I don't think—" Corinne began, but a commotion in the hallway cut her off.

A moment later Natalie Archer burst into the room. I'd met Natalie once or twice and I can't say that she's my favorite member of the Vintage Clothing Society. She's probably mid-sixties, solidly built with a perpetually sour expression on her face. From what I'd seen of her, she bulldozed her way through life and she was in fine form that morning.

"You *have* to do something, Simone. And no, this can't wait. The ball is in a week. This space issue needs to be resolved now."

"I'm in a meeting, Natalie. We can talk about your concerns later."

Natalie dragged a chair away from the table and sat, resting her purse on her lap and clutching it tightly with both hands. "This can't wait," she said again. "I've tried to talk with Colleen, but she won't listen to reason."

"Corinne," Simone corrected her.

Natalie's frown deepened and the grip she had on her purse tightened. "I don't care what her name is. I care that she has taken away so much space we won't have room to display anything at the ball. I've tried to narrow down my selection, but it's simply not possible."

"I realize that space is an issue," Simone said with a lot more patience than I would have shown. "But I'm sure Corinne has explained about the flood at the hotel."

Natalie dipped her head slightly. "She told me about that, yes. But that's certainly not my fault. It's no excuse—"

Simone didn't wait for her to finish. "Then I'm sure you are aware that we've had to change the location of the ball for this year. And that means that everyone is having to make adjustments." Interrupting someone in the middle of a sentence might not seem like a big deal, but Simone is always perfectly polite. The stress of the ball must be getting to her.

"Not *everyone* is being affected adversely," Natalie

insisted. "You know how small some of these shops are. They can get by with less space. I can't."

"The space is allocated equally," Simone said. "Everyone pays the same amount and everyone's footage is being cut equally."

"I'm willing to pay more," Natalie said.

"That's not the issue," Simone said firmly. "I'm sure you wouldn't want me to cut your space if someone else made the same offer. Now if there's nothing else—"

"There most certainly *is* something else," Natalie said. She gave me a look clearly intended to send me packing. "But perhaps we should discuss this privately."

Seriously? She'd barged into my meeting with Simone, not the other way around. The lady had some serious entitlement issues. Still, I reached for my purse, intending to leave, but Simone stopped me. "Rita and I are in the middle of a meeting," she reminded Natalie. "If you absolutely must talk to me right now, you'll have to do it in front of her."

Natalie let out a heavy put-upon sigh, I guess to make sure we both knew how unreasonable we were being. "Fine. Then here it is: You have to do something about that girl. She's rude."

A muscle in Simone's jaw twitched. "Which girl would that be?"

"The receptionist or whatever she is. The one who was just in here. Colleen."

"Corinne." Simone's correction was a bit crisp this time.

"You know who I mean," Natalie said with a flick of her wrist. "Now, really, Simone, you know I'm usually extremely forgiving and tolerant of other people, but that girl's attitude leaves a lot to be desired."

I would have laughed at Natalie's list of her admirable traits, but I was pretty sure that would offend her. And it's not a good idea to bite the hand that feeds you. Offending someone like Natalie Archer might not be in Zydeco's best interests.

Somehow, Simone managed to keep a straight face. "Corinne is a valuable employee," she said. "She's doing exactly what I instructed her to do. I realize that you're unhappy with the changes we're having to make, but that's not Corinne's fault."

Natalie leaned forward slightly. "You're not saying we should blame Orra, are you? Poor thing! She didn't mean to die the way she did, and she certainly didn't intend to cause trouble for the rest of us."

"Of course not," Simone said. "Orra's heart attack has nothing to do with any of this."

"Except that it frees up her share of the space. And that space should go to someone who needs it. That's all I'm saying."

Simone looked horrified, and I had to admit I was pretty shocked myself but Natalie's real motive for barging in was becoming clear. "Won't Dominique use the space?" I asked. "If the Vintage Vault paid for the opportunity to display, they may still want to use it."

"I doubt that," Natalie said. "What would be the point? Surely the store will go out of business now. Dominique has her hands full dealing with all the legal issues."

"Oh?" Simone said. "You've spoken to her?"

"Only for a moment. She called to tell me there will be a small, private memorial for Orra on Monday. I suppose I should attend, but frankly, it's at the most inopportune time."

Simone and I exchanged another incredulous look.

Natalie tilted her head to one side, seemingly oblivious to our reactions. "You've heard the rumors, I assume. About Orra and the Toussaint necklace?"

Simone's gaze flicked toward me. "I've heard some talk, but I hardly think—"

"They say some cook found it. One of the caterers for the Belle Lune Ball, I heard."

Simone glanced at me again, but I gave my head what I hoped was an imperceptible shake. If Natalie didn't know about my connection to the necklace, I didn't want to tell her. And I certainly didn't want her to know that the necklace was in the room with us. It would be just like her to keel over and die just to get attention.

"I suppose," Natalie went on, unaware of my silent exchange with Simone, "there will be a big hassle now over ownership. Nothing is ever as easy as it should be."

"I don't think anyone has come forward to claim it," I said cautiously. "So maybe it won't be a problem."

Natalie cut an irritated look at me. "If you think that, my girl, you're living in a fantasy world. The ownership of that necklace has been hotly debated for a hundred and fifty years or more. The question won't go away now that the rubies have resurfaced."

I offered a tiny smile. "Well, maybe the current family will be more reasonable than their ancestors were."

"One can hope," Natalie said. "But I doubt it. The Merciers and their kin aren't what you'd call reasonable. Never have been."

I was about to ask what she meant by that when Simone took charge again. "We're getting off topic," she said. "I'm afraid Rita and I are both so busy we can't afford to get off track."

Natalie took the reprimand in stride and picked up where she'd left off. "My concern isn't solely about the changes Colleen is making to the hotel space. I'm deeply concerned about the way she treats a charter member of the society like myself. I don't think anyone can discount the contributions I've made."

"No one wants to do that," Simone assured her.

Natalie acknowledged that with a thin smile. "That's good to know, but it doesn't change the facts."

"As I said, Corinne is just doing her job."

Natalie's smile evaporated. "Simone, dear, I don't think you understand how . . . rude Colleen is. If you *must* keep her, perhaps someone should have a talk with her. Explain to her how things work around here. Teach her a few things about how to get along."

"With you."

"With everyone." Natalie rearranged the death grip she had on her purse. "Really, Simone, if you won't see to the matter yourself, you'll leave me no choice but to go over your head and discuss this with Evangeline. That girl is not the best face for the society. Even you must be able to see that."

Simone stood abruptly. "I think we're finished here," she said. "Feel free to talk to my mother if that's what you want to do, but I must ask you to leave now."

Natalie's expression hardened with disapproval and, I thought, some embarrassment. Still clutching her purse in both hands, she stood and lifted her chin. "You disappoint me, Simone. I expected better." And with that, she strode out of the room.

Simone remained standing until Natalie disappeared, then sank into her chair and laughed uneasily. "I shouldn't have lost my temper, but she's such an awful woman I couldn't help myself."

"You were a lot nicer to her than I would have been," I said. "What has she got against Corinne anyway?"

"Who knows? That woman is so full of herself, she thinks everyone should do her bidding." She rubbed her forehead and sighed. "I'm sorry for the interruption."

"That's not a problem," I assured her, and we got back down to business. But all through the meeting, my mind kept drifting back to what Natalie had said about the necklace. So far nobody had approached me about ownership, but I wondered if that was about to change.

Seventeen

⚜

After my meeting with Simone, I walked through the French Quarter toward the parking garage. Even though it was nearly noon, only a few tourists were evident. The sky was clear and a cool breeze made the walk pleasant. At least it would have been pleasant if I weren't so uncomfortably aware of the necklace in my bag. I had to find a safe place to keep it, and fast. I certainly couldn't keep lugging it all over town with me until Monday when the bank reopened.

I'd almost reached my destination when I remembered that the New Orleans Historic Voodoo Museum was somewhere nearby, which meant I might be able to get a look at the portrait of Beatriz Toussaint wearing the necklace. I googled the museum's address on my phone, saw that it was open until six, and decided to make a detour before going back to work.

I found the museum in the middle of the block, on the first floor of an old building with wrought iron balconies and flower boxes filled with pansies blooming on the upper floors. I stepped inside, paid my entrance fee, and looked around curiously. It seemed that every inch of space was filled with something, from statues and bottles of potions to postcards, books, and dolls in every shape and size. Dozens of pictures were hung on the walls, and I wandered slowly until I came to the painting I'd been looking for.

The portrait was smaller than I'd been expecting, but every bit as opulent as I'd anticipated. An ornately carved frame accented with gold-leaf surrounded the image of a very young woman with dark hair piled artfully on her head and huge almost-black eyes. Whatever doubts I still harbored about whether or not the necklace was genuine vanished as I looked up at the lovely woman in the portrait, and she stared soberly out. I fancied that I could see the sadness she must have felt knowing that her husband routinely slept with another woman.

She wore an elegant burgundy gown, no doubt chosen to match the magnificent ruby necklace at her throat. All three rows of rubies seemed to gleam on the canvas, capturing whatever light had been in the room at the time. The intricate setting matched that of the necklace in my bag, and for a moment I imagined "my" necklace almost vibrating in response.

Remembering that I'd saved a copy of Zoey's picture of the necklace onto my phone, I decided to compare the two. I'm not a jeweler, but to my untrained eye the two necklaces certainly appeared to be identical.

I walked out of the museum determined to make sure that justice was done—both for Beatriz and for Delphine. I just didn't know what that would turn out to be.

After collecting my car, I drove to a home improvement store and shelled out a few dollars for a lockbox, but it did little to make me feel better. If I could lift the mini safe, so could anyone else. Anyone who wanted to steal the necklace could easily walk off with the whole lockbox. The most it would do was slow someone down for a few minutes. But at least it was something.

I had work to do, so I took the lockbox to Zydeco, where I found the whole staff hard at work, including Zoey. Seeing the cake-decorating crew there on a Saturday didn't surprise me. We put in whatever hours are needed to get the job done. But finding Zoey sorting through the paperwork on Edie's desk caught me off guard. I gave her another point on my mental scorecard and lugged the lockbox into my office.

She followed me, knocking on the door frame to get my attention. "Estelle said it would be okay if I came in with her today," she said when I glanced up. "You don't mind, do you?"

"Not a bit," I assured her. "Are you working on anything special?"

She shook her head and hooked a lock of hair behind an ear. "That reporter called again. I didn't talk to him, but he sure is pushy. He said you can't tell me not to talk to him."

Frowning at that piece of news, I cleared a spot on my desk and put the lockbox there. "I guess he's probably right," I admitted, "but I'd rather you didn't."

"How come? I mean, I'm not going to say anything stupid."

"I'm sure you wouldn't," I said. "I'm still trying to figure out what's going on. Assuming the necklace is genuine, that means it's worth a lot of money. I'd rather not advertise the fact that I have it." At least not until I could make sure the necklace was safe.

Zoey nodded thoughtfully, then jerked her chin toward the metal box on my desk. "What's that?"

"A lockbox," I told her. "Someplace a little more secure than what I'm currently using."

Zoey actually cracked a smile at that. "You mean your purse?"

"Yeah. Not the most secure location in the world." I pulled the wooden box from my bag and checked to make sure it would fit into the lockbox, but I hesitated before actually putting it inside. "Did you ever hear from your friend's mother about the curse?"

"Jennifer's mom?" Zoey nodded and came into my office. "Yeah. She's totally into all that stuff. She says that it's, like, really well documented. There's even a portrait somewhere of Armand's wife wearing it."

I nodded and opened the wooden box, gently setting aside the lid and removing the velvet-wrapped necklace. "I just went to see the portrait myself," I told her. "I'm pretty sure the necklace is a match. But that doesn't solve anything. In fact, it raises more questions than it answers."

Zoey craned to see the necklace and let out a soft sigh. "I don't think I've ever seen anything more beautiful. Have you?"

I motioned for her to sit down, then did the same, tucking the velvet out of the way so we could both see the rubies. "I can't say that I have," I agreed. "It's stunning."

Zoey sighed again. "I wonder what it would be like to wear something like that. I mean, how special would you feel with that around your neck?"

I thought about the look on Beatriz's face in the portrait. "I guess it would depend on how you got it," I said. "It looks amazing on Beatriz in the painting, but she only had the necklace because she demanded it. I think that might take some of the shine off."

"You're probably right," Zoey said, her voice still hushed. She fell silent and we both stared at the necklace for a little while before she spoke again. "I know you'll probably say 'no,' but do you think I could try it on?"

I didn't like knowing that I'd been such a Debbie Downer with Zoey. "I don't think it would hurt anything," I said, ignoring the soft whisper of warning that zipped through my head. *There was no curse. Trying on the necklace wouldn't hurt Zoey.* "Come on, let's go find a mirror."

She trailed me to the bathroom and watched me eagerly as I lifted the necklace from its bed of velvet. At my direction, she lifted her hair and I fastened the necklace around her neck. Both our gazes shot to the mirror, where the three rows of rubies glittered back at us. Zoey's eyes were huge, but soft and almost doe-like as she looked at her reflection and I gave myself a mental high-five for letting her have this moment.

Zoey seemed transfixed by her own face, and I could certainly understand why. The rubies seemed to smooth out her complexion and give it a soft, golden glow it didn't usually have. The gentle curve of her lips and the gleam of appreciation in her eyes transfigured her right in front of my eyes. I could see the stunning young woman she would be if she would only spend a little more time taking care of herself.

"You look beautiful," I whispered.

Zoey turned her head to look at me. "It's amazing, isn't it?" She turned back to her reflection and her smile faded slowly. "You'd better take it off now. I don't want to break it or anything."

She was probably right. The setting was old and hadn't been used in so long, it could be extremely fragile. I unhooked the necklace and placed it carefully on the velvet then smiled at Zoey. "Maybe after all the excitement of the Belle Lune Ball dies down, we can get a picture of you wearing it."

She grinned broadly. "Seriously? You'd do that?"

"Sure," I said. *What could be the harm?*

Zoey went back to work and I picked up the necklace, intending to go back to my office. But my inner Cinderella surfaced and whispered that I should try the necklace on myself. I didn't even argue with her. Instead, I carefully fastened the rubies around my own neck and took a good, long look at myself in the mirror. Like it had with Zoey, the necklace improved my complexion and darkened the color of my eyes. It fit perfectly, and with the right gown (and on the right occasion), I thought I could be a knockout.

I still didn't believe in the curse, but for that moment I believed in magic.

I dropped by the bank first thing on Monday morning. I filled out some paperwork and shelled out a little cash, and finally locked the necklace away for safekeeping. Relieved to have it out of my hands, I spent the rest of the day at work, trying to finish all five cakes so we could get a jump on the food for the banquet. As I'd predicted, we were flooded with calls about the necklace. I ignored them all. It was bad enough listening to my friends discussing the story about it that had run on last night's news.

Predictably, Zoey had little to say on the subject, but Estelle more than made up for her, pointing out inaccuracies in Carlo Mancini's story that her niece no doubt could have corrected. Ox thought the reporter should have said less about the curse. Sparkle thought he should have said more. Dwight said that he'd seen a link to the video on Facebook and Isabeau said it was a shame I hadn't had time to fix my hair and makeup first.

A little after five that evening, I drove away from Zydeco. I had every intention of going home, slipping into my most comfortable pajamas, and spending some quality time with Ben and Jerry, but when a white SUV pulled out of a parking lot just ahead of me, my conversation with Carlo Mancini came rushing back again.

According to Carlo, Orra had finished her appraisal of the necklace before she died. Apparently she'd told Dominique, who had shared that bit of information with Carlo. That bothered me on several levels—the main one being, why would Orra have told Dominique instead of me? Before I got too worked up over that, I thought it might be a good idea to find out if the story was even true. Carlo might have been playing me, looking for a bigger story.

And besides, I really ought to pay my respects since I hadn't gone to the memorial service. If I didn't go now, I might not get another chance to talk to Dominique until the Belle Lune Ball. And if Natalie Archer was right about the Vintage Vault's future, I might not be able to find Dominique at all after that.

I might not find her tonight either. I had no idea if the Vintage Vault was still open or if Orra's death had closed it down. But it was the only link I had to Dominique and curiosity was eating me alive, so I decided to take a chance.

The Vintage Vault was dark when I arrived and the front door—half of which was covered with plywood—was locked. I was just about to leave when I thought I saw someone moving around in the back of the store. Hoping I'd found Dominique and not a burglar, I knocked on the front door.

The figure stopped moving, stood still for a moment, and then came toward the door. I breathed a sigh of relief when I recognized Dominique. She wore jeans and a T-shirt, and her dark hair was pulled back from her face with a headband. Dark circles created deep shadows under her eyes, and her face was pale and drawn.

She stopped a few feet from the door and called out, "Sorry. We're closed until further notice."

"It's Rita Lucero," I shouted back. I moved a step backward into the fading sunlight so she could see me better. "I left a necklace here for an appraisal?"

Dominique nodded. "I know who you are, but I don't have your necklace. The police took it."

"Yes, they told me," I said. "I'd just like to talk to you for a few minutes."

Dominique hesitated for a moment, then closed the distance to the door and flipped the lock. "I guess you can come in," she said as she opened the door for me. "The lawyers said I can't open for business, but I don't think there's any law against talking." She offered me a brittle smile and motioned for me to come inside. As soon as I'd cleared the doorway, she locked the door again. "What is it you want?"

Now that I was closer, I could see that her eyes were bloodshot. Apparently, Orra's death had hit her hard.

Aunt Yolanda would have known the right thing to say. I felt myself floundering, but I decided to ease into the conversation gently. "First, let me say how sorry I am for your loss. I guess you and Orra were pretty close?"

Her gaze dropped to the floor briefly. "Yeah, we were. There was only the two of us here."

"I understand she had no family."

Dominique gave her head a brief shake. "No. Not anymore. Her husband passed about twenty years ago. She lived alone after that."

"I'm sure she was grateful for your friendship," I said, hoping that thought would give her some peace. "I'm sure it's been rough for you."

Dominique nodded and folded her arms across her chest. "Yeah. It has been. I had to go through everything here by myself for the police. It's been hell and I've barely slept since Orra—since it happened."

My heart went out to her. I'd thought a lot about Orra since the break-in, but I hadn't really considered how the burglary and Orra's death would've affected Dominique. "Do you have friends or family that could help you with any of the work here?"

Dominique shook her head. "No, but the worst is over, I think." She glanced around the store, taking in the crowded shelves and racks of vintage clothing. "With Orra gone, all of this will be sold or given away. I suppose I'll have to help with that. They *should* ask me to help anyway. There's nobody else who knows this shop the way I do."

"I guess that means you won't be able to keep the store open?"

Bitterness flashed across Dominique's face. "Not unless Orra suffered a pang of conscience and gave it to me in a will, but nobody has found a will yet so I'm not counting on that."

"You won't be at the Belle Lune Ball?"

"Oh, I'll go," Dominique said. "My ticket is paid for and I have a great dress, but the lawyers won't let me do the exhibit. I can't remove anything from the premises. The store and everything in it have to go through probate. That probably means that Sol Lehmann will finally get his greedy little hands on Orra's stuff."

In the rush of cake making and Miss Frankie's disappearance, I'd almost forgotten about Sol. Just how greedy was he? He'd certainly seemed eager to buy my one and only piece of real jewelry, and it seemed that the Toussaint necklace wasn't the only item he wanted. "He was here the day I dropped off the necklace, wasn't he?"

"Sure was." Dominique's mouth twisted and a hard gleam filled her brown eyes. "He was always sniffing around, trying to see what Orra had acquired and then trying to gyp her out of it. I swear, the man has some kind of radar when it comes to valuable objects. Or should I say his wife does. She's the real boss in that family. Be warned, Sol will probably be coming after you, offering to take the necklace off your hands."

"As a matter of fact—"

Dominique's eyes narrowed slightly. "Don't tell me. He's already come knocking on your door."

"Not quite," I said. "But he did see me having lunch with a friend. He cornered me there and offered to buy the necklace."

"Well, that figures. Whatever he tells you, don't believe him. I swear, that man would cheat his own mother."

Harsh. I wondered if that were true. "Orra said something similar to me when I was here. I take it she and Sol knew each other quite well."

Dominique picked up a silk scarf from a nearby table and folded it neatly. "The vintage business is a small one. Everybody knows everybody, whether you want to or not. How much did he offer for it?"

The question sounded innocent enough, but for the first time I wondered if Dominique had an interest in the necklace for herself. Was that why she hadn't told me that Orra had finished her appraisal? "He said something about wanting to display the necklace at the Belle Lune Ball."

Dominique let out a harsh laugh. "Yeah? Why doesn't that surprise me?" She folded another scarf, her movements sharp and jerky. "Look, I can't tell you what to do, but if you want my advice, I'd be careful around him and his wife." She picked up another scarf and eyed me curiously. "But you didn't come here to talk about Sol Lehmann, did you?"

"No, I didn't," I admitted. "I met a reporter the other night. He said you told him that Orra had completed her appraisal of the necklace before she died. Is that true?"

Dominique smoothed her hands over the scarf and nodded. "Yes. I'm sorry, I know I should have told you, but everything was so crazy that night, and then later—" She smiled almost sheepishly. "By then the police had the necklace and it didn't seem to matter so much anymore."

I wasn't sure if I believed her, but I didn't argue. "So it's true that Orra believed the necklace I brought in was the genuine Toussaint necklace?"

"Yes," Dominique said. "She called me about eight, I think. I was home watching TV and I thought she'd gone home, too, but I guess she'd stayed here. She said that she'd had a look at the necklace and she was convinced it was the real thing."

I'd been having dinner with Calvin at that time. I realized

with a jolt that if we'd lingered an hour longer, I might have seen the burglar on my way to my car.

Coulda, shoulda, woulda. I hadn't been in the neighborhood when Orra died. I hadn't had a chance to save her life. And I couldn't turn back the clock and get a different outcome. I needed to focus on the things I could affect now. "I wonder why she didn't call me?"

Dominique looked away for a moment then slowly brought her gaze back to my face. "I know it sounds bad, but she wanted to buy the piece from you. When she called, she asked me to make a list of high-ticket items I thought we could sell quickly. We didn't have enough money in the store's account to offer you anywhere near what that necklace is worth, but Orra desperately wanted to own it."

I hadn't expected that. Maybe I should have. "You're saying that she was planning to drag out the appraisal process until she could get the money together?"

Dominique nodded. "Not entirely aboveboard, I guess, but not illegal. She knew there was a chance you'd turn her down, but she was hoping that if she offered you cash, you'd accept the offer."

"And she'd be able to buy it before anyone else knew it was available." And she'd seemed like such a sweet old lady.

"Yeah, but that didn't work so well. Sol spotted the necklace when he was here that day. He badgered Orra for a long time after you left, asking to see it, promising he wouldn't tell anyone that Orra had it if she'd just let him take a look."

"And did she?"

"No. And believe me, he wasn't happy about that."

No surprise there. "Do you think there's any chance that Sol was the person who broke in here that night?"

Dominique chewed her bottom lip while she considered that. "I guess he could have. It doesn't really seem like Sol's style, but I wouldn't put anything past him."

I thought about mentioning the second, anonymous 911 call, but I decided to keep that piece of information to myself, at least until I knew whether or not I could trust Dominique. I wondered if Sol might have called for help after he realized that Orra was having a heart attack. Maybe—but if he was as greedy as Orra and Dominique claimed, would he have run off without the necklace?

"How did Orra seem when she called you? Was she feeling ill?"

"Not that I know of," Dominique said. "She didn't say anything about that to me." She stopped talking, gave her answer some thought, and bobbed her head firmly. "I'm sure she was feeling all right. She just sounded excited about the necklace."

"So there was nothing unusual about her phone call? Nothing at all?"

"I wouldn't say that," Dominique said with a halfhearted smile. "She wasn't in the habit of calling me at home, so that was a bit different, but it wasn't unheard of. What's this all about? Orra's gone and I don't have your necklace, so I really don't see how I can help you."

"I'm not sure what it's about," I admitted. "I just keep thinking that Orra's death was somehow brought on by the burglary, and I think the police are wrong to close the case without even trying to find out who broke in."

Dominique laughed softly. "You really didn't expect them to waste their time, did you? Everybody knows that Orra died because of the curse."

I was getting *so* tired of hearing about that stupid curse! "There's no curse," I insisted. "Orra died because somebody wanted to steal something from her. Maybe it was the Toussaint necklace. Maybe it wasn't. I don't think we'll ever know for sure."

Dominique frowned thoughtfully. "What else could it have been?"

"I don't know. I'm sure you have a few things of value around here. If the burglar was somebody looking for drug money, it probably wouldn't have mattered what he took."

"We both know it wasn't that," Dominique argued. "The thief didn't actually take anything. Whoever broke in was after one thing and Orra died trying to protect it."

I shifted uncomfortably as a heavy weight of guilt settled on my shoulders. I told myself again that I wasn't responsible for Orra's death . . . but if I hadn't left the necklace with her, she might still be alive. "Do you have any idea who might have broken in? If it was someone looking for the necklace, I should know who to watch out for."

Dominique glanced at the sheet of plywood covering the broken glass in the door and let out a deep sigh. "I don't know. I wish I did. It *could* have been Sol, but it could have been almost anybody."

"But you and Sol and I were the only people who knew the Toussaint necklace was here. That whittles down the list of suspects pretty far."

"Well, it wasn't *me*," Dominique snapped. "Orra could have told somebody else. Or Sol might have. I'm sure he told his wife, and Orra may have called someone for a second opinion. I don't know why you're worried about that. I mean you *know* how the curse goes, right? Anybody who tries to own the necklace will come to harm—anybody but Delphine and her descendants, that is. Orra wasn't a Mercier so the necklace got her. Period."

"The Merciers are safe?" I asked, surprised by the revelation. Why hadn't anyone mentioned that before?

With a shrug, Dominique adjusted the headband holding back her hair. "Sure. You don't think Delphine would curse her own family, do you?"

I guess that seemed logical. If I believed in curses at all, of course. "Did Orra say anything else when she called you that night?" I asked. "Maybe she mentioned someone or said something unusual . . . Something that didn't seem odd at the time?"

"If she did, I don't remember," Dominique said. "Believe me, I've tried and tried to remember. She called and told me about her appraisal of the necklace. She asked me to put together the list. I mean, the only thing that was out of the ordinary was the other call that came in while we were talking, but that wasn't anything."

"What phone call?"

"The phone rang while we were talking," Dominique said. "By the time she clicked over to answer it, the person had hung up. It was nothing, no big deal."

I wasn't so sure. Dominique might be right, but I had an uneasy feeling that I couldn't explain away. "Did you tell the police about that call?"

Dominique shrugged. "I think so. I'm not sure."

"Did Orra call you from her cell phone? Maybe we could check her incoming call log to see if it recorded the number."

"No, I know she called from the landline here at the shop because it showed up on my caller ID. And that's why I knew she got the call. I heard the second line ringing. You can't always hear if a call comes through on call waiting."

"You heard the phone ring?"

"Yeah. We've got a couple of lines, so when one is busy, the next incoming call cycles to the second line. That's what happened that night, I guess." She straightened a plastic tray filled with vintage handbags and gave me an impatient look. "I'm sorry I can't be more help, but there's really nothing to tell. Orra didn't have any family, and she really didn't have any friends. I don't know who broke in here, and frankly the sooner I'm done with this place, the better. It gives me the creeps now, especially after dark."

She shot a meaningful look at the windows and I realized

that the sun had set. "Of course," I said. "I'll let you get back to what you were doing." I thanked her for her time and she let me out, locking the door behind me. She might think that my visit had been a waste of time, but I didn't agree. I'd learned that Orra wasn't as sweet as I'd first thought and that she'd planned to string me along until she could gather enough money to buy the necklace. And I'd learned that Dominique had known how valuable the necklace was before Orra died.

Both Orra and Dominique had warned me about Sol Lehmann and his wife. Had one of them come back after the Vintage Vault closed for the day, intent upon taking the necklace for himself? Or was Dominique just trying to shift the focus from herself?

I wondered about that other phone call Orra had received that night. Dominique had dismissed it as nothing, but my gut was telling me it was significant. There had to be some way to find out who called the shop that night. The police could have tracked it easily enough, but they weren't investigating. The phone company would certainly have a record of calls, but it's not like I could just pop in and ask to see the list.

I'd learned a lot, but it was just enough to make me run into another brick wall. I should be smart and put the whole thing out of my mind, but that was easier said than done.

Eighteen

After my stop at the Vintage Vault I still had time for my rendezvous with Ben and Jerry, so I drove home, determined to relax and stop thinking about the necklace, at least for one night. Comfy PJs? Check. Cherry Garcia? Check. The TV remote and a good book? Check, check. I settled in and called up the oldest episode of *The Blacklist* on my DVR list. I was breathless with anticipation by the time that episode ended, but too tired to watch another one.

I tossed the empty ice cream container into the trash and carried my book upstairs to my bedroom, where I made a pretense of reading for a while. The book was good, but between sheer physical and mental exhaustion, my ability to focus was shot.

I must have fallen asleep somewhere in the middle of the page because when I woke up sometime later, the book was open on my chest and my bedside lamp was still on. I blinked a few times to clear my eyes and checked my phone to see what time it was. One in the morning. Wouldn't you know it? I had a chance for a good night's sleep, and here I was, wide awake.

I felt around for my bookmark, finally gave up, and stuffed a clean tissue in the book to mark my place. Just as I reached for the lamp, a noise outside caught my ear. I live in an eclectic neighborhood filled with a few homes like mine and a variety of mom-and-pop stores. Noises late at night weren't uncommon and I'd grown used to most of them, but there was something about this one that seemed out of place.

I set my book aside and listened more closely. Was it the wind, or something else? The Thai restaurant next door had been closed for at least two hours, but someone might have been working over there. Then again, maybe not. My heart beat a little faster and my hands grew clammy. Miss Frankie's claims that I was headed for trouble and Dominique's warning that only the Merciers were safe from the curse rang in my ears.

Annoyed with myself for letting all of the woo-woo talk get to me, I climbed out of bed and turned out the light. I waited for a moment to let my eyes adjust to the darkness then moved closer to the window. I wasn't going to let myself become paranoid over the necklace, but I didn't want to be foolish either. If someone was out there, I wanted to know who it was.

Bad things happen to good people all the time. A smart woman wouldn't stick her head in the sand and pretend that all was well. Better to be safe than sorry and all that.

I slid my fingers between slats on the blind and wedged open a space large enough to see out of. Shadows danced across the lawn as the winter breeze fluttered through the trees, but I couldn't see anything to cause alarm. I sighed with relief and nearly stepped away from the window when a different kind of movement caught my attention.

Instinctively, I shrank back and held my breath. Whatever

it was, it had more substance than the shadows I had been watching. Was it a neighborhood animal on the prowl, or had it been more sinister than that? I stood there for a while, scarcely daring to breathe. My senses were on high alert and I alternated between thinking I should go for my cell phone to call for help and telling myself that Miss Frankie and the others who believed in the curse had finally gotten inside my head.

After what felt like forever, the shadow moved again. This time I was able to make out more of its shape. Definitely human. Definitely skulking around and obviously up to no good, but I couldn't tell anything more than that. It could have been a small man or a large woman, or maybe the other way around. I didn't exactly wish the intruder on the owners of the Thai restaurant. They seemed like nice enough people. But if the shadowy figure wasn't out to harm them, it was probably after me—or at least after the necklace.

That thought frightened me, but realizing that I could be looking at the person who had sent Orra Trussell into heart failure made me furious. Anger won out over fear. Maybe I should call Carlo Mancini and ask him to let the viewing public know that the necklace wasn't here for the taking. I grabbed my cell phone, rammed my feet into a pair of flip-flops, and dashed down the stairs. I dialed 911 as I ran, gasping out the answers to questions from the emergency operator.

She warned me to stay in the house, but I was too furious to listen. I disconnected and threw open my door, lurching outside in a burst of anger. Not my brightest move, but all I could think was that by the time the police arrived, my unwanted visitor would probably be miles away. I didn't have any idea what I'd do once I got outside with the prowler. I just knew that I couldn't let that shadowy figure get away.

The operator called back after I hung up, which I would have anticipated if I'd been thinking clearly. I'd already blown the element of surprise, but the annoyingly cheerful ringtone made sure the intruder knew I was there.

I paused on the front step just long enough to answer and heard someone moving quickly through the bushes and then a couple of crashes that sounded like metal containers falling over. I actually considered racing after the intruder, but the cool night air and the reality of how foolish that would be, along with very stern warnings from the operator not to engage the prowler, finally caught up with me. Disappointed by my failure, I sank down on the step. I was still there a few minutes later when a shadow emerged from between buildings half a block down. It raced away and disappeared around the corner, and I still hadn't been able to get a good look at whoever it was.

A few minutes later, the police rolled up. Two uniformed officers took my statement and looked around a bit, but since there was no evidence of a break-in or other crime, they didn't seem all that interested. In fact, they tried to convince me that I'd just spotted someone who'd been out drinking and then gotten mixed up on their way home.

Even telling them about the necklace that was now at the bank and its possible link to the break-in at the Vintage Vault didn't stir their interest. Whether the police believed me or not, I was convinced that my late-night visitor was the same person who had spooked Orra Trussell the week before. But again, I had no way of proving it.

I didn't sleep well after my late-night visitors left. Frustration mixed with a bad case of nerves makes it hard to relax. At some point I finally fell into a dreamless sleep broken all too soon by the blare of my alarm. I would have happily slept longer, but we had so much work to do for the Belle Lune Ball I couldn't indulge.

Carrying the largest cup of coffee I could find on my way to work, I dragged myself through the door a few minutes after seven. The rest of the staff was already hard at work, so I grabbed my chef's jacket and joined the fray.

We worked nose-to-the-grindstone all day, barely pausing long enough to order lunch delivery and wolf down sandwiches. I'd already finished the peacock dress and accessories, which left me free to hand-paint fondant that Isabeau had used to cover another dress form cake. She had draped and folded it artistically to give the illusion of a free-flowing cotton. I spent hours painting tiny flowers onto the fabric, matching the pattern to the shapes Isabeau had created.

Ox and Dwight took on the tasks of shoes and a handbag to match while Sparkle and Estelle put the finishing touches on a third dress form cake, this one resembling a tailored suit with matching pumps and hat, topped off with a string of pearls.

By the time we went home on Wednesday, all five dress form cakes had been finished, photographed, and moved into the cooler. We'd made some stellar cakes in the past, but I thought these were our best work yet. I printed copies of the photos for Miss Frankie and dropped them off on my way home.

She made all the right noises over the work we'd done, and I did the same when she showed me the gown she planned to wear to the ball. I watched her closely for signs of an emotional breakdown, but she never mentioned the Toussaint necklace and neither did I, so my visit passed uneventfully. Which was fine with me. Frankly, I didn't have the energy.

On Thursday, we spent the day chopping and dicing and chiffonading everything we could prep in advance without compromising quality. Friday we'd stir and mix and cook everything except those items we had to prepare on Saturday.

By eight that night, we had bowls filled with golden cubes

of sweet potato, mounds of chopped cilantro and chiffonaded sage leaves, hills of ginger sliced into coins, containers filled with diced and sliced onions of several varieties, mountains of cauliflower florets, along with chopped carrots, celery, kale, and cashews. I'd spent days collecting recipes from various sources, and I was proud of the menu I'd put together. By the end of the day tomorrow, all that chopping and chiffonading would be turned into Roasted Parmesan Potatoes, Pork Chops with Pear Chutney, Pasta with Pumpkin and Sausage, Creamy Cauliflower Soup, and Classic Meatloaf. We had half a dozen other dishes on the menu as well, including several that I hoped would appeal to vegan and vegetarian palates.

Once we were satisfied that we'd covered all our bases, we made sure everything was covered and stored before dragging out into the parking lot. Then somebody suggested a stop at the Dizzy Duke, and miraculously we all found a second wind.

We made our ways there separately, some on foot and others in our cars. I fired up the Range Rover and drove the two blocks so I could make a quick getaway later. And yes, I'll admit that after spotting the prowler on Monday night, I wasn't eager to walk the dark streets of New Orleans.

I was alert and slightly on edge even just walking the few feet into the bar. I said hello to Gabriel and spent a few minutes flirting (a pick-me-up I highly recommend) before joining the others at our usual table. Calvin offered to go to the bar with our orders and the rest of us spent a few minutes getting settled. I grabbed a chair at our regular table and hooked my bag over my knee so that it hung between my legs. Which is why I felt my phone vibrate a few minutes after we'd arrived. I snagged the phone and saw Edie's name and a picture of JD on the screen. I groaned softly, hoping Edie wasn't having another mommy crisis. I wasn't sure I could survive a breakdown just then.

I answered, but the music, conversation, and laughter

made it impossible to hear. I could tell that Edie was talking but I couldn't hear what she was saying. "Hold on a minute," I shouted. "I'm going outside." I grabbed my bag and slung it over my shoulder, then pushed through the crowded barroom and out onto the sidewalk.

"There," I said as the door muffled the noise behind me. "I can hear you now. Is everything all right?"

"Everything's fine," Edie assured me. "Actually, I called to ask you a favor. I should have known you'd be at the Duke. It could have waited until tomorrow."

"You've got me now," I said. "Go ahead and ask."

"I need a babysitter for tomorrow night. I know this is bad timing. Really, I do. I know you're completely swamped getting ready for the vintage clothing thing on Saturday, but River has this work dinner and he really wants me to go with him. I don't know . . . maybe he's not so bad. I told him I'd go with him if I could find a sitter. If you can't do it, I'll *completely* understand."

She was right, it was terrible timing. I'd been wanting her to soften up where River was concerned, and I didn't want to throw up a roadblock, but with only two days until the ball, I couldn't see any way I could say yes.

"I wish I could," I told her. "You know I would if there was any way, but the Belle Lune Ball—"

"You're right," she said. "I shouldn't have asked. It's just that all my friends are at Zydeco and you're always my first choice."

A cheer went up from the crowd inside the Duke and I moved a little farther from the doors. I think she said something else, but I didn't hear it. Something hit me from behind, hard enough to make me stagger forward. "Hey!" I started to turn, wanting to see who'd run into me but I didn't get very far. Whoever it was shoved me forward again, harder this time.

I lost my balance and fell to the ground. Pain shot through

my knees, but I was far more aware that my assailant was trying to wrench my bag from my shoulder. I wrapped both arms around the bag and rolled onto my side, hoping the strap wouldn't break and praying that I was strong enough to win the tug of war. Not that I had much in there, but it was the principle of the thing. And I really liked that bag.

Instinctively hoping to minimize any physical damage coming my way, I curled into a fetal position, head down, legs drawn up, arms curled inward. In that position I couldn't see much, but I thought my assailant was tall, or at least taller than me. And strong. It was all I could do to hang on while he—or she—shoved and tugged and jerked on my bag.

On the plus side, my attacker seemed much more interested in the bag than in me. On the negative, I was convinced my attacker was after the necklace.

I heard someone shouting from a little distance away and footsteps pounding toward me. I almost wept at the prospect of help, but most importantly, my attacker let go of my purse strap and hotfooted it away. I sat up gingerly just as Carlo Mancini drew up beside me.

His chest heaved from exertion and he looked worried, but I could only wonder why he was there in the first place. Guess I didn't exactly trust him.

Two more people reached my side only a few seconds after Carlo came to the rescue. One young man helped me to my feet, and then he and his buddy raced off in the general direction I thought my attacker had taken.

Carlo stayed with me. He studied my face carefully and asked, "Are you all right?"

"I'm fine," I said, giving my bag a quick once-over to make sure it hadn't been damaged. To my relief, it seemed intact. "What are you doing here?"

Carlo laughed. "That's some kind of thank-you. I just saved your life."

Yeah. Maybe. I tried to appear gracious. "Thanks. So what are you doing here?"

Carlo's grin faded. "Tell me, do you treat all your knights in shining armor this way?"

"That presumes I have knights in any kind of armor hanging around," I said. "But to answer your question, no. Only the ones that make me suspicious. Where did you come from?"

Carlo jerked his head toward the end of the street. "I was parking when I saw that guy attack you. Not that I knew it was you. I just saw a lady in distress and came to help. Would you rather I let the guy hurt you?"

"Was it a guy?" I asked. "I couldn't tell."

"I assumed so, but I couldn't swear to it." He motioned toward a metal bench near the curb. "You want to sit down or something?"

I nodded and took a step in the right direction. My right knee twinged and my left knee throbbed. Mancini must have seen me wince because he took my arm and helped me hobble across the narrow sidewalk. I hated feeling beholden, him being such a jerk and all, but I did manage what I hoped sounded like a sincere "thank you" as he helped me get settled.

"You probably ought to call the police," he said helpfully.

I wasn't so sure about that. Another complaint might make the police take me seriously, or it might just convince them I was a complete nut. I could have called Sullivan, but he would only tell me to stop inviting trouble. "Yeah," I said. "Maybe. Right now I just want to catch my breath."

Mancini nodded and sat beside me. "So I take it you don't know who just attacked you."

"I don't have a clue," I said. "I came outside to take a phone call, and the next thing I knew, I was on the ground." I suddenly realized that I'd been talking to Edie when the guy hit me. "Speaking of my phone . . . where is it?"

I patted my pockets while Carlo returned to the scene of the crime to look for it. After a moment he leaned down and pulled something out of a planter box. He held my phone aloft with a grin. "Found it!"

I held out my hand and wiggled my fingers impatiently. Edie was probably worried sick. "Is the call still connected?"

Carlo shook his head and gave me the phone. I found two missed calls from Edie and a text message asking if I was all right. I texted back blaming the disconnect on a dying battery and promised to call back later.

"Everything all right?" Carlo asked.

I could almost see him salivating at the prospect of a juicy news story. "Yeah. Fine. Just peachy, in fact."

"Great. It looked like your friend was after your purse."

Score one for the ace reporter. "Some friend. But yeah, that's what it felt like."

"Probably a mugger, then."

"Yeah. No doubt."

"Unless it was something else."

I slid a glance at him from the corner of my eye. "Like what?"

"I don't know. You have anything valuable in there?"

"Just the usual," I said. "Wallet. A little cash. A couple of credit cards."

Mancini fell silent for a moment but he didn't leave, which warned me he had more questions. He finally coughed up the first one. "Did you happen to see my story on the evening news?"

"Yeah. It wasn't bad."

"Not bad? It was terrific. I thought you even came across as almost likable."

Funny guy. "I'm sure that was thanks to your amazing skills as an editor."

"Probably." His lips curved slightly.

I rolled my eyes and stretched my legs carefully to see

if my knees were still wobbly. "I suppose you're planning to report on this."

"Well, sure! It's news. Star reporter saves damsel in distress. I just wish I'd had my camera crew with me."

"Yeah, that's too bad." I made no effort to sound sincere. "I'm heartbroken for you. I'm surprised you didn't video it with your cell phone."

"Didn't even occur to me." The smile slid from his face and he gave me a quick once-over. "Are you sure you're okay?"

I wasn't sure at all, but I couldn't just disappear on the Zydeco crew or they'd think something bad had happened to me. I wasn't in the mood for another intervention. "I think I'll be okay," I said. "But thanks."

"Do you need help getting back inside?" He stood and held out an arm, giving a relatively convincing imitation of a gentleman. "I'm going inside anyway."

"Why? This isn't your usual hangout."

"Why not? Seems like a nice enough place."

I ignored the arm and got to my feet. To my relief, my knees behaved themselves this time. "I suppose it's a free country. Do me a favor, though, okay? Don't tell the people I work with about what happened out here. They worry about me."

"With good reason, it appears."

"Whatever." I hitched my bag onto my shoulder. "Just keep this between us, okay? Seriously. No news reports." The crew from Zydeco would be hard enough to live with if they found out. I didn't even want to think about what Miss Frankie would say.

"I'm not sure I can agree to that," Carlo said. "It would be a great follow-up to the first story."

"Except that it's not a follow-up. I just happened to be standing in the wrong place at the wrong time."

"Then you're not afraid that the curse is responsible?"

"Not even slightly." I stopped in front of the door and

stared him down. "It seems a whole lot more likely that somebody is looking for some good press."

Carlo's mouth fell open. "You think I staged the attack to get a story?"

"It occurred to me."

He clamped his mouth shut and the humor in his eyes evaporated. "In case it escaped your notice, lady, I saved your ass."

I still wasn't sure if he'd done the saving or if he'd latched on to the two young men who'd helped me, but I didn't want to antagonize him into airing the story about the mugging, so I smiled to take some of the sting out of my accusation. "Look, I believe you, okay? I just want to make sure you keep this little incident quiet. It's not news. Nobody would care except my friends and mother-in-law. So how about we both keep quiet? You don't report this and I don't wonder aloud how you happened to be here at just the right time. My mother-in-law rests easy and your reputation isn't bruised."

Mancini gave me a cold stare, but I thought that he was considering my offer. I just hoped there wasn't a law against blackmailing the press. I could be in big trouble.

After a while Mancini gave a shrug and reached for the door handle. "Yeah. Whatever. This one's between us. But don't count on it happening a second time." He pushed past me and strode up to the bar, clearly pissed off at me.

Which was fine with me. Whatever it took to keep him from worrying Miss Frankie. As for calling the police, I decided against it. I was pretty sure they'd call what just happened coincidence, but someone wanted that necklace badly enough to break into the Vintage Vault, badly enough to stalk me at home, and now badly enough to assault me. It was one coincidence too many for me.

Nineteen

⚜

Still shaking after the would-be mugging, I ducked into the ladies' room at the Dizzy Duke to make sure I looked presentable. I wasn't sure I could trust Carlo Mancini to keep his mouth shut, but just in case he hadn't said anything to the Zydeco crew about what happened outside, I didn't want to raise questions by looking like I'd just gone a couple of rounds with the welterweight champ.

One or two spots on my arm had started to sting, which made me think I'd sustained a few scrapes. I'd probably develop a few bruises, too, but for the most part I looked surprisingly unscathed.

I brushed the dirt from my pants and shirt, cleaned the noticeable scrapes on my arms, and washed my hands. I applied a little lip gloss and gave my hair a toss, then returned to our table, where, to my surprise, nobody seemed at all concerned by my absence. Maybe Carlo Mancini had kept his word. Gabriel gave me a deliciously sultry stare as

I walked by so I had to figure he didn't know, and nobody at my table seemed interested in the slightest.

I saw that the reporter had snagged a stool at the bar. He lifted his beer bottle in salute as I sat. I answered with a nod of thanks. Mancini and I weren't destined to become best friends forever, but I had to admit a tiny sliver of appreciation had wedged itself in with all the annoyance.

Ox was in the middle of a story about a family camping trip and Calvin was supplying the details Ox omitted. The story earned laughs from everyone else, but my run-in with the would-be purse thief had soured my enjoyment of the evening. I wanted to go home and nurse my bruised ego, but I was too unnerved to walk back to the Range Rover on my own.

Gradually, as the evening wore on, the stories and laughter began to relieve my tension, and by the time we left, I was feeling almost back to normal. But I still locked my doors as soon as I got in the car and circled my block at home twice to make sure nobody was lying in wait for me. Face it, there had been plenty of time for the mugger to beat me home. He could have been hiding anywhere.

My nerves ramped up again and I started to wish I'd told the others about the mugging. One of them would have followed me home and made sure I got inside safely. As I drove down the dark street, I wished I had someone watching out for me.

I might be nervous, but I couldn't very well drive around all night, so I finally bit the bullet and pulled into a parking space. I laced my keys between my fingers and quick-walked to my front door.

I let myself inside and flipped the lock and deadbolt with trembling fingers then leaned against the door and tried to steady my breathing.

I hated feeling afraid. Even more, I hated knowing how vulnerable I was. After a long time I squared my shoulders and climbed the stairs, and I vowed that I would find some way to get my life back.

It wasn't until Friday afternoon, when I went to the Monte Cristo Hotel to get key cards that would grant us access to the rooms we'd be using, that the necklace intruded into my hard-won peace of mind.

I'd just finished talking to the Monte Cristo's excitable manager, Tommy Sheridan, and was on my way across the shabby-chic lobby when a square woman wearing an expensive-looking suit stepped into my path. "Ms. Lucero? Can I have a minute?"

I managed to stop walking before I ran into her, but I don't think she appreciated the effort that took.

She held out a hand for me to shake. "Natalie Archer," she said. "We met the other day at the Vintage Clothing Society offices."

"Yes. Of course." I slipped the key cards into my pocket and shook the hand she offered. "How are you, Mrs. Archer?"

She smiled ever so slightly. "Harried. There's so much to do and so little time left before the banquet. I'm sure you feel the same."

"Yes I do, but all we have to do is get through the next two days. Then it will all be over."

Natalie's smile faded and she ran an assessing look over my face. I'd been working all morning and I was almost certain I looked frazzled, but there was nothing I could do about that now. "I wonder if you and I might chat for a few minutes."

I couldn't imagine what she wanted to talk to me about. Did she think I could convince Simone to give her the display space she coveted at the ball? "I'd love to," I said, which was only a *tiny* white lie. "I'll give you a call after the event on Saturday."

"I meant now," Natalie said. "This really needs to be decided before the ball."

Mmm-hmm. Just as I thought. Maybe I should hear her out. If she was trying to snag the Vintage Vault's unused space through me, Simone would want to know. "I guess I can spare a few minutes," I said. "What's on your mind?"

Natalie glanced around the lobby. Nobody seemed overly interested in us, but she frowned and shook her head. "Not here. Could you stop by my house later this evening?"

"I don't think that will work," I said. "I'll probably be working until midnight or later. This may be my only opportunity to break away until after the ball."

Natalie glanced around again, sighed loudly, and nodded toward a couple of chairs flanking a small wooden table near the window. "Fine. Let's grab that spot before someone else gets it."

I followed her across the lobby and sat down across from her. She linked her hands in her lap and crossed her ankles like a proper Southern lady. "Are you aware that I'm the last remaining descendant of Gustave Toussaint?"

I blinked in surprise. "I was not." Plus, her claim didn't jive with what Miss Frankie had told me about the family. My mother-in-law had left me with the impression that Gustave had left a long line of descendants in the area, not a sole scion. In spite of Miss Frankie's recent odd behavior, I believed her. She had no reason to lie. I couldn't say the same for Natalie.

"The fact is, Ms. Lucero, that necklace you found belongs to me."

Something buzzed up my spine. Was it a warning, or just curiosity? "If what you say is true, I can appreciate that you feel you have a claim to it, but I'm not at all clear about who owns it. I'm sure Delphine Mercier's descendants could lay claim to the necklace, too. And it *was* found inside property belonging to my mother-in-law, which may open the door to a third claim."

"Hardly a valid one in either case. And it was Miss Frankie who first brought the find to my attention. I think you'll find that she wants nothing to do with it."

Miss Frankie had told Natalie about the necklace? Why hadn't she mentioned that to me? I made a mental note to ask next time I saw her and tried to stay focused on my conversation with Natalie. She was right about Miss Frankie not wanting the necklace for herself, but . . . "Why are you just telling me this now? You could have said something at Simone's office."

Natalie's eyes widened in shock. "This is a private matter."

Yes. Of course.

Natalie took a deep breath and let it out slowly. "I understand your confusion, Ms. Lucero. People can—and will—say things. Some of those things may sound legitimate to someone who isn't familiar with the history of the family. But trust me, the necklace is mine."

Trust her? Was she serious? I couldn't imagine her as the mugger who had attacked me outside the Dizzy Duke, but that didn't make her innocent. She could have hired someone to steal the necklace from me.

"You might be right," I said, "but I'm not prepared to simply hand the necklace over to just anyone who says it belongs to them. I need a chance to research and perhaps consult an attorney." That was a good plan, actually—Thaddeus Montgomery had been Miss Frankie's attorney for as long as I could remember, and probably for several decades before that. I liked and trusted him.

Natalie's mouth pinched in disapproval. "I was hoping we could avoid involving lawyers in this dispute."

"I wouldn't call it a dispute," I said. "But I don't think that trying to resolve this without attorneys would be wise.

Why don't you give me the name of your lawyer? I can have mine call yours early next week."

My offer sounded presumptuous. *I'll have my lawyer call your lawyer!* Aunt Yolanda would have set me straight if she heard me talking like that, but I was learning how to hold my own with the Natalie Archers of the world. They responded to confidence and authority. If I showed the slightest sign of uncertainty or weakness she'd chew me up and spit me out.

"If that's the way you feel, I suppose I have no choice." Natalie made a pretense of reaching for her handbag but stopped short of actually picking it up. "Do you really want to postpone the inevitable? Hear me out, Ms. Lucero. Please. I was thinking that the Belle Lune Ball might be the perfect time to make the exchange. It would not only garner a lot of interest from those attending the ball, but it would be to our mutual advantage to handle it then."

Now I was really curious. "How do you figure that? How could it be advantageous to me?"

"Not to you personally, but to your bakery, certainly. It would be good press for your little shop. I have contacts everywhere. I could arrange coverage by all of the local media and your business would certainly benefit from the attention."

"*If* your claim is legitimate," I said. "Zydeco could take a big hit if it turns out the necklace actually belongs to someone else."

She recoiled as if I'd slapped her. "You doubt my word?"

I couldn't figure out how to say "Duh!" without offending her even more, so I jumped over the question completely. "There seems to be a lot of interest in the necklace. At this point, I don't know who is legitimately connected and who's not. I really can't make a decision until I know more."

Natalie's mouth tightened so far it almost disappeared. "I could provide you with my family tree as proof, but I don't know if that would satisfy you."

"All that would do is establish that you're descended from Gustave Toussaint," I pointed out. "It still wouldn't prove that you have a legitimate legal claim to the necklace."

"Gustave was the last known owner of the necklace," Natalie said. "I don't know what more you think you need."

Standing, I smiled apologetically. "That's the problem, Mrs. Archer. Neither do I. I'm sorry, but that's my final word on the subject. I'll discuss this with my attorney as soon as I can, but it won't be until after the weekend."

Natalie stood to face me. "I suppose there's nothing more I can say to convince you?"

"Not today."

"I'm disappointed in you, Ms. Lucero. If you think you can play favorites and get away with it, you'll soon realize just how wrong you are." And with that she strode away. Her shoulders were squared, her stride long and angry. She ignored someone who attempted to speak to her as she passed and barked something at the next person who tried to get her attention.

I took a deep breath and let it out slowly, and I wondered if Natalie Archer was right. A public ceremonial turnover of the necklace might have been good for business. Likewise, getting on the bad side of someone rich and powerful would no doubt be very bad for business. I still couldn't imagine Natalie Archer prowling around my house in the dark or trying to steal my bag outside the Dizzy Duke, but I had the feeling she was a powerful adversary—one I couldn't afford to underestimate.

Twenty

⚜

"What was that about?"

Startled by the unexpected voice behind me, I let out a little squeal of alarm. Apparently I'd been so busy watching Natalie Archer bulldoze her way across the room I hadn't heard Simone come up behind me. I shrugged lightly. "Nothing, really. Except . . . What do you know about her?"

"About Natalie?" Simone looked a little surprised by the question. "Don't let her get to you. Her bark is far worse than her bite. Just don't let her think that she's made you nervous. I swear the woman can smell fear. She's been a member of the Vintage Clothing Society for as long as I can remember, though, and she's got money and influence, but she can be a real pain in various body parts. Why?"

"She just told me that she's a direct descendant of Gustave Toussaint. She wants me to turn over the necklace to her at the Belle Lune Ball in front of witnesses and reporters. She tried to convince me it would be good for business."

Simone's brows knit. "Are you going to do it?"

I shook my head. "Even if she's who she says she is, I couldn't agree. I'm not handing over a small fortune just because she *thinks* it belongs to her. Do you think her claim is legit?"

Simone held up both hands as if to ward off my question. "Oh no you don't. I'm not offering an opinion."

I laughed at the mock horror on her face. "Why not? It would be just that—an opinion. I'm not asking you to make a decision for me. But maybe you can help in another way. I don't know anything about tracing a family tree. How would I go about verifying her relationship to Gustave Toussaint?"

The clouds in Simone's lovely dark eyes cleared. "That's the beauty of having money, Rita. You hire someone to figure it out for you. Talk to Miss Frankie's attorney. I'm sure he'll know what to do."

"I certainly hope so," I said, trying to shake off the negative feelings Natalie had left in her wake. "I think I've just found my way onto Mrs. Archer's bad side. She warned me not to play favorites. What does she think I'm going to do, take her side over Miss Frankie's? She should know better than that."

Simone looked surprised. "Does Miss Frankie even want it?"

"Well, no, but that doesn't mean she doesn't have a claim."

"Maybe, but I'm sure Natalie wouldn't consider Miss Frankie's claim legitimate. In her mind, it's her family against the Merciers. She's probably far more concerned that you'll side with Ox against her."

Wait a minute. What? "What does Ox have to do with anything?"

Worry flashed through Simone's eyes. She'd known Philippe years before I did—was once nearly engaged to him—and had also been close to Ox, something Ox had neglected to mention in all the discussions I'd had with him about taking the Belle Lune Ball contract. I'd felt hurt and betrayed, but I thought we'd gotten past all that. "The house . . ." Simone said. "The building Philippe bought for Zydeco used to belong to Ox's family."

I think my jaw hit the floor. "But I heard it belonged to an old woman named Miss Carrie. I thought Philippe bought it from her estate after she died."

Simone nodded. "He did, but Miss Carrie was a distant relative of Ox's. That's how Philippe found out about it. The house was in disrepair and the whole neighborhood had been rezoned for commercial use. The family didn't want to go to all the expense of restoring and repairing and all that, so they sold it to Philippe."

My heart beat hard against my chest and I felt as if the floor had opened up beneath my feet. "Why didn't Ox ever tell me?"

Simone lifted one thin shoulder. "I don't know."

I tried desperately to process what she'd just told me, but I couldn't seem to make sense of it. This wasn't the first time Ox had tried to "protect" me from an unpleasant truth. But what kind of friend holds back a piece of information like that? Why hadn't he told me about Zydeco?

"No wonder he was so upset when Miss Frankie asked me to be her partner instead of him," I murmured, more to myself than to Simone. "He'd been there from the beginning. He'd even helped Philippe find the building. Ox must hate me."

"I'm sure he doesn't," Simone said gently.

"I'm glad you're sure," I said acidly. "I'm not sure of anything anymore. So now you think Ox might also have a claim to the necklace?"

Simone's gaze flickered away. "I wouldn't know. But he might."

"Well, even if he does," I said, "it's no more legitimate than any claim Miss Frankie or I might have. His family doesn't even own the house anymore."

Her gaze flickered back, skimming across my face but not

really landing there. "Well, then, there's nothing to worry about." She put a hand on my arm and finally managed to make eye contact. "Why don't we just forget about all of that?"

I wasn't convinced that Simone was telling me everything she knew, but I didn't think she'd say anything more right then. I'd have to talk to Ox about it later. Not that *he'd* be any more forthcoming, but at least I could try.

I worked up a weak smile and said, "You're right. It's pointless to stew over it. I was just picking up the key cards for the rooms Zydeco will be using on Saturday. Do you want to go with me to check them out?"

"I thought you'd never ask."

We took the ancient elevator to the second floor and checked the spaces I'd been assigned. It wasn't that I'd expected them to magically double in size since the last time I'd looked, but I was disheartened to see that they were as small as I'd remembered. We spent a little while checking and double-checking measurements, reconfiguring the layout in our imaginations, and suggesting and discarding different ideas. By four, we were right back where we'd started. The only possible workable solution was the one we'd already agreed upon.

But I was still thinking about what Natalie had said when I drove away from the hotel, and Simone's information had left me feeling edgy. Ox and I had been friends for a long time. Maybe I owed him a chance to tell me his story first. Though he'd had more than two years to do it already. Two years working side by side in the very building, and he hadn't said a word.

I decided on another approach—I'd talk to Calvin instead. If Miss Cassie had been a mutual relative, maybe he'd be more forthcoming with some information. I was pretty sure Ox wouldn't like me going behind his back, but I was upset enough not to care. What did it say about our friendship that I felt more comfortable talking to Calvin after just a week than I did with Ox after a decade or more?

I knew that Calvin was working at Mambo Odessa's shop in the French Quarter that afternoon so I aimed the Range Rover in that direction. I didn't want to wait for him to come to Zydeco. Besides, I wanted to talk to him somewhere Ox wouldn't overhear the conversation.

Mambo Odessa's tiny shop is located on Dauphine Street. It's an old wooden building with peeling white paint and bright blue shutters huddled between two tightly closed neighbors. Only a few people were out and about in the French Quarter that afternoon. Here and there a delivery truck blocked the narrow streets, slowing my progress once I turned off Canal Street.

Rather than circle around looking for a parking space, I pulled into a nearby parking structure and turned my keys over to the valet on duty. I pocketed the claim ticket and headed down the uneven sidewalk toward Mambo Odessa's.

I passed a family with a couple of small children meandering toward Jackson Square. On the next block, two old men argued good-naturedly. Only a few gift shops and restaurants were open for business, and in the heat of the day, the whole neighborhood felt sleepy and innocent. Come nightfall, the now quiet streets would fill with music, alcohol, and wide-eyed tourists. All those tightly closed shutters would fly open to reveal bars and nightclubs and strip joints. The Quarter would shake off its sleepy family atmosphere and roar triumphantly to life. The Quarter at night is energetic and interesting, but I like it best in the daytime.

Now that I was here, though, I wasn't sure this was such a great idea. I don't believe in voodoo, but there's something about Mambo Odessa that makes me tread carefully. She's . . . different. Not necessarily in a bad way.

I'd been to her shop once before. Instead of the dim lighting and displays of shrunken heads I'd expected, Mambo Odessa's shop had a light, airy feel. Sunlight poured into the shop, illuminating the very normal-looking collection of soaps, oils, and candles that were designed to enhance fortune, health, good luck, or love. Along with those, displays of jewelry and jujus and several shelves filled with educational books and DVDs invited visitors to browse for a while. Of course, she also carried the requisite gris-gris bags filled with herbs and roots, and one wall was covered with dolls dressed in brightly colored costumes and feathers. (I didn't know what the dolls were for and I wasn't going to ask.)

Mambo Odessa, wearing a caftan in shades of red, yellow, and orange, stood behind the counter. A matching turban covered her head, and she wore several strings of beads around her neck. Or maybe they were bones. I didn't want to look too closely. As always, she also wore a pair of small round sunglasses.

She came out from behind the counter, smiling as if she was expecting me. "Ah. Rita. You are here. You have questions for me, no?"

Maybe it's the way she knows things she can't possibly know that leaves me feeling off-balance. It's a struggle not to look like a deer in the headlights when I'm around her. "Actually, I was hoping to talk with Calvin. Is he in?"

"Not at the moment. I sent him to pick up a few things. Why don't you come in and sit down? We can talk."

She motioned me toward a small wrought iron table and matching chairs. I hesitated for a moment, but she floated across the room, apparently convinced I'd do what she wanted.

I could have resisted, but who was I kidding? Besides, Mambo Odessa probably knew more about the house Ox's family had once owned than Calvin did. Or maybe neither of them knew anything. I was assuming that it was their branch of the family tree we were talking about, but maybe I was wrong.

Still, I followed her to the table and took a seat.

"Would you like some tea?" she asked. "I have water ready."

I shook my head. "Thanks, but I'm not much of a tea drinker. And I really don't have a lot of time."

She smiled serenely and sat across from me. "Then by all means, child. Ask what you want to know."

I wasn't sure where to begin. "I'm sure by now you've heard that I found the Toussaint necklace."

Madame Odessa dipped her head once. "Of course. You're worried about what will happen to you?"

"Not exactly." I laughed nervously. "I know you make your living based on people who believe in the supernatural, but I'm not one of them. I don't believe the necklace is cursed."

"Oh, but it is, child. That much I know for sure."

Aunt Yolanda had always told me to pick my battles. This wasn't a battle I wanted to have with someone who may or may not think she was capable of putting a curse on me. I skipped to the next question. "What do you know about the curse, then?"

"I know that it's powerful," Mambo Odessa said. "And I know that it's full of anger and hatred. That curse won't go away until the damage is undone."

That wasn't good news, especially since I didn't know what it meant. "What damage are you talking about? How would somebody undo it?"

Mambo Odessa sat back and regarded me with interest. "Tell me what you know about the necklace's history."

I gave her the Cliff Notes version, touching on all the important points. Armand and his two women. The betrayal Delphine felt when he gave "her" necklace to his wife. The death of Beatriz's unborn child when its mother died. The deaths of Gustave's wife and daughter. Had I left anything out? Nope, I think that covered it.

Mambo Odessa nodded as I talked and let out a sigh when I finished. "You know enough. Delphine suffered mightily after that. She'd lost her patron, and she had no way to care for her children."

"She had three children, right?"

"Yes."

"And they were all Armand Toussaint's?"

"Yes."

I thought about what that meant. "But the baby Beatriz was carrying was her first?"

"That's right."

I wondered if Beatriz had known about Armand's children. Had it hurt her to know that he'd fathered three children by his mistress before she got pregnant? I knew the pain that would have caused me. If Philippe had been producing children with another woman when we were married, it would have killed me.

"Beatriz didn't need to be cursed," I said. "She probably died of a broken heart."

Mambo Odessa touched the beads around her neck. "You have a good heart, child."

The compliment warmed me from the inside out. I smiled and said, "I just think it's so sad. I'd like to be furious with Armand for the way he treated those women, but he was just as much a product of his times as they were. Delphine had to sell herself to get by. Beatriz had to pretend she didn't mind that her husband had another family, and I guess Armand was just living up to what was expected of him. It's not fair to judge him by modern standards, but still . . ."

Mambo Odessa didn't say anything for a while. She just kept fingering the beads on her necklace and staring at the center of the table. Just when I was starting to wonder if she was performing some voodoo ritual, she shifted her gaze to meet mine. "The necklace must go back where it belongs. You know that."

"But where *does* it belong? Gustave Toussaint's last direct descendant—if that's really who she is—says the necklace belongs to her. Or does it belong to Miss Frankie, since she owns the building where we found it? Or is there some long-lost descendant of Delphine's who ought to get it? I wish I knew the right thing to do."

Mambo Odessa pulled her hand away from her beads and touched the back of my hand. "I can't tell you what to do, child. To end the curse, you must decide."

Was she kidding? "But how am I supposed to know what to do?"

"Stay open to the whispers of the ancestors. They'll tell you what you should do."

"That's not exactly helpful," I said. "I told you that I don't believe in the curse and I'm not in the habit of communing with the dead. But I do believe that somebody is trying to steal it from me. Someone was sneaking around outside my house a few nights ago and I was the victim of an attempted mugging earlier this week. So far, nobody's been seriously hurt, but I'm afraid that might change."

Mambo Odessa's lips curved slightly downward and I realized I'd said more than I wanted to. I hoped she wouldn't tell Ox about my troubles.

Her eyes got a faraway look in them. "Much harm was done in the past," she said again. "You have been chosen to undo the damage."

"Chosen?" A sharp laugh escaped before I could stop it. "Who do you think chose me?"

Her eyes cleared suddenly. "Who else? Delphine Mercier."

A shudder ran through my body. I tried to laugh it off. "Why would she choose me? I'm not even related to her."

Mambo Odessa's lips curved slightly. "You'd have to ask her that question. Would you like to?"

"Ummm. No. Thanks, though." It was definitely time to change the subject. "Speaking of the necklace, I just found out that Ox's family used to own the house where Zydeco is located now. That's really why I came. Do you know anything about that?"

"About the house? You would have to ask Ox."

"Fat lot of good that will do me," I grumbled. "Ox is supposed to be a friend, but it gets harder and harder to think of him as one when he continually keeps things from me. He could have told me about the house a long time ago."

"Nobody is perfect," Mambo Odessa said. "Not even my nephew."

"I'm not asking for perfection," I said to make sure I didn't sound unreasonable. "I'm just asking for some consideration. Common courtesy. A little thing called trust."

"Ah, but trust is a two-way street, is it not?"

What is it with aunts? Why was Mambo Odessa going all Aunt Yolanda on me? "Don't try to blame me for Ox's faults." I got to my feet and fumbled to hoist the strap of my bag over my shoulder. "Thanks for your time."

"Don't be too angry with him," she called after me as I walked to the door. "You need each other."

Yeah, yeah, yeah. I waved a hand over my head and stepped outside. Let her make of that whatever she wanted to. I *was* angry, not only with Ox, but with Mambo Odessa, too. All of her cryptic talk about undoing damage and Delphine choosing me to right past wrongs felt like nothing but an attempt to manipulate me.

I couldn't blame her for defending her nephew. I was pretty sure Aunt Yolanda would bend over backward for me. But she wouldn't pretend that she had some mystic connection to the afterlife to do it. I didn't know anything more about the necklace than I had when I left home that morning. I had a good mind to sell the stupid thing and pocket the money for myself. It would serve them all right.

Twenty-one

⚜

Still fuming, I went back to work and spent the evening caught up in the flurry of activity. Part of me wanted to back Ox into a corner and demand answers from him, but the wiser, more logical part of me was grateful that we were too busy for drama. If I confronted Ox now, it would impact everyone on staff. My hurt feelings were going to have to wait until after the ball.

Putting the needs of the bakery first was the right thing to do, but it wasn't easy. The sound of Ox's voice rankled. His laughter made my insides clench with anger. When he had the nerve to bark an order at one of *my* employees, my blood boiled. As the day wore on, I became increasingly short-tempered with him. The rest of the staff pretended not to notice for a while, but by the time we were ready to lock up and go home, they'd given up the pretense. Everybody was walking on eggshells because of the tension in the room, and the worst part was that it was all coming from me.

Obviously, I couldn't let the situation continue for long, but

I hoped we could at least get through Saturday and the Belle Lune Ball without imploding. Ox and Isabeau left around eleven, with Calvin in tow. Estelle and Zoey headed out shortly afterward, and Sparkle said good night ten minutes later.

I didn't want to be left by myself, but I was torn between leaving with the others and wanting to run through my to-do list one more time before I went home. Cowering had a lot more appeal than toughing it out, but I had responsibilities. I pulled up my big girl panties and told myself to do my job.

My false bravado didn't stop me from being enormously grateful when I realized that Dwight was still here, too. I wasn't sure if he had legitimate work to do or if he was sticking close for some other reason, but it didn't really matter. I wasn't alone. That was the important thing.

I hurried through the list of tasks we needed to accomplish in the morning and added several last-minute items to the list of supplies we needed to take with us to the Monte Cristo. As I started toward the kitchen for a final check of the work we'd done that night, Dwight trailed after me.

He always looks rumpled, but that night he looked as if he'd been sleeping in his clothes for several days. I wasn't entirely sure he hadn't been. His T-shirt was dusted with flour and splattered with unidentifiable globs of food. His hair stuck out all over, stray whiskers ranged out from his beard onto his cheeks and chin, and his jeans were threadbare in places.

I waited for him to say something, but he just lurked in the doorway and watched me work. I finished my mental inventory of the dishes in the fridge, shut the door with a little more force than necessary, and whipped around to glare at him. After holding my tongue (mostly) with Ox, my nerves were already frayed, so it didn't take long to lose my patience. "What?"

I must have surprised him. He jolted upright from his usual slouch and blinked rapidly. "What what?"

"You've been staring at me for half an hour," I said. That

might have been a *slight* exaggeration, but it made my point. "Obviously something's on your mind, so tell me what it is."

Dwight reslouched and scratched lazily at his whiskers. "Just want to make sure you're okay, that's all."

"Why wouldn't I be?"

"I don't know. You seem upset. Is everything okay?"

I knew he meant well and I could have given him an earful about Ox and his secrets, but it seemed wrong to unleash on Dwight instead of going directly to Ox. I shrugged and moved to the stack of boxes near the pantry. "Everything's fine. I'm just making sure we haven't forgotten something important."

Dwight moved a few feet into the kitchen and leaned his elbows on the island. "I already checked and double-checked everything."

"Two sets of eyes are better than one," I said. "Maybe I'll see something you missed."

"Maybe." He scratched the other side of his chin. "Something going on I should know about?"

I was pretty sure I knew where he was going with that question and I didn't want to talk about it. "No. Nothing."

"You upset with Ox or something?"

I shifted a couple of items in the box so I could see better. "Or something," I said. I tried to smile, but my face felt stiff and the result was more of a grimace. I stopped working and leaned against the counter. "I'm fine," I said. "Ox is fine. In fact, everything is fine."

"You don't seem fine."

Everybody's a critic. I tried the smile thing again. "If I were upset with Ox, I'd talk to him about it. Really, there's nothing for you to worry about."

"If you say so. So when are you bringing Edie back?"

The abrupt change of subject caught me off guard. "I haven't decided," I said. "When she's ready."

"You don't think she's ready yet?"

"No, do you?"

Dwight shrugged. "Maybe. Probably. I think she'd come back if you asked her."

Dwight's sudden interest in Edie's state of mind seemed out of character. "What makes you think that? Has she been talking to you?"

"Edie hasn't," Dwight said. "But I had a beer with River the other night and he was talking about it. He thinks she's ready to come back."

If that was true, why hadn't River said something to me? He had my phone number. He could have mentioned his concerns at any time. But just like Ox, he'd clammed up and kept his thoughts to himself.

Maybe it wasn't them, I thought with a pang. *Maybe it was me!*

Worry and irritation rolled around together in my stomach. I wasn't sure which had the upper hand. "Am I hard to talk to or something?" I asked Dwight.

He gave his hand a so-so waggle. "I wouldn't say you're *hard* to talk to."

Not exactly a feel-good answer. "What *would* you say then?"

Dwight shrugged with his mouth. "It doesn't really matter, does it?"

"Yeah," I snapped. "It does. First Ox, then apparently River, and now you. What is it about me that makes everybody clam up? Just *tell* me."

"I don't know if you've noticed," Dwight said, "but you're wound up pretty tightly. You should relax more."

"Seriously? That's your advice?" Even as I scoffed, I recognized that I'd heard people say the same things about my uncle Nestor. Uncle Nestor is a champion worrier, and it's not easy finding the right approach when it comes to discussing touchy subjects with him. But I am *so* not my uncle Nestor.

"How am I supposed to relax when there's so much work

to be done?" I demanded. "And it doesn't help to find out you're all talking behind my back."

"You're the boss," Dwight said. "It sort of comes with the territory."

"I don't *want* it to come with the territory. I want you to like me. I want to be your friend . . . like Philippe was." My voice grew higher and tighter with every word, and when tears pooled in my eyes, I was horrified. I swiped them away impatiently. "What am I doing wrong?"

Apparently disturbed by my mounting hysteria, Dwight straightened his posture again. "Wrong? Nothing. You're great. We all like you."

"Then why won't anybody talk to me?"

"I'm talking to you right now."

I growled with frustration. "You know what I mean. Did you know that Ox's family used to own this building?"

"I knew this place used to belong to somebody in his family," Dwight said cautiously.

"See? That's what I mean. I didn't know that. Not until Simone told me. I saw River just a few days ago. Did he tell me he was concerned about Edie? No!"

"Was Edie standing right there?"

Sort of. She'd been asleep but that was beside the point. I was too worked up for logic. "I'm not a hothead," I said, crossing another of Uncle Nestor's less admirable attributes off the list. "I'm not unreasonable. I try to listen. I try to be helpful. And I certainly don't expect everything to be done my way."

Dwight came *this close* to smiling. "Who said you did?"

"Then what is it about me? Why won't Ox talk to me? I have to pry everything out of him."

"That has nothing to do with you," Dwight said.

"Then how did you know about Ox's history with this house and I didn't?"

"I heard about it back when he and Philippe were setting up the business. You've gotta know it doesn't mean a whole lot to Ox. He's close to his family and all that, but you know he's not the kind of guy who holds on to the past."

"But why wouldn't he say anything about this house once belonging to his family, after we found the necklace?"

"Because it's a nonissue in his mind. He barely even knew the lady who died here, so it's not as if he grew up here or spent summers playing in the garden." Dwight came around the island and put a hand on my shoulder. "Are you really going to tell me that you're tight with . . ." He waved a hand around as if he was trying to snag an idea out of the air. "With your fifth cousin three times removed? Because I don't think their relationship was anything more than that."

I frowned sullenly, but not because Dwight wasn't making sense. "I suppose not," I said reluctantly. "Then you don't think Ox is nursing a secret longing to claim the necklace for his family?"

It was a stretch, even to me, and Dwight's laugh confirmed how ridiculous the idea was.

"No, I don't think that at all. I doubt he's even given the necklace much thought at all. You know how he is."

I nodded as if I did, but I still wasn't sure how well I knew Ox. It was too much to figure out right then, so I finished up and walked with Dwight to the parking lot. His small truck was on the other side of the lot from my Range Rover, but I refrained from asking him to walk me to my car. It would only take me a minute to get there. Nothing was going to happen to me in sixty seconds.

Despite that pep talk, I hurried toward the Range Rover and prayed I was right. Even with the distraction of being really pissed off, it didn't take me long to realize that something was wrong. My heart plummeted and I turned to run back toward Dwight. "Wait! I think I might have a problem."

Dwight stopped just short of getting into his truck. "Another flat tire?"

It was meant to be a joke, referring to an incident the previous year when someone had flattened a tire on my Mercedes (may it rest in peace), but my sense of humor was out of commission. "I think somebody broke into my car," I said, struggling to hold back a flood of angry tears. "Can you turn your truck this way and get some light on it?"

Dwight's smile faded. He cranked the engine and moved the truck around so that his headlights illuminated the side of the Range Rover. I was relieved to see that the doors and bumpers hadn't been crushed, but there was just a big empty space where the driver's side window used to be. Bits of glass glinted on the pavement, and a quick glance inside revealed a lot more glass on the seat and floor.

Dwight got out of the truck and assessed the damage, turning back to me with a dumbstruck look on his face. "Somebody broke in?"

"It sure looks that way," I said. I tried not to let my mounting panic show, but I'm pretty sure I failed.

Dwight looked inside the truck again then back at me. Slowly, his expression changed from shock and awe to suspicion. "What's going on, Rita?"

"What do you mean? Somebody broke into the Range Rover."

"But you don't seem all that surprised."

He might not have been surprised either if I'd told him about the prowler and the mugging. Guilt sloshed around with the anger I was feeling and came out in a terse snarl. "Well, I am. It's not like this happens every day."

"No, but again, you're not . . . surprised. Has this happened before?"

"This?" I shook my head quickly. "No."

"Something else then?"

I tried to laugh, but the sound stuck in my throat. "It's no big deal," I said when I realized that Dwight wasn't going to let the subject drop. "I mean, it's not as if I got hurt or anything. I'm just a little nervous, that's all."

Dwight took my arm and led me back to his truck. He settled me in the passenger's seat, placed a call to the police, and then nailed me with a look that meant business. "What's been going on?"

"Nothing," I said again. "Not really." I wanted to keep a stiff upper lip. I wanted him to believe that everything was under control—especially me. But this wasn't the first time Dwight had been there for me during a crisis, and the look in his cocoa brown eyes was my undoing.

"You know what happened at the Vintage Vault, right?"

"Yeah. Somebody broke in and the owner died of a heart attack."

"Right. Well, I think that whoever broke into Orra Trussell's shop is still after the necklace. Ever since I got it back from the police, things have been happening."

"What things?"

"I think somebody was prowling around outside my house one night. And then somebody tried to mug me outside the Dizzy Duke."

Dwight's eyes flew wide. "You were mugged? Why didn't you say something?"

"I didn't want everybody to worry and get all overly protective," I said. "You know how you all get. And the mugger didn't get anything anyway."

"And you think Ox keeps secrets."

I gaped at him. "That's not the same thing at all."

"If you say so. Have you told the police about the other things?"

"Yes and no," I admitted. "I called after I spotted the prowler lurking outside my house, but I didn't report the mugging."

Dwight snorted softly. "I think you have your priorities backward. If you were going to pick and choose when to call the police, I'd say to do it after you were physically assaulted."

"If I'd known that was coming, I might have skipped the first call. The police weren't all that worried about the prowler. I didn't think they'd do anything about the mugging."

"So you didn't even give them a chance."

I made a face at him. "They'll get a chance tonight. We'll see what they say."

Dwight rolled his eyes in exasperation. "Don't you think you should call Sullivan?"

"I'm thinking about it," I said. I didn't mention that I hadn't exactly confided in Sullivan about the other incidents and—since he hadn't called or come over to lecture me about my personal safety—I figured he didn't know. Maybe I was being naïve, but I wanted to keep it that way.

The police finally showed up about forty-five minutes after Dwight placed the call, and I swear they were working in slow motion. It seemed to take forever for them to look over the scene of the crime, call in our driver's licenses and plates to check for warrants and question both of us about the incident. (How many ways can *you* say, "I didn't see anything"?) After that, they filled out some paperwork and left, but I still had a vehicle without a window to deal with.

Dwight and I rigged a replacement window out of clear plastic from the storage room and packing tape, which I just *knew* was going to leave residue on my brand-new car. Dwight called a friend of his and arranged for the Range Rover to be towed in for repairs and gave me a ride home, promising to pick me up bright and early in the morning.

I didn't sleep well. First the prowler, then the mugging, and now someone breaking into my car. Seriously? Did someone really think I was keeping a valuable ruby necklace in my glove box?

On the way back to Zydeco the next morning—which came *way* too early to suit me—Dwight and I hashed out a new plan for hauling everything we needed from Zydeco to the Monte Cristo and back again that didn't include the Range Rover in the lineup. With a little creative adjusting, we managed to come up with a plan that wouldn't require anyone to make extra trips, which made me feel slightly better. The Range Rover was gone when we pulled into the parking lot, which I told myself was good news . . . assuming no one had removed our makeshift plastic window and hotwired it.

Luckily, Ox had retrieved a business card and a copy of an invoice that the tow truck operator had left on the loading dock door, so I was able to stop worrying and get to work. The plan was for half the crew to deliver and set up the cakes while the other half stayed at Zydeco and spent the morning sautéing, roasting, and baking. They would transport the hot food later in the day, close to time for dinner service.

Ox had offered to remain behind and oversee the dinner preparations with Isabeau and Estelle. Calvin stayed, too, since he'd be needed to help carry the heavy food items and other equipment. The cakes were heavy, too, but I had Dwight, Sparkle, and Zoey on my team. It took a while to load all five cakes into the vehicles that would transport them, and in the process of moving them, two of the dress form cakes developed small cracks in the fondant—an annoyance and a minor time suck, but not a catastrophe. Once we had all the cakes loaded, we drove in a caravan to the hotel, where Dwight and I started the long and tedious process of carefully offloading and then hauling each cake to the second floor in the antique elevator while Sparkle remained on the street with the remaining cakes and two vans.

Eventually, we got the cakes inside the hotel and the vehicles stowed at a nearby parking garage, and we were able to get down to work. The next few hours passed in a blur as we moved the cakes into the ballroom, covered the tables with pale gray tablecloths, patched the cracked fondant, secured a few unstable decorations, and positioned the shoes and accessories for each dress. I was aware of Simone and her crew bustling about as they decorated the ballroom for the event, zipping in and out between members of the hotel staff, who delivered long banquet tables for the displays and rounds for the dinner service. While Dwight and Sparkle finished with the last cake, I supervised setup of buffet tables in the hallway, making sure they were spaced far enough apart to allow for easy traffic flow.

Early that afternoon, the arrival of the band Simone had hired added to the chaos as they hauled guitars, a keyboard, drums, amplifiers, and other gear I couldn't identify and set up their equipment on a small raised platform at the far end of the ballroom. While they performed sound checks and tuned their instruments, Simone's team hung strings of fairy lights, positioned vintage decorations between the display tables, and dressed each table with gleaming stemware and polished silver. Centerpieces of cut flowers in old-fashioned milk bottles added to the vintage feel.

Tommy Sheridan bustled in and out throughout the afternoon, checking on his crew, touching base with Simone and me to make sure we had what we needed. By the time Natalie Archer and the other members who had purchased display space began to arrive at three, we had finished setting up all five cakes.

The peacock feather dress shimmered in the lighting Simone had arranged. The tailored suit looked so real I wanted to try it on, and the simple cotton dress with its painted flower print looked almost translucent. The beaded evening gown sparkled, and the shirtwaist dress with oxford pumps looked like something straight out of *The Grapes of Wrath.*

Dwight roped off each cake to prevent anyone from

bumping into them while they worked, and Sparkle and I began trailing large extension cords from the outlets in the wall to the buffet tables, taping down each cord for safety as we went. Two or three times I heard Natalie bark an order at one of the other members, but for the most part, she seemed to be on her best behavior. I just hoped it would last.

By five o'clock, the displays were set up and artfully arranged, the items for the silent auction clearly designated and bidding sheets provided for each item, and the ballroom glittered and gleamed. Simone and the others who were attending the ball vanished, presumably to dress for the evening, and like clockwork, Ox and his team arrived with the food.

I hoped for Simone's sake—and for my own—that the evening would be a rousing success. We'd both worked long and hard, planning and then changing plans right up until the last minute. I wanted the silent auction to raise an obscene amount of money for charity, and for the food and the cakes to be enthusiastically received. This was the largest job I'd ever undertaken, and I was both nervous and excited.

At last the witching hour drew near and people began to arrive. My nerve endings hummed as I watched group after group of glittering, smiling people step off the elevator and survey the scene in front of them. I heard a few gasps of delight when people saw the cakes and several murmured comments that sounded like approval, and a tingly warmth spread all through me.

Gabriel, looking jaw-droppingly handsome in a tuxedo, spotted me as he arrived and came over to greet me. Finding out that my favorite bartender came from a family with ties to the elite had surprised me at first, but I was slowly getting used to seeing him at events like this. He gave me a hot Cajun smile and kissed my cheek, murmuring something in my ear about wanting to claim a dance later. *As if.* Not that I didn't want to. I'd danced with him before and I can honestly say the man knows his way around a dance floor, but there was no way he'd get me out there when I was on the job.

As he melted into the crowd, I turned my attention to the elevator again. I was a little bit nervous about seeing Miss Frankie and Bernice. Actually, I didn't worry about Bernice, but I didn't know if Miss Frankie was back to normal or if she was still freaked out about the Toussaint necklace. At least the necklace was one thing I *didn't* have to worry about since it was safely locked up at the bank.

At last the flow of arriving ball guests dwindled, people assumed their seats in the ballroom, and Evangeline Delahunt, looking elegantly glamorous in dark blue silk that floated delicately when she moved, stood in front of the podium to welcome the crowd. Simone had reappeared at some point, even more stunning than her mother in a pale pink evening gown that must have been made of silk, her dark hair gently waved in a style I always associated with Hollywood starlets from the 1930s.

I, on the other hand, was wearing industrial black slacks and my chef's jacket over a black tank top, a pair of sturdy, comfortable shoes, and had my curly hair tamed and held back in a severe bun. I felt anything but glitzy. But I wasn't there as a guest, and my perks would come in the form of a paycheck and (hopefully) a bigger customer base that would more than make up for anything I might miss out on.

Evangeline welcomed the crowd, gave a short speech about the charity they were supporting with tonight's event, and officially opened the buffet lines. Ox, Isabeau, and I stood near each of the buffet tables, ready to answer questions should any of the guests wonder about ingredients or have health concerns. I picked up some buzz about the necklace and a lot of chatter about the food as people passed by, but I was too busy for the next half hour to do anything else, including keep an eye out for my mother-in-law.

It wasn't until the lines at the buffet had dwindled that I

spotted Miss Frankie and Bernice at a table near the front of the room. Miss Frankie must have been watching for me because, as soon as I noticed her, she waved me over. I hesitated for a moment, wondering if Evangeline would think it inappropriate of me to mingle with the guests. Maybe she would, but I knew Miss Frankie too well to think that she would give up if I ignored her. To avoid a scene, I slipped carefully between tables, skirting the cash bar and avoiding a couple of collisions with members of the hotel staff who were providing beverage service with the meal.

I was thrilled to see that everyone seemed to be enjoying the food, and ecstatic to see the ongoing interest in the cakes. Several people had left their tables to snap pictures of the cakes with their phones, and the bits and pieces of conversation I picked up as I moved through the room all seemed enthusiastic.

Miss Frankie greeted me with a brief hug from her chair and a kiss on the cheek. She looked wonderful in a champagne-colored gown, matching shoes, and a diamond necklace I'd seen her wear only a couple of times before. Her auburn hair had been teased and sprayed into its usual style, but tiny sparkling gems peeked out from bejeweled combs in her hair here and there.

"It looks like everything is going well, sugar. The food is wonderful and the cakes are absolute works of art!"

I grinned from ear to ear and took the empty seat beside her, wondering if the gems in her hair were real diamonds. "It is going well, I think."

"You've done well. I'm proud of you."

Her praise filled me with warmth. "And the rest of the staff," I prompted. "They did most of the work."

"Well, of course they've all done well. They're wonderful. But you led them." She put a hand on mine and patted it gently. "You've done us all proud."

"You sure have," Bernice chimed in. She was wearing a dark blue velvet gown that made her hair seem extra snowy white. "Everybody is raving about those cakes. They look even better in person."

"It's our best work yet," I said, glad to see that Miss Frankie was acting like herself again. "When this is all over, I'd like to give the whole staff a bonus," I said. "They've all gone above and beyond getting ready for tonight."

Miss Frankie nodded. "Certainly. If you think we can afford it, and if you think they deserve it, go right ahead. It's a good idea to keep people happy in the workplace." She fell silent while a trio of women approached the evening gown cake. One snapped a photo of the other two, then they changed places for another two shots before finally wandering away.

Miss Frankie sent me an "I told you so" look.

Bernice came close to giggling out loud. "You're going to be famous before the night is over. Evangeline always invites the press, so I'm sure the right people are taking note of what you've done."

I started to remind them that Simone was responsible for most of the decorations, but Miss Frankie spoke up before I could finish. "It's a good thing you got rid of that necklace. Otherwise, who knows what might have happened tonight? What did you do with it anyway?"

Gulp! It was one thing to keep key pieces of information to myself, but quite another to tell an outright lie. "It's at the bank in a safe-deposit box."

Miss Frankie closed her eyes briefly. When she opened them again, sadness infused her expression. "Oh, sugar. You still don't understand, do you?"

I turned in my chair to face her more fully. "I *do* understand, Miss Frankie," I said, my voice low to keep us from being overheard. "I know why the necklace upsets you so much, but I also know that there is no such thing as a curse.

And if you'll just stop for a minute and think rationally, you'll have to admit you know it, too. Besides, I'm only hanging on to it until I can figure out who the rightful owner is and then I'll turn it over, I promise."

She gave me a skeptical look. "And just how do you intend to figure out who the rightful owner is?"

"I thought I'd start by talking to Thaddeus Montgomery."

Miss Frankie looked surprised, but she recovered quickly and gave a thoughtful nod. "I suppose talking to Thaddeus is a good idea, but I think he'll tell you that the necklace rightfully belongs to the Toussaint family."

"Maybe he will," I said, "but at least I'll know for sure. I mean, the Merciers must think they have *some* claim on it."

"I can't imagine why," Miss Frankie said. "Delphine never actually owned it."

"No, but it was promised to her, and that's why the whole mess got started in the first place." I swept a glance over the room again, noticed several more people snapping pictures of the cakes, and then caught a glimpse of the human bulldozer several tables away. She was talking to a young woman with dark hair who looked vaguely familiar. Both women looked a bit angry—but then, that seemed to be Natalie's default emotion.

"That reminds me," I said. "Do you know Natalie Archer?"

Miss Frankie followed my gaze. "Of course I do, sugar."

"She says that she's Gustave Toussaint's only heir. Is that true?"

Miss Frankie frowned. "Well, bless her heart. Natalie knows she's not Gustave's only descendant. There's her brother, too, and at least a dozen cousins. I'm sure she's just confused."

Yeah. I'm sure that was it. "She also says that you told her about Zoey and me finding the necklace. Is *that* true?"

Miss Frankie patted the back of her hair nonchalantly. "Yes, I did. I went to speak to her the day you were so worried about me. I heard about what happened to Orra, so I knew you hadn't taken my advice. And since I knew that Natalie was one of the Toussaint heirs, I decided she ought to know. We had lunch."

Lovely. Miss Frankie and Natalie, ladies who lunch. Considering how worried I'd been, I supposed I *should* have been relieved to learn that she'd been with Natalie and not visiting Mambo Odessa or some other voodoo priestess. But it was hard to feel relieved about anything where Natalie was concerned. "Sounds like a long lunch," I said with a halfhearted grin. "Why didn't you just tell me that's where you were?"

"I didn't realize I had to account for every minute of my day," she said. "And it was a wonderful lunch. We had a lot to talk about. Natalie and I have known each other for years. I went to school with her brother."

As if that explained everything. "That's nice," I said, "but now she expects me to just hand over the necklace to her on her say-so. She had some grandiose plan about me giving it to her tonight in front of the press."

Miss Frankie slid a sidelong glance at me. "Has she been bothering you?"

I shrugged. "A little, I guess. But it's nothing I can't handle. Just please tell me if you've spoken to anyone else who might come forward with a claim. I'd like to be prepared."

Miss Frankie patted my shoulder gently. "Natalie means well, bless her heart. Although she can be a trial at times. Do you want me to call Thaddeus for you? I'd be happy to arrange a meeting."

I shook my head, wanting to keep Miss Frankie as far from the necklace or anything having to do with it as humanly possible. I *so* didn't want another freak-out. "I'll take care of it. After tonight, I'll have a couple of days to breathe before we have to gear up for Mardi Gras." And I intended to lay the Toussaint necklace to rest.

Twenty-two

I'd been away from my post for too long, so I stood to excuse myself just as Sparkle appeared on the edge of my vision. I saw her look around, spot Miss Frankie and me, and begin weaving her way toward us. She didn't say a word when she reached me; she just shoved her phone under my nose and waited for my reaction.

I wasn't sure what I was seeing at first, but after a moment the confusion cleared and I let out a tiny shriek. "Is this what I think it is?" I asked.

Sparkle's face remained completely stoic, but her dark eyes glittered with excitement. "Yeah. Zydeco's trending. Cool, huh?"

Miss Frankie moved a little closer, trying to see the phone screen. "Trending? What does that mean? Is it good?"

"It's very good," I told her. "It means that people are talking about us online."

"Lots of people," Sparkle added. "They're posting pictures

of the cakes, of the buffet, of the dessert bar . . ." Her voice trailed off, but I thought I detected a hint of a smile. "I just thought you'd want to know."

"I did," I assured her. "Thanks." A little bubble of euphoria surrounded me at the thought of Zydeco being a trending Twitter topic. And in a good way! I didn't ever intend to admit it aloud, but I'd overextended myself and my staff by accepting this contract. I was more than a little relieved that it was working out so well. Better than I could have expected, in fact.

"We have hundreds of new Twitter followers, too," Sparkle said. "All in the last few hours."

I mentally upgraded my opinion of social media, but just then Natalie spoke to the young woman at her table and rose to her feet and I forgot all about Facebook and Twitter. The young woman turned toward me and I saw her full-on for the first time. I caught my breath when I realized that I was looking at Dominique. She looked completely different in a jade beaded gown and matching headband in her dark hair. It was the hair that made her unrecognizable to me. Somehow she had removed every trace of curl so that it fell in silky straight lines to her chin.

I nodded a greeting, which she returned with the hint of a smile before she turned away to watch Evangeline resume her place at the podium. Evangeline introduced the members who were running for board positions in an upcoming election and turned the microphone over to Natalie.

I held my breath, hoping Natalie wasn't going to blindside me by mentioning the Toussaint necklace. I needn't have worried. Turned out, she was only up there to deliver a memorial to Orra, complete with pictures taken of her at various events over the years.

Based on my limited experience with Natalie, the heartfelt tribute stirred and surprised me. Most of the people in that room seemed touched by Natalie's presentation, and several were mopping their eyes with their napkins as the homage wound to a close. I thought Orra would have been pleased by the outpouring of what appeared to be genuine grief.

Only one couple seemed unaffected by the tribute—Sol Lehmann and his wife exchanged glances several times as Natalie spoke. Neither seemed upset over Orra's untimely death; in fact, I was almost positive that I'd caught Mrs. Lehmann rolling her eyes over a couple of Natalie's more sentimental comments.

I reminded myself that failure to show grief or sadness didn't automatically mean that the Lehmanns had tried to steal the necklace from Orra, but it certainly didn't make Sol or his wife appear *less* guilty. Which is why, when Mrs. Lehmann excused herself from the table and stepped out into the hallway, I decided to follow her. It was probably too much to hope that I'd catch her riffling through my handbag looking for the necklace, but a girl can dream.

Mrs. Lehmann headed straight for the ladies' room, not my handbag, which was kind of a letdown. I'd been so *sure* she was going to make another attempt at stealing the necklace.

After she disappeared into the lavatory, I hesitated for about three seconds, then went in after her. I wasn't ready to write her off as a suspect just yet. And I was tired of looking over my shoulder, wondering when the jewel thief would strike again. If Sol Lehmann and his wife were responsible, I wanted to prove it. It would be easier to confront her now than to find a time and place later.

I did a little reconnaissance and determined that there was no one else in the bathroom with us—at least assuming those were Mrs. Lehmann's black pumps I could see beneath the stall door—and that there was no other way to leave the room. Satisfied that she hadn't ducked out the back way, I busied myself in front of the long mirror and waited.

She didn't make me wait long. Mrs. Lehmann came out

of the stall, glanced at my reflection as she walked toward me, and gave me a vague smile when we made eye contact in the mirror.

I smiled back and mumbled a greeting—the kind that's socially acceptable under awkward circumstances. I waited until she'd activated the water faucet and reached for the soap dispenser to strike up a conversation. "You're Mrs. Lehmann, aren't you?"

She stopped mid-pump but her smile was a couple of watts brighter. I guess she thought I was a potential customer. "Yes. Do I know you?"

"I don't think we've ever met," I said. "My name is Rita Lucero." I watched her closely, looking for a guilty flinch, a flicker of recognition—anything to convince me that she knew who I was.

I got nothing. She gave the soap dispenser another pump and smiled. "I'm Miriam." She ran a glance over my chef's jacket and plain black pants. "Are you one of the caterers?"

Either she had never heard my name before, or she was doing a good job pretending to be oblivious. I bet on the latter. "Actually, I'm one of the partners at Zydeco," I said, wondering if that bit of news might get something out of her.

She looked surprised as she put her hands under the water stream again. "I hope I didn't offend you. I just assumed you were one of the workers."

"Not at all," I assured her. "I'm definitely one of those, too." I glanced at the door and changed the subject before she could finish washing up. "That was a nice tribute Natalie gave in there, wasn't it?"

Miriam's lips quirked slightly. "Yes. Very."

I knew I was being pushy, but I didn't want her to get away before I could ask a few questions. "Did you know Orra Trussell well?"

"I suppose. As well as anyone here."

"Well, it's nice that she had so many friends. Someone told me that she had no family."

Miriam's lips quirked again. "I wouldn't say that she had *friends* here. *Colleagues* might be a better word."

"Oh!" I tried to act surprised. "So you weren't friends with her? That seems so sad."

"Save your sympathy," Miriam said. "You reap what you sow."

"Oh!" I said again. "Natalie's tribute left me with a different impression."

Miriam looked away from what she was doing. "She made Orra sound like a saint, didn't she? Don't get me wrong, I'm sorry Orra's dead, but she wasn't a saint by any means."

"I only met her once," I said. "I didn't know her at all, but she seemed like a nice woman."

"That's the impression she wanted people to have," Miriam said. She pulled her hands away from the sink and shook the excess water from them before heading for the paper towel dispenser. "Most people fell for the act."

"I wish I'd known that before I went to the Vintage Vault," I said, hoping to encourage more gossip from Miriam. "I left a necklace with her for an appraisal. Was she not trustworthy?"

Miriam dried her hands and tossed the towels, but this time when she looked at me, she seemed more focused. More alert. She completely ignored my question and took the bait I'd dropped. "Sol was telling me something about a necklace that Orra was appraising. The Toussaint rubies, I believe. You're the one who left it at the Vintage Vault?"

I nodded. "Actually, your husband approached me about buying the necklace. He didn't tell you about that?"

"We're supposed to be partners," she said with an eye roll dramatic enough for a teenage girl. "He's *supposed* to tell me everything, but he doesn't. You know how men are."

Did I ever. Seemed like all the men in my life were experts at keeping things bottled up. "Sol didn't discuss the Toussaint necklace with you?"

"Oh, we've discussed it. Plenty of times, in fact. Every jeweler in the South has been waiting for that piece to turn up again. Of course, not everyone thought it would be found. Some people believed that the stones were removed from their settings and sold off separately years ago, but most of us thought that it would be found eventually."

"I had no idea it was so well known."

"Oh, yes," Her eyes narrowed speculatively. "So what kind of deal did you and Sol strike?"

"We didn't make a deal. I'm still trying to decide what to do with the necklace. I'm not sure I even have the right to sell it to anyone."

Miriam's smile faded. "You found it, didn't you?"

"Well, yes, but it originally belonged to the Toussaint family . . ." I let my voice trail away and hoped that I sounded genuinely confused.

"Don't let anyone bully you, my dear. You found the thing. You can do whatever you want with it." Miriam opened her purse and produced a business card. "Before you strike a deal with anyone, please call me. I can make you a much better deal than anyone else, including my husband."

Interesting. Clearly Miriam and Sol weren't working together. I took the card and slipped it into a pocket. "Thanks. I'll keep you in mind," I said, but Miriam was already halfway out the door.

I tucked my disappointment away and waited a few seconds before I followed her. By the time I emerged, she had already disappeared but I guess it didn't really matter. I had a feeling she wasn't the jewel thief, after all.

But crossing Miriam Lehmann off the list of possible suspects brought another name up to the top. Dominique had painted a far different picture of Sol and Miriam's working relationship than the one Miriam had shared with me. Had Dominique deliberately misled me? And if so, why?

People were dancing by the time I got back to the ballroom. Gabriel waltzed by with Bernice on his arm and mouthed, "You're next," when he knew I was watching them.

My insides did their usual flippy thing at the look in his eyes. Under other circumstances, I would have waited right there for him to come back, but I had no intention of making a spectacle of myself. I turned away reluctantly to check on the behind-the-scenes staff, which was what I was being paid to do.

I walked past the buffet tables, pleased to see that most of the food was gone, and started down the hall toward the staging area. I spotted Zoey sitting on a bench outside the prep rooms. Carlo Mancini stood over her, punching and swiping on his tablet. Anger bubbled up inside me, but I wasn't sure which of them I was angriest with.

Zoey saw me coming and her face blanched. She shot up off the bench and backed away from Mancini as if she'd suddenly discovered he had the plague. "I really have to get back," she murmured. "I have to work."

She slipped back into the prep room before Mancini could stop her. He turned slowly to face me, a deceptively calm smile on his face. "It seems you make young Zoey nervous. Why is that?"

I wanted to snatch that goatee right off his smug face, but I was pretty sure he'd jump on an angry outburst from me like a hungry duck on a junebug. Since I didn't want to feed him any kind of story, I returned his smile with one of my own. "I don't know what you mean. Zoey is a conscientious employee who knows she shouldn't be having personal conversations when she's supposed to be working, that's all."

"Or granting interviews to reporters you've forbidden her to talk to?"

I gave an icy laugh. "She can talk to whoever she likes, as long as she's not speaking for Zydeco. I'm the only one who can do that."

He glanced at the door behind him and shrugged. "Fair enough. I understand you may be presenting the Toussaint necklace to its rightful owner tonight. Any comment?"

The door flew open while Mancini was asking his question and I caught a quick glimpse of Calvin holding a gray plastic bin, on his way to start disassembling the buffet tables. Not wanting to interrupt the conversation Mancini and I were having, however, he eased the door almost shut again, but I could see a sliver of his dark arm and white sleeve.

It was nice of him to want to protect me, but considering Mancini's question, Natalie Archer was in more danger than I was. How *dare* she claim that I was going to give her the necklace? I ground my teeth in frustration. Was she trying to back me into a corner?

"My only comment would be that you have your facts wrong," I told Mancini. "The necklace isn't even on the premises."

Mancini's eyes found mine. "Where is it?"

I laughed and shook my head. "Like I'm going to tell you. Sorry. That information is private."

Mancini shrugged. "Can't shoot a guy for asking."

"I know. What a pity. Now if you'll excuse me," I said with a meaningful glance at the door. "I have work to do."

Mancini stepped aside with a slight bow and I moved past him into the staging area. The rooms had seemed small when I'd looked them over before the event, but they were actually larger than I'd been expecting. Even so, we'd managed to take up every inch of usable space and several sections looked as if something had exploded nearby. It would take us forever to clean up after the ball was over.

Calvin was still hovering near the door. He gave me a worried once-over when I surged inside. "You okay? Was that guy bothering you again?"

I waved away his questions and scanned the chaos to make sure everything was under control. "Don't worry about him. He's like a gnat—annoying but not dangerous. I think he's gone, but if he isn't, just ignore him."

Calvin nodded and carted his plastic tub out of the room just as I noticed Zoey in the far corner. I skirted a stack of boxes and rounded a table before I realized that she was talking to Estelle. They both turned to look at me and the scowl on Estelle's face made my step falter.

I pasted on a smile to show that I came in peace. "I have some great news," I said. "Sparkle says that Zydeco is trending. I guess a lot of people are tweeting and posting pictures online."

Zoey perked right up, but Estelle eyed me skeptically. "That's good," Estelle said. "Is that what you came to tell us?"

"Not exactly," I admitted. "I saw that Carlo Mancini was nosing around and I wanted to make sure that everybody was all right."

"All right?" Estelle asked. "Or keeping our mouths shut?"

I winced inwardly. "Okay, look, I'm sorry. Obviously I've offended you, Estelle, but that was never my intention."

Estelle sniffed to show her disapproval. "What was your intention? Why did you give Zoey the gag order?"

"It wasn't a gag order," I said defensively. "I just wanted some time to figure out what was going on."

"So you stuffed Zoey into a corner and did all the talking yourself."

Harsh! I glanced at Zoey, but she was back to her old self—staring at the toes of her shoes and pretending she wasn't even there. "I never intended to stuff you into a corner, Zoey. I just wanted to control the information that was getting out there. Obviously, I went about it in the wrong way."

Zoey glanced away from her shoes and almost made eye contact. "It's okay. It's no big deal."

I was glad she understood. I could only hope her aunt would calm down and quit giving me the stink-eye. "So what did Mancini ask you?" I asked, trying to sound nonthreatening. "Did you give him an interview?"

Zoey shook her head. "I told him he had to talk to you."

"What did he want to know?"

Zoey shrugged. "Just where the necklace was now and what we were going to do with it. Stuff like that." She lifted her eyes to meet mine. "I couldn't tell him anything, could I? I don't know."

"The necklace is safe," I assured her, but I was cut short by the buzz of my phone and a message from Ox telling me that Evangeline Delahunt was looking for me for pictures. "I'll tell you all about it tomorrow," I told Zoey. "I promise. Let's just get through the rest of tonight."

Zoey almost smiled and I thought even Estelle looked a little less annoyed as I hurried away.

At last the evening came to a close, adrenalin stopped pumping and exhaustion set in. Disposing of the food and packing away the dirty dishes took a while. Isabeau, Sparkle, and Estelle went out to clear the dessert bar while Ox and Dwight began breaking down tables. Calvin and Zoey packed boxes onto a couple of rolling carts and started hauling them out to the Zydeco van.

I stayed in the staging area and continued packing dishes and equipment away into boxes so they'd be ready when Zoey and Calvin came back. My arms and legs felt heavy and weariness tugged at my eyelids, but we'd been given so many positive comments by attendees, I was on an emotional high. Humming lightly, I stacked a couple of chafing dishes into a large box.

As I turned back for more, Natalie Archer poked her head into the room. "Ah! There you are. I've been looking for you, Ms. Lucero."

I tried to look pleased to see her. "Mrs. Archer. How can I help you?"

"Give me five minutes of your time. I won't take more than that."

"That sounds reasonable enough," I said. "Come on in." I didn't like the woman, but she was an old friend of Miss Frankie's so I tried to at least be civil. Besides, if I could get Natalie talking, maybe I'd learn something helpful, like who she hired to steal the necklace.

Natalie scowled and peeked a bit farther into the room. "A private word, if you don't mind."

I could have pointed out that we were alone, but she could see that for herself. Or maybe she thought I had minions hiding in the boxes. I shrugged and put the pans I was holding into an empty box. "As long as it's only a few minutes," I said and followed Natalie out the door.

Most of the party goers had left the hotel by that time. A few lingered, clustered in small friendly-looking groups around the now-empty space. Natalie marched past all of them, leaving me no choice but to follow. She passed several conversation nooks that apparently didn't meet with her approval, and finally settled on two chairs near the stairs.

Since the stairs were still blocked due to the broken pipe, nobody would be able to come up behind us and we could see anyone who approached from the front. I got the feeling she didn't want anyone to overhear what she had to say.

She took one chair and I took the other. I spoke before she

could, hoping to find out what I wanted to know before she took control of the conversation. “I thought your tribute to Orra was lovely,” I said. “You must have cared about her a great deal.”

Natalie smiled—I think. Her lips moved, anyway. “Orra was a colleague, and that’s what one does in circumstances like these. Anything less would have been inappropriate.”

How touching.

“But that’s not what I wanted to discuss with you,” she said.

Surprise, surprise. I never thought it was. I smiled all friendly-like. “Of course not. What can I do for you, Mrs. Archer?”

“You can tell me where you stand on the necklace. I’ve spoken with my attorney, and he assures me that my claim will stand up in any court of law.”

Considering how formidable she could be, I wasn’t surprised. Her attorney was probably afraid to give her bad news. Or maybe she was making it all up. Either way . . .

“My position hasn’t changed,” I told her. “As I said before, I haven’t had a chance to talk to my attorney. Now that the ball is over, I’ll try to contact him early next week.”

“That seems completely unnecessary,” Natalie said. “You can speak with my attorney. He has promised to be available night and day.”

I almost laughed, but managed to contain it. “That’s kind of you. I’m sure your attorney will present your case in the best possible light, but I would prefer to discuss it with someone more . . .” How to say “not under your thumb or being paid by your dollar”? I decided on, “. . . impartial.”

Natalie’s eyes grew cold. I swear, I could almost hear her bulldozer engine revving up. “I assure you, my attorney is fair and honest. Everything he does is aboveboard.”

“I’m sure that’s true,” I said. “But I still want to talk to my guy. You’d feel the same way if our positions were reversed.”

She shook her head as if I'd saddened her terribly. "I suppose I might," she said in a tone that clearly suggested otherwise. "Will you at least tell me if you've had other offers?"

"As a matter of fact, I have," I said. "Several, in fact."

"May I ask who the other parties are?"

Sol, Miriam, and maybe Dominique. I wondered if I could count the attempts to steal the necklace as offers. The jewel thief made four. "I prefer not to divulge that information just yet."

"I see." Natalie smoothed her hands over the fabric of her skirt. "I'm disappointed, Miss Lucero, but I suppose there's no rushing whatever your process is."

"I'm afraid there isn't." And now that we'd settled that, I tried to steer the conversation back to what I wanted to know. "I spoke with Miriam Lehmann earlier. She painted a very different picture of Orra than you did in your comments."

Natalie looked supremely uninterested. "That doesn't surprise me. Miriam means well, but she would say anything if it got her what she wanted. I suppose she's one of the parties who offered to buy the necklace from you."

"We discussed it for a moment," I admitted, then pivoted the topic. "I'm curious to know how many people knew that the necklace was in Orra's possession the night she died. I'm told that news travels fast in vintage clothing circles. How did you hear?"

Natalie actually smiled. "Why should I answer your question when you refuse to answer mine? If you tell me who else has offered to buy the necklace, I will consider telling you what you want to know."

Wow. How generous. "So you did know that Orra had the necklace at the Vintage Vault that night?"

"I didn't say that. But let's not play games with one another. I do hope you're not considering an offer from the Merciers."

Strangely enough, I hadn't received a single offer from the Merciers, but I didn't think Natalie needed to know that. "Again, Mrs. Archer, I prefer not to discuss that."

"The necklace is not theirs, you know. Armand gave it to his wife, which is what he should have done. I don't know how Delphine managed to kill them both, but I am quite sure she did. Her kin shouldn't benefit from her crime. I'm certain there are laws against that."

Okay, *that* was a new angle I hadn't previously considered. "You think Delphine actually murdered Armand and Beatriz?" I knew that there were current laws on the books that prevented a criminal from profiting from a crime, but I didn't know how those laws might apply to this situation.

"Whether she poisoned them herself or caused them to die by the curse, she was guilty," Natalie insisted.

Guilt by curse? Hmmm.

I stood to indicate that I considered the conversation over. "I'll contact you after I've spoken with my lawyer," I said again. "That's really the best I can do."

Natalie got to her feet slowly. "Aren't you at all curious how Beatriz Toussaint's necklace came to be hidden in your place of business?"

The question hit me like a two-by-four upside the head. I like to think that I'm pretty quick on the uptake, but as it happened, I hadn't even considered that question. Why *was* the necklace in the stairs at Zydeco? If the Toussaints were in possession of the necklace for the first fifty years or so, who had hidden it in Miss Cassie's old home?

"Are you suggesting that someone stole the necklace from Gustave's family?"

"I think that's fairly obvious, don't you?"

"You don't think Gustave might have given it away after his wife and daughter died?"

"He wouldn't have done that," Natalie said firmly.

I tried to do some mental calculations, but no matter how I diced or sliced the numbers, I couldn't make Natalie old enough and Gustave young enough to have been alive at the same time. "What makes you so certain?"

"Gustave lost his uncle, his aunt, his wife, and his daughter, all because of Delphine's curse. He would have died before he willingly gave the necklace away."

"You might be right," I said. "Or maybe he decided he'd lost enough. Maybe he hid it himself."

"Impossible."

Improbable maybe. Certainly not impossible. But before I could respond, I saw Miss Frankie making her way toward us. Frankly, I didn't know whether to cheer or groan. I supposed that would depend on which personality she'd brought with her.

"Rita, dear," she said when she drew closer. "I've been looking all over for you. I wanted to tell you again what a wonderful job you did tonight."

She sounded like the sane version, but I couldn't be sure. I stood up to greet her and Natalie did the same. "Yes," Natalie said. "It was lovely."

Miss Frankie beamed and put an arm around my waist. "Isn't Rita somethin'? I love her like she's my own flesh and blood." She kissed my cheek and moved to stand by Natalie, still all smiles. "You know how it is, don't you, Natalie? I'm sure you feel the same way about your girls. Now . . . I've been meaning to ask you about something." She slipped her hand under Natalie's elbow and led her away. "It's about my garden . . ." Her voice trailed away as they walked toward the elevator.

I grinned and said a quick prayer of thanks that the real Miss Frankie had returned.

Natalie said something, but they were too far away for me to hear it. But I thought that she looked less like a bulldozer and more like a sad, aging woman. I even felt a twinge of sympathy for her. But just a twinge. I still had no idea who was responsible for the attacks on me and I couldn't risk feeling sorry for anyone.

Any one of these ordinary-looking people might have frightened Orra so badly she'd keeled over on the spot. Any one of them might have tried to hurt me. I couldn't lose sight of that.

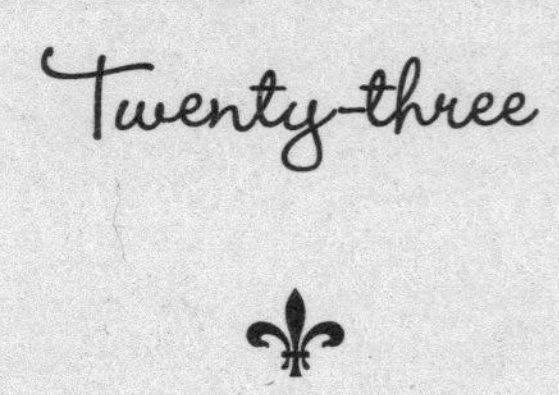

Twenty-three

By the time we finished up at the Monte Cristo, the Range Rover's window had been replaced and my credit card payment processed. I caught a ride to the repair shop with Ox and Isabeau, where the Range Rover and its shiny new window waited for me.

I cruised home, cranking the stereo to keep me awake. Even so, I was so tired I barely remembered how I got from one side of town to the other.

Finding a parking space on the same block as my house is always cause for celebration. Finding one directly in front of my house almost never happens. Someone must have been watching out for me, because the spot right in front of my house was open when I pulled up. I did a little victory dance as I gathered up my things and trotted up the front walk, happy to be home and thrilled to have the successful Belle Lune Ball behind me. I was so caught up in my internal celebration, I was halfway up the walk before I realized that the front of the house looked different. It was another moment before I comprehended that my front door wasn't completely closed.

I stopped walking abruptly and stared at the door dumbly while I tried to process what I was seeing. Had I left the door open when I left that morning? I didn't think so. True, I'd been in a hurry and distracted by all the work in front of us, but finding the broken window on the Range Rover had spooked me. I was confident that I'd paid enough attention to shut and lock the door when I left for work.

I dropped the bags I'd been carrying and pulled my cell phone from my pocket to dial Sullivan's number, realizing belatedly that my battery had died sometime during the evening.

Terrific.

Now what? I briefly considered checking the house to see if the intruder was still there, but at the last minute common sense prevailed. I could have gone back to the Range Rover, but without a cell phone, I'd be sitting there all night. I wasn't going to just drive away and leave the burglar alone in my house. Abandoning the idea of charging into a potentially dangerous situation, I walked next door to the Thai restaurant instead.

Its walls were covered with dark wood paneling and a collection of ornamental carvings. Wooden wind chimes played as the door swooshed shut behind me. The restaurant was empty of customers, but a small woman with a serious face scurried toward me, waving both hands in front of her. "Sorry. Too late. We're closed. You go away now. Come back tomorrow."

"I'm not here to eat," I said. "I live next door. I think somebody broke into my house and I need to use your phone to call the police."

She glared at me suspiciously. "You live where?"

I hooked a thumb in the right direction. "Next door. My name's Rita Lucero," I said, suddenly remembering my manners. "I've been working all day and just got home. I found my front door open."

"Open?"

"I think somebody broke in. May I use your phone? And maybe wait here until the police arrive?"

"You can call," she said, motioning me toward an old-fashioned black phone on the counter. "But I don't think you can wait here. We're closed."

"I don't want to eat," I said again. "I just need to wait until the police arrive. It shouldn't be too long." I could have waited in the car, but suddenly the idea of being alone wasn't sitting well. This time I planned to call Sullivan directly. I try not to take advantage of our relationship, but since my previous calls to the police had met with unsatisfactory results, this time I was going for the big guns.

It took less than three minutes for Sullivan to hear me out and start heading in my direction. Unfortunately, it would take him at least thirty minutes to get there without traffic. I wasn't sure my hostess would be happy about that, but I wouldn't be happy if I had to wait outside by myself in the middle of the night. We couldn't both be happy.

I parked myself on a bright red leather chair and folded my hands on my lap to show that I had no intention of stealing from her. "I don't want to keep you," I said in my friendliest voice. "If you have work to do, please go ahead."

She made a show of straightening a stack of menus, then bustled around doing . . . whatever. I watched in silence since she didn't seem interested in conversation. After a little while, though, the silence began to get to me. That and a wall of exhaustion so strong I needed something to help me stay awake until Sullivan arrived. I decided to try chatting with her.

"Have you had anything unusual happen here at the restaurant?" I asked. She stared at me in confusion so I tried to clarify. "The other night, I thought I saw someone prowling around by my house. You weren't broken into, were you?"

"Here? You saw somebody breaking in here?"

"No, but I saw someone moving around late at night. I thought that he—or she—might be scoping out my house, but then he ran across your property and I wondered if he was trying to break in."

She didn't say a word.

"I heard a noise after he disappeared around the back of the building," I explained. "I thought he might have run into your trash cans, but it could have been something else. You didn't find anything suspicious when you came to work, did you?"

A frown tugged at the corners of her mouth. "When?"

I thought back, trying to remember exactly which night I'd seen the prowler. The week had been so crazy, all the days had blended together. "Three or four nights ago," I said.

"And you think someone broke in here?"

I must have been mumbling. "Not exactly. Just wondering if you remember finding anything unusual one night this week."

"No. Nothing suspicious. Nothing unusual. Animals knock over trash cans sometimes. Maybe that's what you heard."

"It wasn't an animal," I said. "I definitely saw a person. Have you noticed anyone who doesn't belong lurking around the neighborhood?"

She reached beneath the counter for a feather duster and began working it over the ornate decorations on the wall. "Strange people come around all the time," she said. "They're called customers."

Had she just cracked a joke? I laughed in case that's what she was expecting. "You haven't noticed someone unusual watching my house or anything?"

She stopped dusting and scowled at me. "I don't have time to look at what's going on outside. I work."

I decided to take that as a "no," and gave up trying to engage her in friendly conversation. I spent the next twenty minutes trying to stay awake and watching her pretend to work while keeping an eye on me. By the time Sullivan pulled up in front of the restaurant, I was more than ready to get out of there.

Breathing a silent sigh of relief, I hopped up and jerked my chin toward the door. "The detective is here."

She hustled out around the counter and flipped the lock. "You go. Next time come back to eat."

That sounded reasonable, so I promised that I would and hurried outside. She locked the door almost before I got all the way through it and turned out the lights. It didn't matter so much now. One look at Sullivan's six-foot-nothing of Southern boy charm and I knew I was going to be okay.

He motioned for me to go back inside the restaurant. "Stay there. I'll check out the house and then we'll talk."

"Not an option," I said. "She's already locked me out and turned off the lights."

He cut an irritated glance at the darkened front door. "Well, you're not coming inside with me. Not until I know it's safe."

"Fine. I'll wait out here. By myself. In the dark. No problem."

Sullivan made a noise that sounded like a growl. "You're not coming inside with me."

"I'm sure that whoever broke in is long gone," I argued. "It's been half an hour since I called you, and he was probably gone even before I got home."

"Maybe," Sullivan said grudgingly, "but we won't know for sure until I check it out."

I appreciated his concern and I understood his caution,

but I *really* wanted to get inside and curl up on my sofa—assuming it was still there. "Just let me inside," I bargained. "I promise you can search to your heart's content and I won't bother you."

"And if there's someone waiting inside? No, you can wait in your car. You'll be safe there."

"Yeah. Maybe. Come on. He's probably not even in there. It's been a long time since I got home. And if he is, I'll let you take care of him. Please, Sullivan. I've been on my feet all day and I'm exhausted."

I could tell that he didn't want to agree, but I gave him my best puppy eyes and he caved. "Fine," he snarled, "but you wait outside until I make sure the main floor is clear."

"Deal," I said to show that I could be reasonable.

We moved cautiously up the walk and Sullivan gave the front door a quick once-over before disappearing inside. It felt like I'd been waiting a couple of hours when he reappeared at the door and waved at me to come in. He motioned me toward the living room, where cushions tossed onto the floor and signs that the furniture had been shifted convinced me that the intruder had been searching for something. I had a good idea what he'd been after.

I replaced the couch cushions and settled myself on it with a weary frown. "How is the kitchen?" I asked around a jaw-cracking yawn.

"It's been tossed," Sullivan said. "Our friend was definitely looking for something. Upstairs looks clear, too, but I'm going to make sure. Stay here. Do *not* move."

Ordinarily, I might have argued with him, but I was too tired to move. If the intruder *was* still in the house, I'd be tempted to promise him the necklace just to get rid of the thing.

Nodding agreeably, I curled my legs under me.

Sullivan grunted—shorthand for "Well, all right then," and moved soundlessly up the stairs. I was a little unnerved at the thought of him checking my messy bedroom for intruders. The whole house could have used a little TLC, but I couldn't work up enough energy to care.

Sullivan was back shortly, but instead of talking to me, he turned on several lights and gave the front door a more thorough inspection. "Looks like somebody took a crowbar to this," he said after a while. He leaned in close and scowled, then plucked something from beneath two splintered pieces of wood. "It appears that we're dealing with a nice thief," he said, holding the item up by one corner.

"What is it?"

"A fifty-dollar bill."

I blinked in confusion. "The robber *left* money? That's a switch."

Sullivan nodded. "Looks like you're taking me to dinner. How about sushi?"

I grinned, or at least I tried to. "Sure. I'll pencil it in."

Sullivan laughed and trotted back to the kitchen. When he came back, the bill was in a baggie. "We might be able to pick up a print or two from this," he said. "It's worth a shot."

"Go for it," I said, yawning again.

He perched on the other end of the couch. "Is this about the necklace you found?"

"I sure hope so," I said. "Otherwise, I have two crazy people after me."

"You're going to have to explain that," he said, putting a hand on my calf and rubbing gently. "But first, tell me what to pack for you. You'll stay with me tonight."

"It's okay. He's not coming back." I offered up the token protest, but I couldn't work up any real conviction.

"Maybe not," Sullivan said, "but you're not staying here. The door won't lock and I'm not leaving you unprotected. So either I camp out here on your sofa, or you come with me. You choose."

"Fine. You win." I sat up and tried wiping some of the sleep out of my eyes. It was one thing to let Sullivan search my messy bedroom for intruders, but another thing entirely to let him rummage through my underwear drawer. I might not have minded quite so much if the drawer had been filled with dainty, lacy scraps suitable for an overnight stay with a gentleman friend, but my comfortable cotton briefs were strictly utilitarian.

"I'll grab what I need," I said. "Back in five."

It actually took a little longer than five minutes for me to find everything I thought I'd need, but Sullivan didn't seem to notice. He was on the phone when I came downstairs, arranging for someone to secure my house overnight. It pays to have connections.

When he'd finished settling everything to his satisfaction, he led me to his car, a seriously impressive red Impala, and drove me to his apartment. I'd been there before, but never as an overnight guest. I might've been more nervous if I hadn't been so exhausted. As it was, Sullivan set me up in his bedroom and took the couch for himself. I don't know how he fared, but I fell into a deep, dreamless sleep almost as soon as my head touched the pillow.

Twenty-four

⚜

Sullivan woke me around ten the next morning. Or maybe I should say the aroma of fresh coffee woke me and brought Sullivan into the bedroom with it. He'd also put a couple of bagels on a plate and added a tub of whipped cream cheese, but the coffee made everything else unimportant.

Sighing gratefully, I took the mug he offered me and scooched up against the headboard to make room for him. He left the tray at the foot of the bed and brought his broad shoulders and impressive physique into the bed with me. My heart flipped around for a moment and heat raced through me when his thigh brushed mine. He kissed me thoroughly and then settled back with a satisfied smile.

"Nice way to start the morning," he said. "We should do this more often."

"Agreed, but I vote we try it under better circumstances."

Sullivan kissed me again. "Deal. I thought I'd go back over to your place this morning and check it out in the daylight," he said. "Want to come along, or would you rather stay here and catch up on your sleep?"

I laughed and sipped coffee, hoping the caffeine would kick in quickly. "I'm awake now," I pointed out. "And you should know me better than to think I'm going to stay behind."

His clear blue eyes twinkled. "You never know. You might've been willing to let me check it out on my own. Pigs might be flying around outside, too."

I grinned. "I suppose there's even a chance that hell is frozen over. You let me know if it is and then I'll think about staying behind."

"Pretty much what I thought you'd say." He crossed one foot over the other, making himself comfortable. "Now that you've had some sleep, why don't you tell me what happened when you got home last night."

The smile slipped from my face. "There's not much to tell," I said. "Everything from the time I finally left the Monte Cristo is pretty foggy. I don't even remember actually driving home."

"That might not be something you want to tell a cop."

"I wouldn't tell just *any* cop," I said. "And for the record, I might be awake but I'm not coherent." I took another bracing sip of caffeine and tried to remember the details. "I parked the car on the street and started toward the door just like always. I was exhausted, so I'm not sure what I noticed first. But I could tell that something wasn't right. It was dark, so it took a few seconds to realize that the door was open. I knew I hadn't left it that way, so I tried to call you on my cell but my battery was dead so I went to the restaurant next door."

Sullivan nodded as I talked. "So you didn't actually go look at the door?"

"Nope. I behaved myself."

"Who says you aren't teachable?" He winked as he said it and something warm and pleasurable scampered up my spine.

"Nobody, I hope." I put my mug on the nightstand and wrapped my arms around my knees. "Until last night, I was convinced that whoever was after the necklace was involved with the Vintage Clothing Society. But all of the suspects were at the ball last night so it couldn't have been one of them."

"Not necessarily," Sullivan pointed out. "You were working. I'm sure you stayed later than most of the guests."

He was right, of course. My thinking was still foggy. "No, of course not. I know Natalie Archer was there almost until the end, but I had to go collect my car at the shop, so I guess any one of them could've still gotten to my house, broken in, and searched it, all before I got home." I shuddered just thinking about it. "Could they have still been inside when I got home?" And my nerves gave way to anger. "I almost wish I'd walked in. I'm really getting tired of this."

"I'm sure you are, but don't start taking chances. This guy hasn't been violent yet, but it's not worth taking a chance."

I looked away, hoping he wouldn't see guilt on my face. I hadn't told him about the attempted mugging at the Dizzy Duke, and I wasn't sure I wanted to tell him now. If he thought the wannabe thief was a real danger, I'd have a harder time convincing him to let me tag along when he went back to the house.

"Why don't you tell me about these suspects of yours?"

"Well, there's Orra Trussell's assistant, Dominique," I said. "She knew that Orra had the necklace in her possession, and I get the feeling that she's ambitious. I think she'd be happy to inherit the Vintage Vault now that Orra is dead. Maybe she saw the necklace as her chance to get ahead. Maybe she went back to the Vintage Vault to steal the necklace and startled Orra. I mean, she has no alibi—unless the police can prove that she really was home when Orra called her that night."

"I wouldn't hold my breath," Sullivan said. "But Dominique wouldn't have needed to break in, would she?"

"No, but if she wanted to make it look like someone else

stole the necklace, she couldn't very well just unlock the door and take it."

"True. Okay, so Dominique. Who else?"

"Sol Lehmann and his wife, Miriam. Sol was at the Vintage Vault the night I dropped off the necklace. He's offered to buy it from me, and so has his wife. They don't seem to be working together, but who knows? I don't trust either one of them. And then there's Natalie Archer. She claims to be Gustave Toussaint's descendant, and insists that the necklace belongs to her. But she *was* at the Monte Cristo almost as long as I was. I don't think she could have made it to my house before I got there."

"Has she offered to buy the necklace?"

I shook my head. "No, and I don't think she will. She seems to believe that the necklace is rightfully hers. She's not going to pay to get it back."

"But would she steal it?"

"I wouldn't put it past her," I said. "But if she's behind all of this, she must have an accomplice."

Sullivan filed that away and asked, "Anyone else?"

"I don't think so."

Sullivan polished off his coffee and set his cup aside. "Well, we won't figure out who broke in from here. Can you be ready in ten minutes?"

"Make it fifteen," I said as I scampered off the bed and headed toward the shower. Usually I take pride in my independence. I don't need a big, tough man to protect me. But I'm not a fool either. Whoever wanted the Toussaint necklace was becoming more aggressive all the time, and I liked knowing I wasn't alone.

Sullivan and I spent more than an hour checking my house for clues that might tell us who had broken in while I was working, but we came up empty. We talked to a few of my nearest neighbors, hoping to find someone who'd seen or heard something unusual. Most of the shops had been closed, and the neighbors who lived on my street had either been sleeping or away from home at the time of the burglary.

Since it was Sunday and we had no big jobs coming up, Zydeco was closed. I expected everyone on staff would take the day off to recuperate, and that left me free to spend the morning with Sullivan. We stopped at a local bistro for soup and sandwiches and ate in my kitchen while a friend of Sullivan's repaired the splintered wood and installed a new lock. By two that afternoon, the house was livable again, though Sullivan suggested that I continue to stay at with him, at least until we figured out who was responsible for the damage.

I won't even try to deny that the idea of hiding at Sullivan's house was tempting. The break-in had left me feeling exposed and vulnerable. Every pop, crack, and creak in the house made me jump. But if I ran, then whoever was responsible for all of this would win, and that wasn't okay.

Sullivan and I argued mildly until he was called out on a case. He left reluctantly, and only after making me promise that I'd check in with him every hour. I agreed, mainly because I knew that if he was working, he'd be too busy to lecture me, and also because I was a little nervous about staying alone in the house. But that was exactly why I had to stay. I lived on my own, which meant that I didn't have the luxury of curling up in a fetal position every time something made me nervous.

Determined to keep my chin up, I puttered around the house for a while after Sullivan left. I washed a load of towels, stripped my bed, and put the bedding through the wash as well. I straightened the kitchen, dusted the living room, and ran the vacuum over the floors.

With the housework finished—at least as finished as it was going to get—I found myself getting restless. What was I doing? Letting the jewel thief turn me into a victim? It wasn't like me to just sit around, waiting for him or her to strike again. There had to be something I could *do.*

But what?

First thing tomorrow, I'd contact Thaddeus Montgomery and get his legal opinion about Natalie's claim, but I was too edgy to wait until then. I wondered if someone from the Mercier family was behind the break-ins. I could try to track down the Lehmanns or Dominique or even Natalie Archer, but I had no idea where to begin looking for any of them on a Sunday afternoon.

I had a feeling that talking to Ox about the issues between us would get me about as far as talking to a brick wall, but at least I knew how to find him, so he seemed like the most logical place to start. I shot off a text asking if he was at home. A volley of texts later, I'd arranged to stop by for coffee.

Ox and Isabeau live in a third-floor apartment facing a pool that's shared by everyone in the complex. The building itself is made of brick that is slowly giving way to the elements. It's sheltered by a canopy of massive tree branches, but tiny bits of crumbled brick always seemed to litter the sidewalk, convincing me that the building was on its last legs.

I climbed a set of metal stairs and knocked on the door. Ox answered almost immediately, looking more curious than annoyed by my visit. I took that as a good sign.

He wore a pair of sweatpants and a white T-shirt. The shadow of whiskers darkened his cheeks and chin, and a fine layer of stubble covered his head. He saw me glance at it and followed my gaze with a hand. "Haven't bothered to shave yet."

"Sorry to cut into your day off," I said as I trailed him into the kitchen.

He shrugged and motioned me toward the table then set to work filling two mugs with coffee. "It's okay. Isabeau's out shopping and I'm just kicking around the house."

I shrugged my bag from my shoulder and settled it on an empty chair. "Thanks for letting me stop by. I wouldn't bother you on your day off if it weren't important."

Ox sat heavily and put his feet up. "What's up?"

Sitting there with him brought all those feelings of betrayal rushing back, but I wanted to start the conversation on a good note so I said how pleased I was with the work we'd done for the Belle Lune Ball. We chatted for a while, sharing comments we'd heard from guests, but inevitably that conversational well ran dry and Ox called me out. "Yeah, it was a good night, but you didn't come here to talk about that. Why are you really here?"

I gave up on the small talk. "Why didn't you tell me that your family once owned the Zydeco building?"

Ox shrugged. "It never came up. You think I should have said something?"

If there was a more frustrating man on the planet, I'd never met him. "You don't?"

"What difference would it have made? Philippe bought the house and turned it into a bakery. My family didn't have anything to do with it when he died."

"Maybe not, but it would have been nice to know."

"Why?" Ox sat up straight and rested his arms on the table. "Seriously, Rita, what difference would it have made? So some second cousin of mine's great-aunt owned that building. So what? You think Miss Frankie would've made a different decision if she'd known that? For that matter, do you really think she didn't know?" He was scowling, but his tone wasn't hard or cold. That was a plus.

"I have no idea what Miss Frankie did or didn't know," I admitted. "But what about when Zoey and I found the necklace? Why didn't you say something then?"

"Why would I?"

"Because apparently that necklace is a very big deal.

Everybody wants to get their hands on it. Somebody wants it badly enough to go to a lot of trouble for it."

One of Ox's eyebrows quirked upward. "What kind of trouble?"

Yeah. Okay, so I hadn't exactly been completely honest with Ox either. I took a fortifying breath and let it all out in a rush. "Someone's tried at least three times to get the necklace from me. I think it's the same person who broke into the Vintage Vault."

"What do you mean? Tried how?"

"Somebody was prowling around my house a few nights ago," I confessed. "Then somebody attempted to mug me outside the Dizzy Duke. Then there was the busted window on the Range Rover, and last night somebody broke into my house."

Ox's quirky eyebrow took a nosedive. "You never said a word."

"I didn't want the lectures," I admitted. "But trying to steal my purse is one thing. Breaking into my house is something else entirely. Although to be fair, whoever it was did leave a fifty-dollar bill to help pay for the damage. And before you start lecturing me, I didn't do anything reckless. I called Sullivan last night before I went into the house."

Ox rubbed his face with his hands then moved one to the back of his neck and rubbed the muscles there. "I'm glad to hear that, at least. Did you get a good look at the person who tried to steal your purse?"

I shook my head. "I didn't get any kind of look. I was hit from behind and went down like a lump. All I could do was curl up in a ball and hang on to my bag for dear life. If Carlo Mancini hadn't come along, I'm not sure I could have outlasted the guy."

"Mancini was there?"

I nodded. "Yeah. For some reason he's really interested in the necklace. Anyway, he chased the guy away."

"You're sure it was a guy?"

"Not one hundred percent," I said. "It could have been a very strong woman."

"Did Mancini see anything?"

"Not that he shared with me. But I don't think he did. Otherwise, he never would have agreed to keep it quiet."

Ox cut a sharp glance at me. "He did?"

"Yeah. I didn't know whether or not I could believe him, but I've been keeping an eye on his news stories and I haven't heard anything about it so far. I think I would have if he'd run with the story."

Ox stood and walked to the sink, where he stared out the window for a long moment. "You have any idea who's behind this stuff?"

"Not really," I said. "I don't have proof of who's involved, but *somebody* is after the necklace and I'm tired of sitting around waiting for the next shoe to drop. That's why I'm here."

Ox whipped his head around to look at me. "What? You think I did it?"

"No! Of course not. I'm just . . . I'm at a loss. I need to figure out who's doing this so I can get my life back to normal." I slumped down in my chair and turned my mug in a slow circle on the table in front of me. "You're good at thinking things through. I thought maybe you could help me. There's one thing that puzzles me. Natalie Archer brought it up. How *did* the necklace get into the stairs in our building?"

Ox gave me a sidelong look. "Your guess is as good as mine. As far as I know, the thing disappeared before Gustave Toussaint died."

"And yet somehow it ended up at Zydeco, which your distant relative used to own. Is there anyone in your family who might be a little—" I broke off, unsure how to say what I was thinking.

"Unhinged?" Ox supplied for me. "Whacko?"

"'Passionate' sounds better," I said with a grin. "Or dishonest. So what do you think? Anybody in your distant family who might have stolen the necklace?"

Ox turned his back on the window and leaned against the counter, one foot crossed over the other. "Probably too many to count. But if they stole it and hid it, I wouldn't have heard anything about it, would I?"

"Maybe not. Or maybe you've heard someone talk about it. Maybe the subject has come up at a family reunion. Maybe you just know because you're family. I mean, if somebody's a little off-kilter, doesn't everybody in the family know about it? It doesn't come as some big surprise, does it?"

One side of his mouth curled in a halfhearted grin. "No, it doesn't. But the problem is, *most* of my family is unhinged. You've met Mambo Odessa, right? Do you think she's normal?"

"She's a lovely woman . . . for a voodoo priestess."

"She thinks she can talk to dead people. Does that sound normal to you?"

"I guess that depends on your definition of 'normal,'" I said. "So you're saying there are more people like her in your family?"

"More people like her than like me, that's for damn sure." Ox came back to the table and sat. "But do I think that some long-dead uncle's cousin's brother-in-law was crazy enough to steal the necklace? I couldn't say."

I sighed and leaned my head back against the chair. "I guess that means you don't think some grandmother's sister's niece could be trying to steal the necklace back? And here I was hoping you'd know who was behind all of this."

"Yeah. Well. Sorry. Wish I could help, but you know how it is."

I digested that for a moment before saying, "Do you think there's anyone alive who knows how that necklace ended up in the house?"

Ox lifted one shoulder. "I doubt it, but who knows? You

really want me to spend my day off calling crazy relatives to ask?"

I could tell that he wanted me to say no, but I nodded eagerly. "Please?"

Ox groaned low in his throat, but he didn't refuse, which was good enough for me. I polished off my coffee and carried the mug to the sink. "Thanks, Ox. Will you let me know if you find out anything?"

"You'll be the first person I call," he said grudgingly.

I pretended not to notice. "Thanks! I owe you one. I'll see you at work tomorrow."

I wasn't angling for an invitation to stay, and I didn't want to intrude on Ox's day off, but I wanted to rattle around on my own even less. I rinsed my cup, half expecting Ox to invite me to stick around.

He didn't.

So I hiked up my big girl panties, and let myself out the door. From the corner of my eye, I saw Ox pick up his cell phone as I shut the door behind me and the look on his face made me glad it wasn't my number he was calling. Maybe it was a good thing he hadn't asked me to stay.

Early evening shadows stretched across the street as I left Ox's apartment. I slid behind the wheel of the Range Rover, but I couldn't make myself crank the engine. I hadn't learned anything really helpful from my conversation with Ox, but at least it was a new trail to follow.

It didn't feel right to leave Ox doing the legwork while I went home and watched TV, so I decided it might be time to pay Sol Lehmann a visit. I wondered if he knew that Miriam was working against him, and whether knowing that his wife was planning to outbid him would make him feel. I had no idea where the Lehmanns lived, but with the magic of the Internet at my fingertips, I might be able to find out.

I'd just launched the browser app on my phone when I spotted Ox leaving his apartment building. He was talking on his phone, so intent on his conversation he didn't see me sitting there. He turned away from me and jogged down the sidewalk to his truck and roared away from the curb with a screech of tires.

Instinctively, I scooted down on the seat so he wouldn't see me as he drove by, but I'm not sure he would have noticed me even if I'd jumped out in front of him. He looked determined, even angry, and I wondered whether one of his "crazy relatives" had said something that set him off.

On impulse I pulled into traffic, made a U-turn, and tried to catch up with him. I was afraid I might have lost him, but I could see his truck several cars in front of me. I didn't want him to spot me in his rearview mirror like I'd noticed Mancini's white SUV, so I hung back, hoping my Range Rover wasn't so familiar that he'd pick me out of traffic.

He sped past a golf course, hung a right on State, and another on Claiborne, eventually merging into traffic on I-10. It was a little harder to follow him once he was on the Interstate, but I managed to keep him in sight until he took the exit for Orleans Avenue. By then, I was almost certain that he was heading for the French Quarter and Mambo Odessa's shop so I took a chance, peeled off and made my way there by another route. Hoping to avoid running into Ox in the Quarter, I paid for parking at the Sheraton and hiked the five blocks to Dauphine Street on foot.

The whole time, questions raced through my head. What had Ox found out that made him so angry? Had I misjudged Mambo Odessa? Could *she* possibly be the one who had tried to steal the necklace? Frankly, it didn't seem like her style. She was much more likely to shake some bones and cast another curse.

It wasn't until I was half a block away from Mambo Odessa's that another possibility suddenly appeared on the sidewalk in front of me.

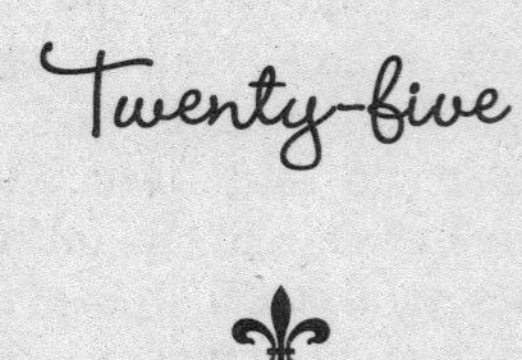

It was hard to see over the heads of the passing pedestrians, but if I stood on tiptoe I could see Ox lean in close, getting right in Calvin's face. I couldn't hear what he said, but I was convinced that the anger I'd seen on Ox's face earlier was directed at his cousin. But did that mean that . . . Calvin? Was *Calvin* the would-be thief?

I'd been shielded by pedestrians who were making their way into the Quarter as night fell until then, but I didn't want to take any chances. I ducked into the open doorway of a noisy bar and waited a moment before I dared peek at the sidewalk. I saw Calvin wave off whatever Ox said with a laugh, and turn as if he intended to walk away. Ox grabbed his arm and Calvin turned around, now as angry as Ox was. He prodded Ox in the chest with one finger. Ox swatted it away.

Chatter and the clink of glass behind me made it impossible to hear, but I had to know what they were saying. Call me cynical, but I didn't think Ox planned on telling me about it.

I waited for a small group of people to pass the doorway and fell in behind them, moving closer to the two men at an annoyingly slow pace.

I was only two doors away from Mambo Odessa's shop when Ox grabbed Calvin by the shirtfront. "What the hell is wrong with you, man? Have you lost your mind?" Ox yelled as he shoved Calvin up against the wall.

Calvin's head hit the wall with a *thunk* that I could hear from where I stood. He broke Ox's grip on his shirt and shoved him hard.

Ox kept shouting. "You break into someone's home? You assault people? Dammit, Calvin, Rita's a friend of mine. What the hell—?"

Calvin shoved a finger in Ox's face. "You know what's wrong with you? You've changed. We were raised to put family first, but you've turned your back on all of us."

I was aware of a small crowd gathering to watch the fight—some people moved in close and others hung back, lining the sidewalk across the street. Ox didn't seem to notice, and neither did Calvin. They were too focused on each other.

Ox slapped Calvin's hand away and said something too low for me to hear. He made another grab for Calvin's shirt, but Calvin was too quick for him. He landed a solid blow to Ox's middle followed by an uppercut that sent Ox reeling. As Ox staggered backward, Calvin broke away and ran hell-bent around the corner.

I didn't know whether to follow Calvin—like I'd be a match for him—or stay where I was and make sure that Ox was all right. Before I could make a decision, I felt a hand on my shoulder. I jerked around in surprise and found Mambo Odessa standing behind me.

I wondered if she'd seen the altercation between her two nephews. The look on her face gave nothing away.

Her lack of apparent emotion broke down the last slim

hold I had on my own anger. I'd been frightened and assaulted, and she didn't even have the decency to look upset. "Did you know what Calvin was doing?" I demanded.

"You think I condone his actions?"

That wasn't what I'd asked and she knew it. "I think you knew that he was the one trying to steal the necklace."

She turned her face toward me, but I couldn't see her eyes behind her sunglasses. "And you think I should have stopped him."

"I think you should have tried."

Her lips curved slightly and she looked away again. "Not everything is black and white, child. Sometimes people do the wrong thing for the right reason and sometimes they do the right thing for the wrong reason."

I wondered which motive she attributed to Calvin, but Ox had recovered, jogged to the corner in a belated attempt to go after his cousin, and now was walking toward us wearing a dark scowl on his face.

Mambo Odessa melted into the crowd, leaving me on my own. It was just as well. I had nothing else to say to her anyway.

I tried to make myself invisible, but the crowd around me seemed to part like the Red Sea, leaving me exposed and easy for Ox to spot. His eyes blazed and his nostrils flared, and the look on his face made my stomach tie itself in knots. "What in the hell—? What are you doing here?"

I refused to let him know that he intimidated me. "Just hanging out," I quipped. "Waiting for you to call and tell me what you found out from your family. I'm going out on a limb here, guessing that you made contact with at least one of them."

He took me by the arm and started walking—fast. I had to run to keep up with him.

"My family didn't tell me anything. I would have called you if they had."

Yeah. And I had some swampland in New Mexico for sale.

"Seems like somebody told you something," I said. "You came storming out of your apartment even before I drove away. It was what? Three minutes after I left your place?"

He stopped walking so abruptly, I almost lost my balance. "This," he said, waving his free hand to encompass half of Dauphine Street and the crowd that was slowly dispersing, "has nothing to do with you or your problem. I needed to talk to Calvin about something."

"About what?"

"Family stuff."

I might have believed him if he'd looked at me while he talked, but his gaze bounced around guiltily, never quite landing on my face. "Family stuff like the Toussaint necklace?"

Ox rolled his head on his neck, a sure sign that he was angry. "Believe it or not, Rita, not everything is about you."

Ouch! "I never said that it was," I snapped. "But if you think I'm going to believe that you came to see Calvin for some reason completely unrelated to the necklace and what's been happening to me, you're the one who's crazy. What's going on, Ox? And this time, be honest with me."

He mopped his face with one hand and turned partially away. It looked like he was struggling with himself over what to tell me, but I didn't care. I'd had it with him and his secrets and his penchant for privacy.

"Be honest," I said again. "Tell me, was it Calvin who broke into my house?"

Ox made eye contact, probably to show me that he wanted to wring my neck for asking. He spent a full minute breathing heavily and growling, probably hoping he could make me cower and change the subject.

Instead, I squared my shoulders and glared right back at him. "Was it Calvin?"

He growled once more and looked away. "I don't know. I think so."

He wouldn't have admitted that much unless he was convinced, but I wondered how he'd figured it out so quickly. More specifically, I wanted to know what he'd seen or heard that I missed. "Why? What made you think it was him?"

Ox leaned against a light post and studied the cobblestones at our feet. "The money he left when he broke in," he said after a long time. He lifted his gaze and met mine again. He looked so miserable, I almost felt sorry for him. "He did the same thing when he was a kid. Broke my mom's dining room window throwing a baseball around. She wasn't home, but he felt so guilty he gave her all the money he had to fix it. He was maybe ten and I think he only had a couple of bucks. He did the same kind of thing a few years later when he put a scratch on his mom's piano. So when you told me about the money he left at your place, it rang some bells, y'know?"

I let out a sigh that felt as if it started at the soles of my feet. Relief over finally knowing who was responsible for the attacks on me and my stuff, I guess. But I was also sad that if Calvin had broken into the Vintage Vault, he'd inadvertently brought on Orra's heart attack. His attacks on me hadn't been truly malicious, and calling 911 to report Orra's distress seemed like something Calvin might have done, but it didn't completely wipe away his part in her death. "So you confronted him. I'm guessing he denied it?"

"He didn't admit it or deny it," Ox said. The hurt and disappointment on his face made the knot in my stomach twist a little tighter. I'd grown up with four boisterous cousins who'd been in trouble more times than I could remember, but I knew how I'd feel if one of them did something illegal or hurt someone intentionally. I didn't know Calvin well, but I was having trouble believing the worst of him, and obviously Ox was struggling with it, too.

"I told him he had to come clean with you," Ox said. "I told him he had to tell the police what he'd done." He touched a spot on his chin and winced. "Obviously, that suggestion went over like a lead balloon."

"I noticed," I said with a tiny smile. "Where do you think he went?"

"I have no idea." Ox put his fists on his hips and shook his head. "If you'd asked me that twenty years ago, I could have given you an answer, but I don't know Calvin anymore. I have no idea where he's gone or what he's capable of."

I didn't like the sound of that. "I guess I need to let Sullivan know," I said, thinking aloud. "I'm not sure what the police will be able to do about it."

"If Calvin's smart," Ox said with a scowl, "he's already on his way out of town. Now that he knows we're on to him, I doubt he'll be back to bother you."

I wanted to believe that as much as Ox did, which explains why I ignored the ripple of uncertainty that ran across my shoulders. I should've known better.

With Calvin on the run, there was no reason for me to hunt down Sol and Miriam Lehmann. Ox and I grabbed dinner at a sandwich shop in the Quarter, po'boys that neither of us finished and a bag of chips apiece. Ox spent the whole time grumbling about Calvin and convincing both of us that his cousin's reign of terror was over.

It was full dark by the time I drove home, and I was relieved to have answers to at least a few of my questions. I parked half a block away from the house, pondering Calvin's motives and wondering how someone so nice could get so far off the right track as I walked through the yard and climbed to the porch.

Which might explain how I didn't notice Calvin lurking in the shadow of the magnolia tree that separates my yard from the yarn shop next door, and why he was able to get the drop on me.

He was on the porch behind me before I even saw him coming, one hand around my neck while he pressed something hard and cold into my back. I had a sick feeling that it was a gun, but I was still so deep in denial about Calvin that I actually thought he might be bluffing.

"Open the door," he growled in my ear, his voice low and threatening.

Some part of my brain was screaming a warning not to let him inside with me, but the other part was arguing that Calvin was Ox's cousin and basically a good guy, even if he was seriously misguided.

"I need my keys," I squeaked out around the pressure on my throat. "And I need to breathe."

He relaxed his grip a little and again I told myself that he wouldn't really hurt me. I pawed around in my bag until I found my phone. Keeping one hand on it, I produced my keys with a little *voilà* move.

Calvin nudged me closer to the door. I tried to get the key into the lock, but I couldn't see. Plus, my hands were shaking. And it was a brand-new, unfamiliar lock. Whether or not I believed Calvin was a real danger to me, being accosted on my doorstep was still unnerving. I had to let go of the phone and use both hands to unlock the door.

I flipped on the light as I stepped inside and whirled around to give Calvin a piece of my mind. At the sight of an actual gun in his hands, now aimed at my stomach, my heart jumped up into my throat and whatever I'd been about to say froze on my tongue.

He came inside behind me and pushed the door shut with his free hand. "Where is it?"

Anger bubbled up inside me, right alongside the fear. I didn't want to end up a story on the news, but I'd had it up to *here* with Calvin and his quest for the cursed necklace. "Where is what?"

"The necklace. Just hand it over and I'll leave."

I thought about the cell phone lying useless inside my bag and wished I'd kept hold of it. I had a landline, but I'd never get the phone off the hook and dial without giving myself away. But I had to do something. I couldn't just stand here like a lump while Calvin held a gun on me. I tried to think of an alternative. I could scream (which would probably freak Calvin out enough to make him pull the trigger), send Morse code messages with the mini-blinds (which would probably go unnoticed by everyone *but* Calvin), or try to disarm the armed man standing in front of me. I didn't calculate my odds of overpowering him very high, but other than curling up in the fetal position and hoping for the best, it seemed my only even semi-viable option.

I knew I had to keep Calvin talking while I tried to come up with a plan. "Why don't you put the gun down so we can talk?" I suggested in the most soothing tone I could manage.

He waved the gun in my face. "I don't have time to talk. Ox probably called the police on me. Or you did." He ran his free hand over his face, but it was over too quickly for me to try something heroic. "Why do you have to be so stubborn?" he asked, as if our current situation were my fault. "Why didn't you just give up the necklace that night at the Dizzy Duke?"

Yeah. Blame the victim. Good plan. "Well, to begin with," I said, trying not to sound angry, "I didn't know it was you. I thought you and I were friends. For another, I don't have the necklace with me. And I never for one minute thought you were the one who broke into the Vintage Vault. How did you even know the necklace was there?"

He gave me a "Duh!" look. "You told me."

Had I? I tried to remember our conversation the night we had dinner, but too much had happened in the meantime.

"I mean, you didn't tell me what store you'd been to," he went on. "But it wasn't hard to figure out once I went back to look."

"So you broke in and tried to steal it from Orra?"

"I didn't know she was there," Calvin said. "She surprised me as much as I surprised her."

"Except that she had a heart attack and died."

"That's not my fault! She already looked sick when she came out of the back room." Calvin took a couple of jerky steps away and then turned back toward me. "I never laid a hand on her. I even called for help. It's not like I just ran away and left her there."

I wasn't sure Orra would have appreciated the gesture, but I didn't say so aloud. Talking about her seemed to be upsetting Calvin, and that wasn't the reaction I was going for. "Would you please tell me why the necklace is such a big deal to you?"

"Because it's . . . *evil.*" He dashed sweat from his forehead with his gun hand. "It's cursed. You know that. I have to get rid of it. I have to *stop* it."

"Well, yeah, but I don't believe it. It's just metal and stone, Calvin. It doesn't possess any magical qualities."

"I know you don't think so, but I *know* so. My grandma told me all about it. She told me how Delphine cursed it. She told me how Armand and Beatriz died and how Gustave's wife and daughter passed later. They weren't sick. They weren't hurt. They just *died.*"

I didn't argue with him, mostly because I didn't think he'd listen. Whatever had really happened, I didn't think anyone would ever be able to prove how they died. "And you think Delphine was responsible?"

"I know she was. Everybody in my family knows it. We've lived with that stupid curse and the bad things it did for over a hundred years. People died because of it, and in this town people don't forget things like that. All my life people watched us like there's something wrong with us. Like we'd do them in just for looking at us funny. You don't know how that feels."

I'd been about to say something else, but his words hit me then and made me clamp my mouth shut in surprise.

"What do you mean you've lived with it? What does it have to do with you?"

Calvin barked a sharp laugh. "You don't know? Ox didn't tell you?"

Did he really need to ask? "Ox never tells me anything," I snapped. "Why don't *you* tell me?"

Calvin darted a nervous glance over his shoulder. "That necklace belongs to us. It should have been ours all along."

My own nerves were making it hard to think, but a light finally went on in my head. "You and Ox are Merciers?" Was he kidding me?

"My grandma was Delphine's youngest grandkid. She told me all about the stones. And then I found her papers at Mambo Odessa's and I found out the truth."

"Delphine had papers? What papers?"

"Letters. A journal. Auntie Odessa got them from Grandma when she died."

So Mambo Odessa had known about Delphine all along, and presumably so had Ox. I had a lot to sort through, but that could wait. I forced myself to stay in the moment with Calvin and his gun. "What truth did you learn?"

"The house. It was Delphine's."

I blinked a couple of times, trying to follow what he was saying. "What house? Mambo Odessa's?"

"No! Yours. Zydeco. *That* house."

"Miss Cassie's house? *My* house?" My heartbeat ramped up and my mouth grew dry. "But what—? How—?"

Calvin waved the gun in my face again, growing more agitated by the minute. "Yes, Miss Cassie's house. What the hell do you think I'm talking about? You're working every day in the house Armand Toussaint gave to Delphine when their first child was born."

I stared at him in stunned disbelief. How did I not know that? My confused thoughts became white noise, making it harder than ever to follow him. "But how did the necklace get in Delphine's house? I thought the Toussaints had it."

"They did, until Gustave finally gave it to Delphine. It was all in her papers."

Had I heard that right? "When did Gustave give the necklace to Delphine? *Why* did he give it to her? And why didn't she say something? I mean, he gave her what she wanted, didn't he?"

Calvin snorted a laugh. "He gave it to her because he thought he could end the curse that was killing off his family by giving up the necklace. But by that time she was so filled with hatred, she wasn't going to let it drop. She wanted the Toussaints to look bad." Anger and bitterness twisted Calvin's expression. "She'd gone to him and asked for the necklace after Armand died and Gustave inherited the estate. Do you know what he did? He laughed at her and called her a liar. He said there was no way that his uncle, who'd adored his wife, would have given something that valuable to someone who was nothing more than a whore. Delphine told him the curse would kill them all, but he didn't believe her."

No wonder she was hostile toward the Toussaints. "But you just said that he *did* give it to her," I pointed out.

"Years later," Calvin said. "After his daughter died, Gustave finally believed Delphine about the curse. He gave her the necklace to stop the curse and keep the rest of his family from being hurt by it. But it was too little, too late."

"But why—?" I shook my head, still trying to make sense of what he was saying. "If Gustave gave it back to her, why didn't *he* tell people that he'd tried to make things right?"

"Because she didn't give him the chance. She killed him. Poisoned him the very day he brought the necklace to her. She thought he deserved it. And then she hid that damned necklace and never told a soul what she had done. But it's all there, all written down in her journals."

I could tell that the story tormented Calvin, and with

good reason, but the gun in my face made it hard to feel all that sympathetic toward him.

"So why are you doing this? For Delphine, or for the Toussaints?" I said when I could speak again.

Calvin wagged the gun at me again. "I'm doing it to stop the curse. You don't understand. *Nobody* understands."

"I'm trying to understand," I assured him. "You're telling me that you don't approve of what Delphine did?"

"Would you? She put that curse on the necklace, killed people, and then—*then,* when Gustave gave it to her and asked her to lift the curse, she refused. How could she do that? Let her kids grow up thinking that they'd been wronged? Let her grandkids think the same thing? She told them the Toussaints stole their future, took what should have been theirs, and it was all a damned lie. It wasn't until Grandma read her letters that anybody knew what she'd done."

"So Delphine was the one who hid the necklace in the house." I'd felt sorry for her until now. Now I wondered if she'd always been crazy, or if her circumstances had pushed her over the edge.

"That's what she said in her journal. She hated Armand and his family so much by then, she wouldn't even admit that Gustave gave it to her. She wanted that damn thing so much she was willing to kill for it, but then when she got it, what did she do? She buried it and never looked at it again." A trickle of sweat snaked down Calvin's cheek and seemed to remind him that he needed to hurry. "I just need the necklace, Rita. Give it to me and I promise I won't hurt you."

I wondered if he would really just walk away. I couldn't wrap my mind around the idea of Calvin as a killer, but since I was staring down the barrel of a gun, it was pretty clear that I was a lousy judge of character. "I don't want to get hurt, and I don't want you hurt either, but I don't have it with me."

"Don't lie to me," he shouted. "Just hand it over."

One part of my brain wanted to do what he said. The

necklace had been nothing but trouble since the moment Zoey and I found it. I should have been thrilled for the chance to get rid of it. But even if I could hand it over, I'd been through too much to just give it to Calvin now.

"What are you going to do with it?" I asked, hoping I could stretch the conversation long enough to come up with a brilliant plan for survival.

"Does it matter?"

"It does to me," I said. "After everything you've put me through, I think I deserve to know."

"I'm gonna put it in Delphine's vault. Let her spend eternity with it. And I hope it haunts her in the afterlife. I hope she gets what *she* deserves."

Great idea—except for the part about breaking into a mausoleum at the cemetery. "You're not thinking clearly," I said gently. "There's no way you'll get away with that. The police will catch you before you can even get the vault open."

"No they won't. Especially if you don't tell them." He put the gun to my temple and moved his finger onto the trigger. "I don't guess I can just walk away and leave you to call the police after all."

Nervous sweat pooled under my arms and snaked down my stomach. Nobody knew that Calvin was here. Time was running out quickly.

"Killing me won't solve anything," I said. "And burying the necklace with Delphine won't make anything different. What she did was horrible, but it doesn't reflect on you or anyone else in your family."

As I finished what I was saying, I thought I heard a noise outside, a soft brush of something against the concrete that could have been a footstep. But it could also have been my imagination. I tried appealing to him. "Put the gun down, Calvin. You're not like this. You don't want to spend the rest of your life paying for this."

The sound came again, and this time I knew I'd heard it. Hoping to distract him, I shot a glance at the door and whispered, "What was that?"

As I'd hoped, Calvin took his eyes off me long enough to follow my gaze. Saying a prayer for superhuman strength, I dropped and heaved all my weight against his knees. I might have managed to knock him down if I'd been behind him instead of in front, but at least I caught him off guard, and he staggered backward a step or two.

I threw myself against him again. I heard a bang, but my heartbeat was pounding so loudly in my ears, I couldn't tell if it was a gunshot or something else. I heard a roar of pain and felt Calvin land heavily on the floor beside me.

Fear made it hard for me to see, but I scrambled toward his hand, hoping to get the gun away from him before he shot me. I groped blindly for the gun, wedging my knee into Calvin's armpit as hard as I could to keep him from moving his arm.

Calvin bucked like a wild man, heaving his body from side to side. I heard another roar of pain or anger and tried even harder to find the gun. I could hear voices, but I couldn't make out what they were saying until a firm hand gripped my arm and gave me a gentle shake.

"I've got it, Rita. Just call the police."

I blinked in surprise, trying to clear the fog from my brain and my eyes. A strange man stood over Calvin holding the gun. Behind him, wild-eyed and holding a heavy skillet, stood the woman from the Thai restaurant next door.

"Somebody break in," she said. "This time I saw."

I almost laughed aloud. The man with the gun cleared his throat. He wasn't a stranger, I realized. I knew him. He'd come to my rescue once before, too.

"What in the hell are you doing here?" I snapped.

Carlo Mancini shot me a cocky TV news grin. "You're welcome. Now are you going to call the police or what?"

Twenty-six

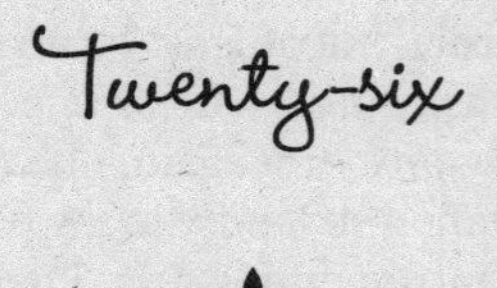

Three weeks later, I stood at the podium in front of a moderate-sized crowd and officially presented the Toussaint necklace to the New Orleans Historic Voodoo Museum in the French Quarter. It seemed only right to let the necklace live out its life next to the portrait of Beatriz. And to share the history of both branches of the family.

The museum's curator accepted the gift and gave a short speech about the necklace and its colorful history. A history that everyone on both sides of the Toussaint-Mercier family—with the exception of Calvin—seemed determined to preserve. I didn't get it, but as long as it didn't affect me, they could hold on to the curse forever if they wanted to.

I was ready to get the necklace out of my hands. I'd had enough of it and the people who wanted it. Giving it to the museum where everyone could see it and hear its gruesome tale seemed like the right thing to do. I just hoped that my decision would appease Mambo Odessa's ancestors, none of whom had whispered anything to me, by the way.

Ox and Mambo Odessa stood on the other side of the podium as official representatives of the Mercier branch of the family. Despite her claims to the necklace—or maybe because of them—Natalie Archer stood just off to the right of the podium, beaming as if the whole thing had been her idea. I had my suspicions about that. I thought her newfound generosity had a lot to do with Miss Frankie, who stood beside her to offer moral support.

Bernice was there, too, standing in the crowd near Sol and Miriam Lehmann. Nobody could have said that the Lehmanns looked happy about the presentation, but they did appear resigned.

The rest of the Zydeco crew, all spiffed up and enjoying the mimosas being passed around by a small staff of waiters, were sprinkled throughout the crowd that had gathered to witness the event that some were calling an epic moment in history. And by "some," I mean Carlo Mancini, who was waiting for an exclusive interview with Zoey and me after the presentation. I figured I owed him something. If he hadn't been so determined to get his story that he'd followed me home, I might not have been here at all.

Even the woman from the Thai restaurant, whose name I'd since learned was Fon, had accepted my invitation. I'd sent flowers to thank her for her part in my rescue and I was taking the Zydeco gang, plus Gabriel and Sullivan (if he could make it), to lunch at her restaurant after we were through here. It might be a bit awkward having both of them together in one room, but I couldn't pick one over the other.

The curator's speech received a smattering of applause, after which Zoey and I posed for a couple of pictures with the curator that would, I was told, be prominently displayed beside the necklace. When the photographer had finished snapping pictures, Mancini stepped up and shoved a microphone in my face, rattling on in front of the camera and asking me an occasional frivolous question—"How do you feel now that you're free of the necklace, Ms. Lucero?" and "Do any of your recent experiences lead you to believe in the curse after all?"—to which I offered equally inane answers—"I'm happy to see the necklace preserved for history, Carlo," and "No, they do not." Zoey, all dolled up in a pair of black slacks a size too small and a flowy shirt that looked brand new, shared her version of the great find and played up her part in spreading the word via social media while Estelle looked on and nodded her approval from time to time.

Once he'd finished with me, I moved to the edge of the crowd, where the crew from Zydeco stood nursing their drinks. Ox looked really good in the suit and tie Isabeau had insisted he wear, while she herself looked stunning in a flowered sundress and a pair of four-inch heels that made my calves ache just looking at them.

I knew he'd been to the jail earlier to visit Calvin, but I didn't let myself ask how their conversation had gone. I'd hated pressing charges against Ox's cousin, and I might not have if Carlo and Fon hadn't witnessed Calvin holding a gun on me. He was awaiting trial at which I'd have to testify and I wasn't looking forward to that *at all.* Whatever happened, I just hoped Ox wouldn't hold it against me.

Edie and River were there, too, as part of the Zydeco crew. Once all the excitement over the necklace and the Belle Lune Ball had died down, Edie and I had finally had a chance to talk about her coming back to work. Judging by the way Dwight was playing with JD, dangling a set of keys over the baby's head and making all kinds of weird goo-goo noises, nobody would mind if Edie occasionally had to bring JD to work with her.

"I think it was a beautiful ceremony," Estelle gushed as

Sparkle handed me a cup of my own. "Although I do think you could have let Zoey be part of the actual presentation."

Zoey rolled her eyes at her aunt. "It's okay. I didn't mind. Really."

Estelle was right, though: Zoey deserved the recognition, not just for her part in finding the necklace, but for her willingness to remain quiet even when she didn't want to. I was growing fond of her and I wasn't ready to send her packing yet.

"Edie's coming back to work in a couple of weeks," I said. "But that doesn't mean I want you to leave. You've done a great job. How would you feel about staying on, at least until Mardi Gras is over?"

Zoey's face lit up and for a moment her insecurities vanished. "You mean it?"

"Of course."

Estelle nudged her with an elbow. "You want to stay, don't you?" Without waiting for an answer, she turned to me. "She wants to stay. It would mean the world to her."

I smiled at Estelle and took Zoey's arm, leading her away from the others so she could make up her own mind. "You don't have to decide now," I told her. "And don't say yes just because Estelle wants you to. She means well, but I want you to decide for yourself."

I wasn't sure, but I thought I detected tears in Zoey's big, dark eyes. "Yeah. I mean, *yeah* I want to. I like it there. At Zydeco. And maybe if I do good enough, you could teach me about cakes? I'd love to make something as beautiful as the dress form cakes were. Pictures of them are still showing up in my news feed."

That surprised me on two levels. The Belle Lune Ball had been an even bigger success than I'd thought at the time. The ongoing popularity of the photos people had uploaded had my head spinning. But the biggest revelation was the one about Zoey herself. "You're interested in baking?"

"Baking. Decorating. Making cakes that look like something. I want to learn how to do all of it. Next time something we make goes viral, I want to be part of it."

Who would have thought? I grinned, remembering when I'd first discovered the world of cake decorating and asked Uncle Nestor if I could attend a culinary school. "I'll tell you what," I said, making the same offer my uncle had once made to me. "You work hard and learn everything you can at Zydeco for two years. Then, if you still want to learn more, we'll talk about getting you into culinary school. How does that sound?"

Zoey lunged at me and wrapped me in a hug so tight I had trouble catching my breath. "You mean it?"

"It's not going to be easy," I warned her when she finally let me go. "It's a lot of hard work and there's a lot to learn. And you're not going to start out at the top, so don't expect that."

"I don't. I won't." She bounced up on her toes, looking younger and happier than I'd ever seen her. "You won't be sorry, I promise."

A big warm glob of fuzzy feel good welled up inside me. I suspected that our real issue would be getting Estelle to back off and let Zoey fight her own battles, but we had plenty of time to work all that out.

It felt good knowing that. Zydeco had gone through a rough patch after Philippe died and I took over, but we'd weathered the storm and things were looking up. Business was better than ever. Our client base had grown just since the Belle Lune Ball, and we'd been asked to do the job again the following year, which was a major coup. Pleasing Evangeline Delahunt wasn't easy, but we'd done it. Of course, I'd accepted the offer eagerly, in spite of Ox's dour predictions that I was diversifying too far by adding these occasional catering gigs to our schedule. He'd come around eventually.

I had no intention of spreading ourselves too thin or taking on too much, but catering the Belle Lune Ball had given me greater confidence in my skills both as a chef and a manager than I'd ever had before. For the first time since I'd accepted the partnership with Miss Frankie, Zydeco felt as if it was really and truly mine and I wasn't interested in taking a step backward either.

I left Zoey talking to Sparkle about her job offer and crossed the narrow courtyard toward Edie and River. Dwight had moved away to talk to someone else and JD was growing restless without his playmate. Edie handed JD to me and I kissed his soft little cheek. "I just offered Zoey a job," I told Edie. "But not yours, so don't worry about that."

Edie laughed softly. "Good. I can't wait to get back to work, but I'm going to hate leaving JD with a sitter. I wish I could do both."

"You don't need a sitter," River told her. "My work is flexible. I can watch him while you're at work. I've told you that before."

She gave him a look from the corner of her eye, but it wasn't full of her usual irritation. "And I told you, I don't want to be a burden."

"What burden?" River asked. "JD is my son." Also said without the usual heat.

There was something different about them. Something softer. More pliable. I didn't want Edie to freak out or anything, so I pretended not to notice. "I'm sure the two of you can figure it out. It's not as if we're completely inflexible at Zydeco either. If you need to bring him with you to work on occasion, I'm sure we can work something out."

Edie grinned at me and for the second time that day I found myself wrapped in a breath-stealing hug. "You're the best, Rita. I mean seriously."

Yeah. That gave me the warm fuzzies, too.

I snuggled JD closely and wondered what life would have been like if Philippe and I had ever decided to start a family.

Almost as if she read my mind, Miss Frankie materialized beside me and sent JD a grandmotherly smile. "He's a sweet little thing, isn't he?"

I nodded. "So precious."

She leaned against me and sighed wistfully. "Maybe someday you'll make me a grandmother."

I laughed aloud. "I wouldn't hold my breath," I said. "I'm not sure that's a road I'll ever take."

"Never say never," she said with a meaningful glance at Gabriel, who was standing on the other side of the courtyard. "Where is your nice policeman today? Couldn't he make it?"

I squirmed uncomfortably at her unspoken suggestion(s). "He's working, but he'll try to make it for lunch. As for the rest, we'll see."

"You can't blame a woman for trying, sugar. Just know that I'd be thrilled if you ever decided to expand the family."

Yeah. Maybe. Maybe not. I guess time would tell. I leaned my head on Miss Frankie's shoulder, relieved that she'd shown no more signs of hysterics and touched by her generosity. I was a lucky woman, blessed with a great family and wonderful friends.

A little seed of excitement landed in my heart. It stirred and grew as I looked at the people around me. I couldn't wait to see what would happen next.

Recipes

Rita's Roasted Parmesan Potatoes

Makes 4 to 5 servings

5 to 6 medium-sized potatoes, skins on (I think red potatoes or russets are best for flavor and texture.)
nonstick cooking spray
3 to 4 tablespoons olive oil
¼ cup grated Parmesan cheese (this is the kind you put on spaghetti, not freshly grated Parmesan.)
1½ teaspoons paprika
¾ teaspoon garlic powder
½ teaspoon salt
¼ teaspoon pepper

Preheat oven to 425°F.

Scrub the potatoes thoroughly, and dice into bite-sized pieces. Line a large baking sheet or jelly roll pan with aluminum foil. Spray the foil with nonstick cooking spray. Spread the diced potatoes on the foil-lined pan and drizzle the olive oil over the potatoes. Using your hands, gently toss the potatoes until completely covered with oil.

In a small bowl, mix together the Parmesan cheese, paprika, garlic powder, salt, and pepper. Sprinkle over the potatoes and use your hands again to make sure the spices coat all the potatoes.

Place the pan in the oven and cook for 35 to 45 minutes, stirring every 10 to 15 minutes so the potatoes cook evenly and don't burn on the bottom. When finished baking, remove from the oven and sprinkle with additional salt and pepper if desired.

* * *

Pork Chops with Pear Chutney

Makes 4 to 8 servings

CHUTNEY

1 shallot, diced
3 tablespoons cider vinegar
2 tablespoons light brown sugar
1 tablespoon unsalted butter
1-inch piece of peeled fresh ginger (sliced into coins)
1 teaspoon Madras curry powder
¼ teaspoon kosher salt
pinch crushed red pepper

1 cinnamon stick
3 pears, peeled, cored, and diced (large dice)
2 tablespoons dried cranberries
2 tablespoons chopped fresh cilantro

PORK CHOPS

8 thin bone-in pork chops, each about 4 ounces
kosher salt and freshly ground black pepper
2 tablespoons vegetable oil

For the chutney: In a medium-sized microwave-safe bowl, stir together the shallot, vinegar, brown sugar, butter, ginger, curry powder, salt, and red pepper. Add the cinnamon stick and stir into the mixture.

Cover and seal with plastic wrap. Heat in a microwave oven on high for 1 minute. Carefully remove the plastic wrap and stir in the pears and cranberries. Re-cover and microwave for 10 minutes more.

Being careful not to let escaping steam burn your fingers, poke holes in the plastic wrap to release the steam. Set the mixture aside.

For the pork chops: Heat a large skillet over medium-high heat. Pat the pork chops dry and season with salt and pepper to taste. Add approximately 1 tablespoon oil to the pan and heat until the oil shimmers.

Lay 4 chops in the pan and sear until golden on one side. (This should take about 3 minutes.) Turn and cook 1 more minute. Remove the chops from the pan and set aside. Keep warm. Repeat steps above with remaining oil and chops.

When all chops are removed from the pan, add the chutney to the pan and stir, scraping up any browned bits from the bottom of the pan using a wooden spoon. Simmer until slightly thickened. Stir in the cilantro. Serve the chops with chutney.

* * *

Creamy Curried Cauliflower Soup

Makes 6 to 8 servings

2 tablespoons extra-virgin olive oil (plus a bit more to serve)
2 medium white onions, thinly sliced
½ teaspoon kosher salt (you may want more to season)
4 cloves garlic, minced
1 large head cauliflower (about 2 pounds), trimmed and cut into florets
4½ cups low-sodium vegetable broth (use regular-sodium broth or water if desired)
½ teaspoon coriander
½ teaspoon turmeric
1¼ teaspoons cumin
1 cup coconut milk
freshly ground black pepper, to season

OPTIONAL GARNISHES

¼ cup roasted cashew halves (see note below)
¼ cup finely chopped Italian parsley
red chili pepper flakes, for garnish

Heat the oil in a large pot over medium heat until the oil shimmers. Cook the onions together with ¼ teaspoon salt until the onions are soft and translucent (approximately 8 minutes).

Turn heat to low. Add the garlic and cook for 2 additional minutes.

Add the cauliflower florets, vegetable broth, coriander, turmeric, cumin, and remaining ¼ teaspoon salt. Bring pot to a boil over medium-high heat, then reduce the heat to low.

Simmer until the cauliflower is fork-tender (about 15 to 17 minutes).

Working in batches, purée the soup in a blender until smooth, and then return the soup to the soup pot. If you prefer, use an immersion blender to purée the soup right in the pot.

Stir in the coconut milk and warm the soup. Before serving, add more seasoning and/or spices to taste.

To serve, ladle the soup into bowls and garnish with a handful of toasted cashews, a few springs of parsley, a sprinkle of red chili flakes, and a dash of olive oil to top.

Note: To toast the cashews: Preheat the oven to 350°F and spread the cashews out on a baking sheet in a nice flat layer. Toast for 5 to 6 minutes, or until fragrant.

* * *

Grandma's Corn Pudding

A true Southern Staple

Makes 8 servings

5 eggs
⅓ cup butter, melted
¼ cup white sugar
½ cup milk (Grandma always made it with whole milk, but use the milk you prefer.)
4 tablespoons cornstarch

1 can corn (approximately 15.25 ounces)
2 cans creamed corn (approximately 14.75 ounces each)

Preheat oven to 400°F.

Grease a 2-quart casserole dish.

In a large bowl, lightly beat the eggs. Add the melted butter, sugar, and milk. Whisk in the cornstarch. Stir in the corn and creamed corn. Blend well. Pour the mixture into prepared the casserole dish.

Bake for 1 hour.